TIPPING POINT

An Adam Drake novel

SCOTT MATTHEWS

Chapter One

THE VILLA SITTING on the edge of an oceanfront cliff on the Hamakua Coast of the Big Island of Hawaii had a panoramic view of the Pacific Ocean to the east. It was owned by a grateful client of Adam Drake's who had made it available to him for a short vacation. He had needed a little R&R after a particularly hellish week.

A band of radicalized female college students, recruited by ISIS, had planned to massacre Catholic parishioners while they worshipped at mass in Portland, Oregon. Drake and an FBI agent, aided by a team from Puget Sound Security where he served as special counsel, had uncovered the plot and stopped the terrorists.

The man who recruited the young women, a Muslim computer science professor at their college, had fled to Roatan, an island in the Caribbean, to avoid capture. When his hideaway was discovered, Drake and his team had flown there in the PSS Gulfstream. Allowed to choose between a trip to Gitmo, if they turned him over to the U.S. Army stationed in nearby Honduras, and voluntarily returning to face federal charges in the U.S., the professor had wisely agreed to return with them to Oregon.

An inquisitive press wanted to know why and how Drake and PSS had been involved, and taking a short vacation allowed him to avoid their questions. The Big Island was the perfect place to vacation. Lush tropical beauty surrounded the secluded villa and he was there in the company of the woman he loved.

Liz Strobel was sitting on the other side of a teak patio table on the villa's lanai, wearing a white bikini and eating a blueberry croissant. She was stunningly beautiful, and he knew he was staring, but he couldn't help it.

When she turned and saw him looking at her, she smiled. "Are you enjoying the view as much as I am?"

Drake winked. "Probably more so. I've always loved looking at beautiful things, the endless blue ocean ... a woman in a white bikini."

"You're such a gentleman. What would you like to do today? We could stay here and relax or go to the botanical gardens."

"Let's see the gardens tomorrow. The guy who owns the best helicopter charter service here is a friend. He flew a helicopter in the 160th Special Operations Aviation Regiment, the NightStalkers. He was air support on some of the missions Mike Casey and I were on in Delta Force. His name is Riley Bishop, and he'll be here at ten o'clock to fly us over the volcano and that incredible lava flow."

Liz reached across and turned his wrist over to look at his watch. "We have an hour and a half. Why don't you get your swimsuit on and join me in the pool? You could use a little sun," she said with a smile.

It was Drake's turn to smile. He was wearing cargo shorts and a blue polo shirt. He'd been wearing less than that the night before.

When he joined her minutes later, she was standing on the far side of the infinity pool. Her chin was laying atop her folded hands and seemed to be resting on the horizon. He dove in and came up beside her.

Brushing his hair back out of his eyes, he said, "Penny for your thoughts."

"I can't get the young women who died last week out of my mind. What makes college students want to be jihadists and kill people?"

"Terrorist recruiters offer them whatever they're seeking. If a woman sees herself as a victim, it's a chance to get back at whoever, or whatever, they feel victimized them—a society that doesn't value them or their religion; men who have abused them; friends who have turned their backs on them. ISIS does it, but terrorist groups have been doing the same thing for a long time."

"Will it ever stop?"

Drake slid his arm around her waist and pulled her close. "Not any time soon. In the meantime, why don't we get out? You could use a little sun to get rid of those tan lines that I've noticed. I'll be happy to put sun lotion on for you."

"Once again, you're such a gentleman."

Chapter Two

TWO THOUSAND THREE hundred and nineteen miles away, in San Francisco, a huge counter protest had been organized to confront a "Free Speech" rally.

A conservative radio host and Fox news contributor had been scheduled to speak on the University of California Berkeley campus at an event sponsored by the student Republicans. The event had been canceled because the university was afraid there would be violence. The "Free Speech" rally was then rescheduled by supporters to be held at Crissy Field in San Francisco.

Counter-protestors had quickly hacked the SFPD and determined that the police were told not to actively confront any of the anarchist counter-protesters. Firearms and other obvious things that could be used as weapons were banned, but searches for them would be randomly made. Knives strapped to a counter-protester's leg would likely not be discovered.

Police barricades would be set up and manned, but they could easily be overrun with a sufficient number of counter-protesters. In recent protests to counter the hate of right-wing Nazi supporters of the president and other white supremacists, the counter-protesters had outnumbered the opposition ten to one. Overrunning police barricades with those numbers, especially if the police were being told not to interfere, wasn't seen as a problem.

On Saturday, at two o'clock in the afternoon, fewer than five hundred people were at Crissy Field to support the "Free Speech" rally organized by a group calling itself "We Are Patriots". Five times that number surrounded the patriots holding signs with black Nazi swastikas circled and crossed out in red. Other signs read, "Resist Racism," and "Haters Go Home."

Three leaders of Antifa, the violent anarchist movement, were in charge of inciting the riot. Counter-protestors were assembling in the parking lot of the nearby Sports Basement Presidio, a massive sports equipment store, from where they would march down Old Mason Street to Crissy Field and close in on the rally from three sides. There would be no way for anyone to escape, unless they jumped in the bay at the rear of the field.

The first three patriot speakers did little to stir up the counter-protesters, but the fourth was being loudly shouted down. As he tried to continue, scuffles broke out between the two sides.

It was time. The Antifa leaders were sent a message. "Go!"

It took five minutes for three hundred black-clad anarchists to run down Old Mason Street and out onto the field. The police on the barricades saw them coming and withdrew, standing behind their police cruisers in riot gear.

The black clads cut through the throng of counter-protesters, shoving them aside on their way to the "Free Speech" patriots in front of the stage. Fighting erupted and the anarchists pulled out saps and collapsible batons to beat people to the ground.

Twenty of the anarchists, wearing black hoodies and balaclavas, also used their knives to slash and cut as many of the patriots as they could. Because the knives were silent weapons, the screams from the victims blended in with the other screaming that was heard.

It took the police take several minutes to react to the violence. Before they could reach the black-clad anarchists, they had to wade through the other counter-protesters. By the time they got there, the orchestrated violence was over.

Beaten and bloodied protesters were on the ground, but the riot police didn't stop to help them. They were chasing after the anarchists running from the field.

The massacre was witnessed live on every major television channel for all the world to see.

It was the first wave of violence the anarchists hoped would start a second civil war. The country was so divided, ideologically, politically and racially, that it wouldn't be long before all the factions would be armed to defend themselves. The more violence that was witnessed on television, like the coverage of the war in Vietnam, the sooner the streets would be filled with citizens demanding an end to it all. And when the government couldn't end it all, people would have to choose sides and try to do it themselves.

It was the way you started a civil war.

Chapter Three

PRECISELY AT TEN O'CLOCK, a maroon helicopter circled around the villa to land on the paved driveway that ran across the property from the road. Drake and Liz had watched it fly along the coast from the back deck. By the time it took them to walk through the villa, the helicopter was down on the driveway with its rotors spinning slowly.

Riley Bishop walked over to greet them. He was wearing a white embroidered Hawaiian shirt, jeans, aviator sunglasses and a maroon baseball cap with gold letters. The letters matched the name on the side of the helicopter, Bishop Royal Charters.

He was shorter than Drake by a couple of inches, with broad shoulders and a barrel chest. He walked past Drake and greeted Liz the Hawaiian way, with a hug and a gentle kiss on her right cheek.

"Casey is right, you are a looker. I'm Riley Bishop, at your service."

Turning to Drake, he greeted him with a strong handshake. "Glad to meet you, Drake. If you're half as good as Casey says you are, this lady's in good hands."

"Mike told me to check and see if your flying skills were as good as his. He said he was worried about our safety flying with you," Drake said, returning an equally strong handshake.

Bishop snorted. "He was never as good as me. That's why he left us to join you ground pounders. Come on and get in. I want to show you my island."

Bishop's helicopter was an Airbus H130 Eco-Star, a single engine, light utility helicopter. Drake saw that it had the high-density cabin configuration with three front passenger seats in line with the pilot's seat. He helped Liz in and then climbed in next to her.

As soon as they were buckled in and had their headsets on, Bishop lifted off and headed out nose-down out over the cliff.

"My pilots have our charters covered for the rest of the day, so we'll take the scenic route over the ocean. It's quicker overland, but there's a petition to ban flights overland on the way to the volcano. It's an economic issue for the charters, but I understand where the petitioners are coming from."

"How long have you lived here?" Liz asked.

"I was born on the Big Island. I moved to the mainland for college and returned when I left the service. I've always considered it my home. Most tourists stay on the Kona side of the island. That's one of the reasons I like it here on the windward side."

Drake pointed down to his right at a large villa on a cliff. "Looks like you're getting a few of the uber rich staying on this side."

"That's the richest resident on the island, Mikhail Volkov, the Russian oligarch. He's not here very often, but he has a lot of guests."

Bishop circled around so they could take a better look at the estate. "I've flown a number of them up here, landing on his helipad on the roof."

He flew back out over the ocean and headed south. When he got closer to Hilo, he descended to fly around the bay and show them the town.

"The bay front in Hilo's been hit three times in the last hundred years by tsunamis, once in 1946, in 1960 and then again in 1975. The one in 1946 was caused by an earthquake in the Aleutian Islands. One hundred and fifty-nine people died. A lot of the buildings closest to the bay were destroyed. The one in 1960 was caused by an earthquake in Chile. Sixty-one people died in that one. Two people died in the 1975 tsunami caused by an earthquake off the coast. There's a tsunami museum on the bay front you should check out while you're here. It's got information about tsunamis all around the world."

"There's a lot of green space and parks down there. Is that a statue of King Kamehameha?" Liz pointed ahead.

"Sure is. That area was called 'New Town' before the 1946 tsunami. It was a Japanese residential community. It was completely wiped out, everything except a Coca Cola bottling plant. It's all park land now."

Bishop flew back out over the ocean and followed the coastline and then turned inland south of the two lava streams pouring red hot lava into the ocean.

"Since the eruption in May, Madame Pele's lava has covered over eight square miles of land. You've seen the coverage on TV, but that doesn't capture the massive loss of land that's occurred. Kapoho Bay and the tide pools just disappeared when the lava reached there. Homes, farms, businesses, just gone."

Bishop's two passengers were awestruck by the fast-flowing streams of red lava that had destroyed everything in its path.

"How are people coping?" Liz asked.

"As best they can. There is some temporary housing, but a lot of the people who have lost their homes and their belongings have left. The state and FEMA have done what they can, but the government can't afford to make people whole again. It's tough, but we'll survive.

"The volcano is a national park and there's a great

museum on the rim. Go at dusk or sunrise to enjoy it, if the park's open. There's also a place I recommend, the Kilauea Lodge, where you can stay. Rooms are usually reserved years in advance, but I can help with that, if you want.

"Lava's been flowing to the ocean since 1970, but not anything like this. There are boat charters that will get you close to where the lava flows into the ocean. That's something else I'd recommend."

Liz put her hand over Drake's. "I'd like to see the volcano before sunrise and the lava flow at night from a boat before I leave. This is just incredible."

"If you want, I can get started on that, if you'll give the dates," Bishop offered. "The lady that handles my charter reservations is a gem. She's also the woman I'm dating."

Drake looked over at Bishop, who was looking down at the lava flow with his lips pressed tightly together. He didn't know anything about the man's personal life. He appeared to be a man who enjoyed what he was doing and loved everything about the place he called home. But he was also obviously saddened by the loss of land below.

Drake thought of his old farm, and the vineyard he was working to restore, in the Oregon wine country southwest of Portland. He loved it, like Bishop loved his island. But someday soon, he knew he was going to have to make a choice.

He could stay on his farm in Dundee and risk losing Liz or move to Seattle. She had given up her career in Washington to take a job with PSS and be closer to him. It was up to him to make a similar sacrifice, if he wanted to continue their relationship.

Drake knew what he wanted to do. He also knew a part of him would be saddened when he did it.

Chapter Four

ACROSS THE PACIFIC OCEAN in Oregon, Zal Nazir, a software engineer, left the Intel Hillsboro campus in his black BMW M5 to meet a man for lunch. The invitation for the meeting had come to him in a plain white envelope, left under the windshield wiper of his car the night before.

The name of a nearby restaurant and bar had been written on the back of an embossed business card, from the Iranian consulate in Ottawa, Canada. Below the name of the Copper River Restaurant and Bar was the time for the meeting, one o'clock in the afternoon.

Nazir wasn't unduly concerned about the meeting. In addition to his work as a software engineer for Intel, he was also the founder of the Islamic Revolutionary Council of America (IRCA). The Council was made up of a select group of Muslim hackers he'd recruited to wage cyber jihad. He had chosen American citizens with clean records and no affiliation with any radical imam or mosque in the country. Their names weren't on any watch list, and they were extraordinarily careful about keeping it that way. They all flew under the radar of the enemies of Islam.

He arrived at the restaurant twenty minutes early and

waited patiently for a table to clear next to a window. He wanted to watch the envoy from the consulate arrive to see if he was being followed. From a window table, he would have an unobstructed view of the parking lot.

When he was seated and had ordered a cup of coffee, he watched as cars left the parking lot and looked for cars arriving. At five minutes to one, a white Ford Taurus drove into the lot and pulled into an empty spot. The rear bumper had an Avis rental car sticker on it.

The man who got out of the car looked to be in his late forties. He had dark, curly hair, a pair of round wire-rim glasses and wore a light gray suit. There was nothing about him that attracted attention as he walked to the entrance. But Nazir knew he was the man he was to meet by the relaxed but alert way he casually observed his surroundings. He had made sure there were no threats he had to worry about before he made his way to their table.

Pausing briefly at the door, he saw Nazir and walked to his table and sat across from him.

Nazir reached across the table to shake hands. "You obviously know my name, but I don't know yours. Who are you and why did leave your card on my car?"

"It's not important who I am, Mr. Nazir. I'm only a messenger. But, to put you at ease, my name is Dana Ghorbani. I work at the consulate in Ottawa."

"What do you do there?"

"Something similar to what you and the Council do."

Nazir sat back in his seat. "What do you know about the Council?"

"Everything. I represent your sponsor, Masoud Jihandar. He has something he wants you to do. America is paying too much attention to us, since it decided to pull out of our nuclear agreement. We want you to create a distraction for them to correct that."

"How am I to do that?"

"We want you to work with someone to start a civil war in America. He's been recruited by our ally in the north and will think he's working for them. He has a relationship with the Antifa anarchists through the student group he founded, Students for Social Justice. You will support his efforts with the skills you and your Council have."

"Why would I want to do that?"

Ghorbani leaned forward and said softly, "Because your sponsor wants you to, Mr. Nazir. We'll be in touch with instructions for meeting your new partner."

Nazir watched him stand up without saying another word and walk out of the restaurant. The sponsor Ghorbani had mentioned was a high-ranking officer in the Iranian Ministry of Intelligence and Security, the MOIS, and the supplier of the resources for the Council.

Starting a civil war in America sounded crazy to him, but he wasn't in any position to refuse cooperation. Not with the consequences he knew that would swiftly follow, if he didn't do as he was told.

Chapter Five

IT WAS noon when Drake and Liz got back to their villa after their tour of the volcano and the island with Riley. There was so much to see on the island and they hadn't been up to the volcano yet. Drake needed to call Riley Bishop and see if he could get them into the Kilauea Lodge for a night before they ran out of time.

Liz was at the patio table beside the infinity pool when he came out with the coffee carafe and the box of malasadas that Kalani, their cook, had left when they were on their tour of the island. Malasadas are sugar-coated, deep-fired Portuguese doughnuts filled with a cream filling and, according to Bishop, the favorite comfort food of Hawaii. He had insisted that they try some before they left.

When Liz saw what he was carrying, she gave him a withering look. "Don't you dare bring those things out here!"

Drake apologized and started to turn when she grabbed his arm. "Just one, and then you can take them away."

He refilled her coffee cup and sat down. "Would you like to stay here and just rest today?"

"That sounds wonderful. I'll call Kalani and see if she's available to cook something special for us tonight."

"Everything she's cooked has been special."

Liz got up to call Kalani. As soon as she was inside, he took a bite of a malasada and checked his phone for messages.

There was one from FBI Agent Williams. "Call me when you have a moment."

Williams answered on the first ring. "Sorry if I woke you up. I never remember the time difference."

"It's nine o'clock here, noon your time. What are you doing in the office on a Saturday?"

"I'm still working the terrorist case and the attack on the Catholic churches. I'm convinced she was working with someone other than Professor Ahmadi, as he claims. I haven't been able to rule it out and now we may have a break in the case."

"How did that happen?"

"One of the shooters had a cell phone in her pocket. It was a burner phone, and it was clean, except for one picture on it. It was a selfie with Mount Hood in the background. I've got an analyst trying to figure out where she was when she took it."

"Why are you buying what Professor Ahmadi's claiming? He's facing a life sentence in a federal prison. He'll say anything to avoid that."

"It's just a hunch."

"Let me know what your analyst finds. We'll be back in Portland next Friday."

"I will. Aloha and all that."

Drake called Riley Bishop to get help with a reservation at the volcano, but Bishop didn't answer.

Liz came back with her phone to her ear. "Come inside, there's breaking news on TV."

He grabbed his coffee and started in then turned around to bring the box of malasadas with him. No use leaving them outside for some bird to enjoy.

The live news feed on CNN was showing a demonstration

and riot in San Francisco. Black-clad anarchists were fighting with a smaller group of people in front of an open-air stage. A banner hanging from the edge of the stage said it was a "Free Speech" rally sponsored by "We Are Patriots".

Drake stepped closer to the screen. People were lying on the ground and a camera zoomed in on a woman clutching her stomach. She was bleeding from cuts on her arms and her white "We Are Patriots" T-shirt was stained with blood.

The camera quickly panned across others who also appeared to be injured, including several people who were still and not moving.

Liz passed him the remote controller and he turned up the sound.

"...a white supremacist rally in San Francisco has once again led to violence with counter-protesters who were just there to voice their opposition to the hateful rhetoric of the racists hiding behind the flag and claiming they had a right to their hate speech. When will the government do something to ban these hate groups and start putting people in jail? These people don't deserve the right to speak. They're nothing more than thugs and common criminals."

"So much for fair and balanced news. What about the anarchists wearing black hoodies and masks?" Drake said out loud.

Liz finished her call. "I couldn't reach Kalani, but there's a call from your father-in-law. He has my number but not yours, he said. He'd like you to call him when you have time."

Drake continued staring as the police and first responders took control of the field where the rally was held. EMTs were running with stretchers from ambulances parked on the road at the edge of the field. From the way they reacted when they reached some of the bodies, it was obvious there were fatalities.

"Did he say why he wanted me to call?"

"I heard the same announcer on his TV in the background that we're watching. He's probably calling about this riot."

Drake walked back out on the deck to call his father-in-law.

"Adam, thank you for calling. I hope you didn't mind me calling Liz first. You should be in my contacts, but I didn't take time to look. Actually, I just wanted to hear how she's doing. I'm still not happy about you and PSS luring her away from my staff here in Washington."

"I'm still surprised she agreed to take the job."

"I think we both know why. The reason I called was to invite you to meet a couple of my friends at our cabin at Crosswaters. We'll be there on Labor Day."

"Does this meeting have anything to do with anarchists rioting in San Francisco?"

"Yes, it does. That and more, I'm afraid."

"Is Liz invited?"

"She is."

"Then we'll see you on Labor Day."

Chapter Six

ZAL NAZIR WAS nervous walking down University Avenue toward the Berkeley Marina where Mason Bradley moored his houseboat. Another conservative pundit was scheduled to speak to the student Republicans at the university the next day and the campus was crawling with cops. Police cruisers were patrolling the major streets and stopping to question anyone they thought looked suspicious.

He kept his eyes looking straight ahead as the car to his left drove by slowly and then accelerated away. Wearing a linen blazer, button-down shirt, a tie and jeans, he knew he didn't look like the usual activist protester, but he couldn't afford to be questioned and identified.

When he reached Marina Boulevard, he turned right and followed Bradley's directions to his two-story houseboat. The riggings of a hundred yachts slapping gently against their aluminum masts provided a relaxing sound that accompanied music coming from some of the yachts.

Bradley's houseboat was dark, as he'd been told it would be. In the soft glow of twilight, there wasn't enough lighting to illuminate his face as he stepped onto the front deck. Bradley was waiting just inside his open front door.

"How far did you walk to get here?"

"I had the cab driver let me out at Tenth and University, not far."

Bradley waved him inside. "Did you feel the tension in the air?"

"Hard not to. There are cops everywhere."

The interior of the houseboat had indirect lighting that was turned way down, providing just enough light for Nazir to follow Bradley.

"First time I've been on a houseboat. I didn't expect it to be this big."

"I rented one when I first came down to the Bay Area and promised myself I'd own a nice one someday. I bought this three years ago."

"I didn't think Marxists coveted material things."

"I didn't think Muslims did either."

"I guess we're both hypocrites."

"Would you like something to drink?"

"Vodka, if you have it."

"Will Grey Goose do?"

"Certainly, thanks."

Bradley walked into the kitchen area and took a bottle of Grey Goose out of a cabinet and poured them each a glass. "I'll let you add your own ice."

When Nazir had added ice to his glass, Bradley motioned for him to follow.

The back area of the houseboat appeared to be Bradley's den. Two dark brown leather armchairs were on one side of the room with an end table between them. A small brass lamp provided a soft light. It complemented the reflected light from the city across the bay that was coming through a wide glass sliding door leading out to a rear deck. A floor-to-ceiling book case took up the wall on the other side of the room full to overflowing. Stacks of books were on the floor at both ends of the bookcase.

Bradley sat down and faced Nazir. "I'm having a difficult time understanding why I'm being told to work with you."

Nazir just nodded his head. "Yes, I imagine you are. You don't know me, and I don't know you. But I believe we both want the same thing. I'm told your Russian friend thinks you could benefit from the skills that my associates and I have."

"How exactly would you and your associates benefit me and what I'm doing?"

"Remember how social media was manipulated in the last election? We helped with some of that. You want to start a civil war. For that, you need both sides to be fighting mad. Your anarchists are ready, but the other side isn't ready to take up arms. I can help with that. I can also provide you with intelligence on what law enforcement plans to put into effect in any given situation."

"How?"

"By hacking into their systems and seeing their plans and listening in on their communications. Tell me what you're planning, and I'll tell you how I can help you."

"All right, I'm willing to give you a try. There's an FBI informant we know about in a Black Panther cell in Portland. To keep from being exposed, he's willing to give the FBI false information about a large cache of weapons and explosives about to be delivered to the Panthers' headquarters. The FBI will have to raid the place. We'll let the Panthers know a raid is coming so they're prepared to defend themselves, especially if we help them a little by having someone shoot one of their members and make it look like the FBI fired first. Black Panthers will take up arms to avenge Portland all around the country."

"Does Portland have the weapons and explosives to defend themselves?"

"They'll have weapons, but not enough to be successful."

"They won't have a chance!"

"That's the point, Nazir! When Black Panther groups arm

themselves and start killing some cops in retaliation, the fascists will come after them with a vengeance. When the bullets start flying, people will choose sides when blood's running in the streets. What do you think you can add to my plan?"

"I can tell you exactly what the FBI is doing all along the way. Now let me ask a question. Is your Russian on board with this? I wasn't told that he was willing to take on the FBI."

"I don't know, and, frankly, I don't care. He says he wants to start a civil war. I'll let you in on a little secret. He's a Russian oligarch. He's no friend of America, don't misunderstand, but what he really wants is to protect his natural gas empire in Ukraine. He thinks he can accomplish that if more progressive socialists are in power who will stop fracking in America. He's former KGB and a communist, but he's also a damn oligarch who enjoys being rich. Me, I'm just an old Marxist who wants a revolution."

Nazir looked at his watch. "I have to leave, I'm meeting someone for dinner. Let me know when the raid is arranged so I can monitor the FBI and maximize its impact on the Black Panthers."

Nazir left the houseboat more nervous than he'd been when he arrived. He was no longer sure what the end game was for Bradley and the Russian. Whatever it was, he had to make sure Bradley never found out he was serving the interests of Iran, especially after tonight, when he was going to carry out his own mission to widen the divide between Muslim Americans and the rest of the country.

The more factions fighting each other was just that much closer to a civil war, the way he saw it.

Chapter Seven

WHEN NAZIR LEFT BERKELEY, he drove to the home in Fullerton, California, that belonged to Hezbollah's West Coast bomb maker. He got there a little after nine o'clock in the evening.

Nazir had never met the man he only knew by his first name, Ebrahim. It was enough that someone he trusted told him he was the best bomb maker Hezbollah had in America and wouldn't ask any questions. The man would only need to know what kind of bomb he needed and what he wanted it to do.

That was the only problem Nazir anticipated, telling the man the truth—that he wanted the bomb to blow up a mosque.

The plan he'd agreed to assist focused on provoking groups and factions to become violent or, in some cases, more violent than they had ever been in the past. The poor working class, consisting mainly of young, white college students who couldn't find a job, would need to rise up against elite capitalists, the One Percenters. The anti-fascists had to fear the rise of Nazis, white supremacists and white nationalists so much that they would be prepared to eliminate them all before it was too late. Blacks needed a few more unarmed youths to be killed by the police, illegal immigrants needed a push toward La Raza and Muslims needed to feel even more oppressed than they already did.

He had decided a mosque would be the perfect target. It would be evidence of a message from the American infidel to Muslims that they weren't wanted, that it was dangerous for them here and that they should go home. It was the same message he later intended to take to the illegal immigrant groups in America.

Ebrahim appeared to be younger than he'd expected but worked with such efficiency and confidence that it was obvious he'd been building bombs for a quite a while. They were in his kitchen, carefully laying out the materiel for the bomb on the table.

"Where did you get the PE8 plastic explosive?" Ebrahim asked.

"Is that important?"

"No, not really, just curious," he said, carefully examining each of the five-hundred-gram blocks of PE8.

"Do you need me to build this for maximum casualties?"

"No, I need it to take down a building."

"How will it be delivered?"

"By air. Can you fit it into something like a shoebox? How long will that take?'

"You brought everything I need, so an hour or two at most."

"I'll leave you to it then."

Nazir left in his BMW, using a Garmin GPS Navigator for directions to scout the mosque in Anaheim. From the Google Map he'd studied, there was a gas station next to the mosque he hoped would be closed overnight. He would park there and operate a drone he brought to deliver the bomb to the top of the golden dome of the mosque.

With the evening *Isha* prayer at nine o'clock, there would

be no one in the mosque later that night. He knew the mosque would have the resources it needed to quickly rebuild, and he wasn't concerned about destroying it.

He drove by the gas station next to the mosque and drove on by before turning around to pull in for gas. While he pumped the little gas that he needed, he saw the hours the station was open on the door into the office. It was open until midnight.

It was going to be a long night. The bomb would have a timer, so he wouldn't be captured on traffic cameras leaving the area immediately after the explosion. He planned on waiting until after midnight to plant the bomb, say two o'clock, and then driving to San Diego International Airport from Anaheim. His Alaskan Airline nonstop flight to Portland left at six thirty the next morning

When he got back to Ebrahim's house, the bomb was sitting on the kitchen table.

"What time should I set the timer for?"

"Three a.m. tomorrow morning."

"So be it."

Nazir watched quietly as the young bomb maker set the timer and then put the bomb in a cardboard box.

"PE8 is very stable," Ebrahim said and smiled. "You shouldn't have to worry about it going off."

"I'm not sure I like the way you said that."

"Just yanking your chain. People are too serious around me."

Nazir picked up the box and turned to leave the kitchen. "Thanks, Ebrahim. Keep your day job, your humor sucks."

At a restaurant in Fullerton called Heroes Bar and Grill, Nazir ordered a bowl of seafood gumbo and a beer. The restaurant was busy until it started clearing out just before midnight. He'd been left alone to enjoy his gumbo and the only person he talked with was the young waitress when he ordered. When he finished, he paid his bill with cash and left to drive around for the next two hours to kill time.

At ten minutes to two in the morning, he pulled into the gas station and backed into a spot next to the service door. Anyone passing by would think the car had been left overnight to be worked on in the morning.

Before leaving Ebrahim's, he'd removed the fuse for the interior and trunk lights. Standing behind the BMW with the trunk lid raised, he held a small AAA flashlight in his teeth while he loaded the bomb into the loading bay of the eight-rotor drone he'd purchased on Amazon.

When the bomb was securely loaded onto the drone, he set the drone on the trunk lid and got inside to sit behind the steering wheel. He held the control panel in both hands and started the rotors spinning. When the drone lifted off, Nazir used its built-in camera to fly it to the top of the dome of the mosque. The drone hovered there as he placed the bomb exactly where he wanted it, and then he flew the drone back to land on the trunk lid of his car.

As soon as he had the drone covered with a blanket in the trunk, Nazir left the gas station and headed south to San Diego. A brother would meet him there to pick up the expensive drone before he returned the rental car at the airport.

He kept the radio tuned to a twenty-four-hour news station, hoping to hear a report about a bomb exploding at a mosque in Anaheim, in the conservative and mostly Republican Orange County of California.

Chapter Eight

DRAKE CAME out of the bedroom with a towel wrapped around his waist and went to the kitchen to make a fresh pot of the Kona coffee Kalani left for them the night before.

Before he loaded the grinder with the coffee beans, he used the remote to turn on the flat screen TV in the entertainment area in the next room.

Live coverage of the smoldering ruins of a mosque in California was being shown. A streaming banner proclaimed it was the work of neo-Nazis in retribution for the massacre at the Free Speech rally in San Francisco.

"Liz, come see this," Drake shouted.

She came out of the bedroom and stood by his side, drying her wet hair with one towel, and another towel wrapped around her body.

"This doesn't make any sense, Adam. Why bomb a mosque? Muslims weren't the counter-protestors at the rally in San Francisco."

"The network has to have a reason for blaming it on neo-Nazis, unless this is just sloppy journalism."

They watched for several more minutes, waiting for an

explanation for the network's conclusion that neo-Nazis were responsible. When they didn't hear one, Liz said, "I'm going to get dressed before I join you for coffee. Are we still driving into Hilo this morning?"

"That's the plan. Go ahead, I'll be right behind you. I want to see what's online about this."

His laptop was on the table and while it booted up he wondered if Antifa was acting up back home. Portland had one of the oldest Antifa groups, and it was frequently in the news for breaking up peaceful demonstrations and rioting in the city. Portland had become America's most politically violent city, largely because of the presence and actions of the group.

Nothing he saw online supported the conclusion that neo-Nazis were responsible for the attack on the mosque. There was plenty of speculation and finger pointing in the media, of course, but the FBI was officially refusing to call any one group a "party of interest" in the bombing.

That was officially. He knew someone who could tell him what the FBI was thinking unofficially.

He took his phone out onto the lanai to call FBI Special Agent Williams.

"Please tell me you're not in the office on Sunday."

"Okay, I'm not in my office on Sunday. I'm driving down a country road looking for the place where the selfie I mentioned was taken. What are you doing?"

"Sitting on the lanai with a towel wrapped around my waist, looking at the ocean and curious about what the FBI knows about the mosque bombing and fire in California."

"Let me pull over so we can talk."

Drake heard the crunch of gravel under the tires of Williams' car as he pulled off onto the shoulder.

"The fire was caused by a massive explosion on the dome of the mosque. The dome collapsed, walls were blown out, and the whole main building of the mosque was destroyed. A plastic explosive I'm not familiar with, PE8, was used. It's a special explosive used for demolition work; it's not something you make at home. We're not sure how they got the explosive on top of the dome, and that's all we know right now."

"Sounds like a pretty sophisticated attack. I assume no one is taking credit for the bombing."

"You assume correctly. There is a tweet from the white nationalist group in Nevada saying it wasn't their bomb. They've offered to let us come in and search their headquarters, but we don't have anything that points to them."

"Do you have any suspects?"

"Not on this bombing. But I think I'm getting close to finding the place where the terrorist took her selfie. It's northeast of the small town of Helvetia with a clear view of Mount Hood. It's difficult to establish the exact elevation of the location, that's why I'm out here driving around."

"Good luck with that. Let me know if you hear anything more about the bombing of the mosque, will you?"

"Sure thing."

Drake was staring at the endless expanse of the dark blue ocean when Liz joined him on the lanai. "Learn anything?"

"I called Wayne Williams. There's a tweet from a white nationalist group in Nevada denying responsibility for bombing the mosque. The FBI believes them. They don't think they're sophisticated enough to have done it."

"Why?"

"The mosque was destroyed by a bomb that used a sophisticated explosive, one you don't make at home."

"If it isn't the group in Nevada, that doesn't mean it isn't one of the other alt right groups. Who else would want to blow up a mosque?"

Drake stood up and put his arms around her neck. "Until I know more, I'll let the media speculate about that. Would you like me to go get that cup of coffee you said you wanted?"

"Are you sure that's what you want to do right now?"

"Why?"

"Because you just let your towel fall down around your ankles."

Chapter Nine

FBI SPECIAL AGENT WILLIAMS parked his car on the side of
a country road. There were no lights on in the old farmhouse
he'd found and there were no cars parked anywhere around it.
There was a big barn, but its main door was closed.

The selfie, found on the phone of the dead terrorist who
had been involved in the attacks on the Catholic churches,
had Mount Hood in the background at sunset. It had
captured the majestic mountain when it was colored a soft
reddish-pink by smoke from forest fires burning to the south
and east of it. Analysis of the projected angle of the photo
from the phone to the mountain and the estimated time when
it was taken had allowed an FBI analyst to approximate a
location.

This farm northeast of Helvetia, Oregon.

Williams got out and walked to the southwest corner of
the property, crossing a small ditch beside the road. Standing
behind the corner fence post, he used his Bushnell hunting
binoculars to inspect the farm and confirmed his conclusion
that no one was home.

When he got back to his car, a new Chevrolet Monte
Carlo SS he bought when he transferred to the Portland Field

Office, he stood beside it and called the analyst he was working with.

"Jim, I think I found it. I've driven by this farm several times at the time you estimated the selfie was taken. The mountain looks like it did minus the coloring from the smoke. The address is 13492 Northwest Cornelius Pass Road. Find out who owns it."

"Give me a minute."

While he waited, he took a string of photos of the farm with his phone. The lighting was bad, but the analyst would still be able to enhance them enough for his calculations.

"Wayne, this is interesting. The place is owned by Chevre Farms, a company registered in Panama. It will take a while to identify the owners of the company."

"Isn't Chevre a goat cheese?"

"It is."

"I don't see any goats."

"Maybe they're inside somewhere. My grandfather had goats on his farm and they slept inside, if they could, when it was dark."

"I'll come back tomorrow during the day. Keep working on the owners of this place."

He started the engine of his SS and listened to the burble of its 370 horsepower V8. Adam Drake could have his German Porsche; he would always be a Detroit iron Chevy man.

If this turned out to be the place where the terrorist Umara and the women with her stayed, what was the connection to the owner of the goat farm? She could have rented the place, but would she do that for just a week or so? She couldn't have realistically thought she and the others would survive the attacks on the churches.

There were no neighboring farms close enough to this one for anyone to have seen the occupants, the farmhouse and barn were set back too far from the road. He could canvass the area in the coming days, but rural neighbors weren't going to love FBI agents going house-to-house asking intrusive questions like, "Did you notice anything unusual about the terrorists living on the next farm over? Did you see or hear them practicing with their AK-47s? Did they have visitors you saw that you could identify? Can you explain why you didn't see anything and aren't willing to involve yourself in our FBI investigation?"

He didn't expect to learn much from any of them, but you had to ask.

Executing a three-point turn on the narrow two-lane road, Williams drove south on the road back to Portland. He was thinking about where he wanted to have dinner when he approached a black Mustang that was pulled off on the other side of the road.

The driver was holding his cell phone out the window in his left hand as if he was searching for a signal. The man waved with his other hand to indicate everything was okay.

When he turned his head back to continue driving, Williams thought he caught a camera flash from the man's phone in his peripheral vision. The man must have had the phone on camera by mistake while he searched for a signal.

After turning his radio on and selecting his favorite FM station, he checked his watch and saw that it was just five o'clock in Hawaii.

He had Drake's number on speed dial and was surprised he had a signal and that his call was going through. The guy on the side of the road was probably using one of the low-cost carriers with mediocre to poor coverage.

"Evening, Drake. Got a minute?"

"Just taking a glass of wine out to Liz on the lanai. Fire away."

"I'm pretty sure we've found where the selfie was taken. It's a farm northeast of Helvetia that's owned by some Panamanian company. We haven't identified the owners yet. I'll get a search warrant tomorrow and see if there's evidence the terrorists stayed there."

"What's a company from Panama doing with a farm out there?"

"The company calls itself Chevre Farms. We're thinking it might be a goat farm or something."

"Why would a Panama company have a goat farm in Oregon? You can raise goats anywhere. Is there anything unique about the place?"

"It's just an old farm, maybe thirty or forty acres."

"I have a hunch you're going to find this company is owned by a company that's owned by a company that's owned by a string of other companies. It will take you a while to identify the owners, but peeling this onion is going to be interesting."

"My thoughts exactly. I'll keep you posted."

"Thanks for the call. I appreciate it."

Williams had peeled the onion of shell companies with terrorist ties before. He knew from experience what Drake was talking about. It would take time, but there was always something that led to the people hiding behind these companies.

Chapter Ten

NAZIR'S spotter made the same three-point turn the dark grey Monte Carlo had made and chased after it until he could see its taillights ahead. Then he made his report.

"A man just left. He's been studying the farm with binoculars. I'm following him. What do you want me to do?"

"Keep following him. Describe him to me."

"Mid-forties, six foot tall, well built. He's wearing jeans, a Portland Timbers T-shirt and white Timbers hat. I took his picture on my phone when he drove by me."

"I want to know who he is and where he lives. Send me his picture. If you need to be relieved at some point, call me."

"His picture is on its way." The spotter ended the call, tapped the camera icon and sent the photo from his phone.

Nazir was sitting in Cat Cora's Kitchen in San Francisco International Airport when his spotter called. He'd left a fantastic chicken curry with peas and a glass of pinot gris on the table and walked to a spot in the restaurant where no one could hear what he was saying.

When he returned to his table, he knew he wasn't going to enjoy the cuisine of the world-renowned chef as much as he had hoped. After taking a quick look at the photo his spotter sent him, his stomach was churning.

Since he started working with the Russian, his old friend, Mikhail Volkov, he'd focused on finding ways to start a civil war in America. Now he was being pulled back into the ill-fated scheme of Professor Ahmadi and Samantha Taylor, or Umara as she liked to call herself, to kill Christians while they worshipped in their churches.

He had recruited Umara as his own asset after his contact and sponsor in Iran's Revolutionary Guards had discovered what she and the professor were doing for ISIS. She'd been seen as a valuable young asset, willing to strike a blow against America, a blow that would be blamed on the Sunni thugs of ISIS.

Her plan to storm Catholic churches was clearly a suicide mission. So, working with an unsuspecting Umara, they had planted files and email correspondence to link the attacks to ISIS and the professor when their plan failed.

But if someone was now snooping around his farm outside Portland, Ahmadi must be trying to avoid the death penalty by telling the FBI that he wasn't the one responsible for his girl-friend's actions. He had watched Ahmadi on TV when he'd arrived at Hillsboro Airport in the custody of the FBI.

He knew it had to be Ahmadi because the face in the photo on his phone belonged to the FBI agent who had taken custody of Ahmadi at the airport.

Nazir waved a waiter over to his table and ordered a double Grey Goose vodka over ice with a lemon twist. He had two hours before they would call his United flight to Portland and he had to decide if he was going to be on it.

The farm was owned by a front company he'd set up in Panama. He knew it would take the FBI time to trace the ownership from there to another of his shell companies in the Cayman Islands, then to the Seychelles, Samoa and Belize. But the investigation would eventually lead back to him.

He could flee to Iran, but he'd never been there and didn't speak the language. He was Persian, his parents had immigrated to America before the fall of the Shah and the Iranian Revolution. The option was available, perhaps, but only as a last resort.

Or he could go underground, like the Weatherman and Mason Bradley had done in the seventies. He could hide in plain sight with a new identity. Mason Bradley had experience with that and could help him.

By the time Nazir finished his Grey Goose, he'd made up his mind. He would go underground and not let the Russian or Bradley know. Members of the Council would help him, and he had adequate resources to make the transition.

It would take a little time to disappear, but he knew he could do it. It would be easier, of course, if he had a little more time to get organized.

And the only way he could think to buy a little more time was to get the FBI agent off his trail.

Nazir ordered another double Grey Goose and called his number two. "Go to my apartment and remove anything that might identify me. I do everything electronically, so there isn't much. I have my laptop and phone. Take my weapons, you know where they are. Leave my clothes. I'm calling Intel and telling them I'm taking emergency leave to care for my aging father. Take everything to the safehouse on the mountain."

"Your parents are dead."

"Intel doesn't know that. I never told HR."

"What's going on?"

"My car is at the airport. I'll drive to the safehouse from there and meet you tomorrow."

"Should I clear out my things as well?"

"This doesn't involve you. Take a sick day tomorrow and then return to work. There can be no sign there's anything out of the ordinary going on. Do you understand?"

"I understand."

"Then I'll see you tomorrow."

Nazir's brain was buzzing with the challenges waiting for him in Oregon. He had decided to derail the FBI investigation by getting rid of the man who was snooping around his farm.

Chapter Eleven

LIZ FOUND Drake sitting in a recliner out on the deck, drinking a cup of coffee, when she got up Sunday morning. From the way that he had tossed and turned in bed, she knew something was bothering him.

She walked to him and put a hand on his shoulder. "I didn't hear you get up."

"I couldn't sleep. Thought I might as well enjoy another sunrise before we leave."

"Let me get some coffee and I'll join you. Want something to eat?"

"Maybe some fruit. I thought we might drive to Hilo today, pick up a bento box and see a waterfall or two on the way back. There are nine of them between here and Hilo."

He wasn't sure what was bothering him, but he knew it had something to do with the phone call from his father-in-law. Three years ago, when he was drinking heavily and depressed following Kay, his wife, dying from a swift and aggressive cancer, the senator had stepped in and pulled him out of his dark hole.

A constituent of the senator's needed help when the man's

secretary was murdered in his office late one night. Drake had agreed and, in doing so, changed his life.

The secretary's murderer turned out to be a terrorist. He was a member of a cell of assassins who had planned on killing everyone on a long list of government and industry leaders, including his own father-in-law. When he'd been able to prevent that from happening, with the help of his friend, Mike Casey, the CEO of Puget Sound Security, the secretary of homeland security and Senator Hazelton had asked him to act as a trouble shooter from time to time, for the government.

Since then, there had been other threats to America's security he'd been instrumental in stopping. But, in doing so, he'd been pulled back into the life of a warrior and made to realize that he missed the sense of purpose as well as the exhilaration of battle he'd experienced again.

By meeting the senator and "a couple of his friends" at the Hazelton summer home in Central Oregon, Drake knew there would likely be another request to help the government with something. Something that, in the past, he had always agreed to.

But by inviting Liz to come with him to the senator's cabin at Crosswater, he knew it meant that she would likely be at risk herself, if she was involved with him. He wasn't sure he could allow that.

He couldn't lose another woman that he loved. That possibility was what had kept him from sleeping last night.

Liz set out a plate of bananas, pineapple, mangos and papaya. "There are croissants if you want one."

Drake picked up a slice of pineapple with his fingers and took a bite. "Incredible how sweet fresh pineapple is."

Liz tried the papaya. "Something's bothering you. Care to share?"

Drake ate another slice of pineapple before he answered. "The senator wants both of us to come to Crosswater to meet a 'couple of his friends'. Do you have any idea who these friends are?"

"I didn't know he was coming to Oregon and I have no idea who he wants you to meet."

"He wants both of us to meet them. I guess that's what's bothering me."

"Why?"

Choose your words carefully, he thought.

"I expect that we're going to be asked to do something that Senator Hazelton and his friends can't do for themselves."

"Why does that bother you? You've done things for him before. That's how we met, remember?"

He did. He remembered vividly the night she'd responded to a call from the senator to go help him. With the help of the advance detail of Secret Service she was working with for the secretary of homeland security's visit to Oregon, the bodies of three terrorists were removed from his farm, where they died trying to kill him.

He'd thought then that she was beautiful but cold, a real Ice Lady.

She was still beautiful, but now she warmed his heart.

"I want you to be safe, Liz. With you now working at PSS, I have some way to make sure you are. Meeting the senator's friends means you might be involved with whatever he needs help with. I'm not sure I want that."

Liz's eyes took on a hard and determined look. "Adam, you know I love you, but you don't have to protect me. I was a good FBI agent. If I don't want to be involved in whatever he's asking us to do, I'll say so. It's my decision to make. I appreciate your concern, but you may have overlooked a fact. I'll be there to watch your back, just like you'll be there to watch mine."

He needed to change the subject and she'd given him the perfect way. He smiled and winked. "You can always count on me to watch your backside."

She drew back to give him a playful slap and said instead, "You're incorrigible, Mr. Drake."

Chapter Twelve

THAT SAME SUNDAY IN WASHINGTON, D.C., Senator
Robert Hazelton, the four-term senior United States senator
from Oregon, was in the study of his Georgetown rowhouse.
He was meeting with Michael Montgomery, the former
director of national intelligence and a member of their "committee for safety".

The committee, small "c", was a private group of five
concerned members of Congress and the intelligence community. Like the Boston Committee for Safety that had formed
before the outbreak of the Revolutionary War and sent Paul
Revere on his famous ride, they were concerned about the rise
of violence in their divided country and the risk of a second
civil war.

"It's been quite a week, Mike. I'm not sure how long it will
take before both sides start showing up at rallies armed and
ready to kill each other."

"One Antifa group is already calling for that. Its website is
openly calling for a Marxist-style revolution. The president's
reluctant to shut the site down because they'll scream that he's
acting just like the Hitler they portray him to be. The media
would quickly agree."

"Do we know who these Antifa people are?"

"Some of them are above ground but most of them are underground, just like in the '70s. That's what some in the FBI are worried about. This happened so fast, after the election, that they have very little intelligence on the leaders."

"Is that true on both sides? From what I've seen, the groups being called white supremacists and Nazis are pretty much out in the open."

"For the most part, but I'm not sure how much longer that will last. Antifa and the anarchists have been vandalizing the homes of some of the leaders. They've also shown up at the homes of prominent Republicans and supporters of the president."

"I saw that. Do we know where these groups are getting their money? The black-clad protesters that have been arrested so far aren't from the communities they were arrested in."

"DHS and the FBI are working on that."

Senator Hazelton got up and poured another glass of iced tea. "Want a glass?"

Montgomery checked his watch. "Three o'clock is a little early, but is it spiked by any chance?"

"Not yet, but it could be. You're a southerner. Would you like a spiked Arnold Palmer?"

"You bet I would. Can I help?"

Senator Hazelton picked up the iced tea pitcher. "No, but you could call Mark Holland. See if he's heard anything from his former counterterrorism colleagues in the NYPD."

He met his wife, Meredith, coming out of their bedroom on the way downstairs. "Mike's wanting something stronger than iced tea. I thought I'd make a pitcher of spiked Arnold Palmer for him. Would you like to help me?"

"Is something wrong at his home? Is Emily okay?"

"She's fine, as far as I know. Mike's worried about the recent violence in the country."

She followed him downstairs. "I'll get the lemonade and iced tea from the refrigerator, you get the bourbon."

When he returned and stood beside her in the kitchen, she asked him what the two of them were up to.

"The committee is going to meet over the Labor Day weekend at our cabin in Oregon. I invited Adam and Liz to come. I know you have the senate wives' luncheon right after Labor Day, but I'd like you to come with me."

"Glad to, I've been attending these luncheons for twenty years, I can miss this one."

He took the pitcher from her and kissed her on her neck. "You sure you don't want some of this?"

"Go finish with Mike. Maybe later if there's any left."

His guest was still on his phone when he got back to the study. The senator poured him a tall glass of the spiked Arnold Palmer and handed it to him.

Montgomery sipped the concoction and whispered, "Thanks."

"If you hear anything else before we get together, call me."

The former DNI put his phone back in his pocket and looked over the top of his glass as he took another drink. "Mark's as concerned as we are. He's monitoring the social media of the active Antifa groups in New York. Something's in the works. The chatter's all about taking things to the next level. A couple of the groups are openly talking about who will kill the most cops, like it's a game. The NYPD is gearing up for a new war on cops."

"I don't understand why Facebook and Twitter won't take these sites down. Free speech doesn't include inciting violence."

"Call Zuckerberg and Dorsey before one of your committees and ask them. Maybe they'll tell you why they're turning a blind eye," Montgomery suggested sarcastically.

Senator Hazelton looked over Montgomery's head at his

collection of first edition works on American political history. The mention of the two CEOs reminded him of the rich elite, both past and present, who financed progressive and socialist movements, talking like revolutionaries. They claimed to want a different America than the one that had made them wealthy 'one percenters'. They were the ones who dominated Wall Street and ran the corporations the anarchists wanted to tear down.

"What do we know about our rich elites? They tend to support these radical groups. What are they saying about the violence?"

"Publicly, I don't know. But if you listen to the talking heads on the networks they run around with, who are sympathetic to anyone who feels oppressed by the existence of any group they've labeled as 'haters', they're probably just as sympathetic."

"Maybe we should ask Mark to see what he can dig up on some of our prominent elites. They seem to be the ones who are the most upset by the last election. Antifa's getting money from somewhere. Let's find out if it's coming from any of them."

Chapter Thirteen

MASON BRADLEY TOOK the 4:45 p.m. Issaquah ferry from the Seattle terminal to Vashon Island. A driver was waiting there to take him to the twenty-million-dollar home of Richard Lyman III, real estate magnate and the wealthiest man in the state of Washington, next to Bill Gates of Microsoft.

Lyman was in Europe and had made his home available to Mikhail Volkov for their meeting. Lyman was a rich socialist who was happy to generously donate in any way he could to anything that advanced the socialist movement. Hosting a meeting in absentia, in his home for Mason Bradley, while the professor was giving a series of lectures at the University of Washington would unquestionably advance the movement, Volkov had promised him.

Bradley sat in the back of Lyman's black Mercedes S 560 sedan enjoying the scenery on the drive south to Quartermaster Harbor. He was constantly amazed by the naivete of the rich one percenters and their disdain for the country. Didn't they realize that if their pet causes were successful, they would no longer be at the top of the food chain? In fact, they would be the first to be lined up against a wall and shot. It would be people like him, who were smart enough to use these useful idiots, who would be in charge.

Bradley followed the driver when they arrived and walked through Lyman's exquisite home to a putting green in the middle of a manicured yard at the rear of the house. Volkov was there with his back turned to them when they approached, concentrating on a twenty-foot putt.

"Just hit the damn thing, Mikhail. I'm thirsty."

Volkov straightened up and inhaled deeply before he turned around and smiled. "Mason, go inside and fix yourself a drink. I'll join you in a minute."

Bradley rocked on his heels, considering a response to the snub, then turned around and marched back across the lawn to the house.

Be careful, Mikhail. You're not KGB anymore, Bradley said under his breath.

Volkov's driver caught up with him before they reached the house. "He's working on his game before a meeting in Brussels next week. If you haven't played with him, you should know he takes the game very seriously. That's why I caddy for him when he plays. Someone has to be there to keep him from killing someone with that club of his when they disturb his concentration."

"Driver and bodyguard?"

"For the last five years. I'm a former Spetsnaz, if you're wondering. He's been very good to me."

"Lucky you."

"He said you're an old friend. You should start acting like one."

Bradley squared off with the younger man. "Is that a threat?"

"If it needs to be."

Bradley tried to stare down Volkov's bodyguard, but the man didn't blink. "Show me where the Scotch is," he said as he turned and walked to the door, "and tell your boss we don't have all night. I have a ferry to catch in two hours."

Volkov joined him in the pool room ten minutes later. Bradley was lining up a difficult shot on the pool table and Volkov waited for him to take it. Bradley pulled back his pool cue over and over again, waiting for Volkov to say something; he finally took the shot and missed it badly.

Bradley walked to the bar and leaned back against it. "I expected you to say something."

"I know. Bring your Scotch and a bottle of Stolichnaya. There are glasses in the library down the hall."

Volkov led the way and waited for Bradley to enter the library. When he did, Volkov told his bodyguard to go watch a soccer match in the entertainment center while they talked.

At the end of the library, two green leather armchairs sat on either side of an ornately carved center table with a green stone top. Bradley sat down in one of the chairs with his bottle of Scotch in one hand and the bottle of Stolichnaya in the other.

"That looks expensive. Is it okay to set the bottles here?"

Volkov was at a sidebar getting two crystal tumblers for them and said over his shoulder, "It's very expensive, I gave it to Lyman. It's an antique Russian Empire bronze table with a Malachite top. You can't hurt it, go ahead and set the bottles there. Things seem to be going well for us, don't you think?"

Bradley filled the tumbler Volkov handed him with Scotch and nodded. "Better than we could have expected. Nazir's people are doing a brilliant job provoking the fascist groups."

"What do you plan on doing next?"

"They haven't announced it yet, but the fascists are planning a rally in Oregon and Washington and a march to both state capitals. We'll be there to shed some blood."

"How do you plan on doing that?"

"I have a shipment of fifty Serbian AK-47s arriving in

Seattle. I'm giving half of them to the anarchists to use and the rest to the Black Panthers."

"Do the anarchists know how to use AK-47s?"

"I'll ask the cells to pick out twenty-five men and send them to a ranch I have access to near a hunting preserve outside Cheney, Washington. They'll train there Wednesday and Thursday and be ready for these marches on Labor Day weekend."

"Do you think the fascist groups will be armed?"

"I'll be surprised if they're not."

"Have we covered our tracks, Mason?"

"I have only one senior Antifa leader I deal with. No one knows his real name. He only knows that I can get the money they need for things. He doesn't know about you or Nazir."

"Will you be in Oregon or Washington?"

"I lecture at the university here in Seattle Monday and Tuesday. Then I'll be back on my houseboat in Berkeley on Wednesday."

"And I'll be at my estate on Long Island for the Labor Day weekend. This could be the spark we need, Mason."

"That's what you're paying us for. Let's hope so."

Volkov filled his tumbler with vodka and leaned over to clink his glass with Bradley's. "Here's to civil war and a new future, my friend."

Chapter Fourteen

DRAKE AND LIZ stood with an arm around each other at a volcano overlook, mesmerized by the sight. A dark covering of scattered clouds captured soft streaks of raspberry from the red lava shooting into the air from the caldera below. Set against the dark blue of the early morning sky, the scene was breathtaking.

They stood silently, watching the volcano until the beauty of the sunrise faded into morning.

Liz leaned over and kissed him on the cheek. "I'll never forget this."

"Agreed, that's a picture that will always be in my mind. Are you ready for breakfast?"

Riley Bishop, their charter pilot, had been able to reserve a deluxe room for them at the Kilauea Lodge for the night before.

Holding hands, they walked to their rented Mustang in the parking lot and drove to the lodge. Built in nineteen thirty-eight by the YMCA, and originally called Camp Hale O Aloha, it had been used by children to visit and experience the volcano and the Volcanoes National Park. More recently, in nineteen eighty-six, it had been purchased privately and refurbished as a lodge and restaurant.

They were seated by the rear windows in the small restaurant by a smiling young Hawaiian woman and given menus before she left to seat another couple.

Drake looked over the top of his menu and saw that Liz had already decided what she was having. "That was quick."

"I haven't had French toast in a long time. This looks good."

When their serving waiter came and took Liz's order, Drake followed her lead. "And I haven't had pancakes in some time. So I'm going to have the buttermilk pancakes, an egg, bacon, orange juice and we'll have coffee."

"That should carry you through until at least noon."

"It might. Have you thought about what else you'd like to do before we go home?"

Liz turned to look out the window with a faraway look in her eyes. "I thought of my condo back in D.C. when you said that. I'm not sure where home is right now."

"Having second thoughts about moving to Seattle?"

"No, but I'm not looking forward to finding a place there. It took me a year in Washington before I found the condo I bought."

"There's no rush. Store your stuff with me. Ask Mike to let you use the company's standing reservation at the Woodmark Hotel. That way you can come to Portland on the weekends and not pay rent for an apartment."

Drake's phone vibrated in his pocket, and when he took it out, he saw there was a message from Steve Carson, the pilot who dropped them off in the PSS Gulfstream G650 on his way to Honolulu. PSS was exploring the need to have an office there to better serve its clients on the Pacific Rim.

We're flying home tomorrow, instead of Thursday as planned. Do you want me to stop in Hilo and pick you up?

. . .

WHY TOMORROW? *Thought you and Tyler had appointments to view properties until Thursday.*

THE ANARCHISTS SAY *they're burning down Seattle, Wednesday. Mike wants all hands on deck.*

I'LL TALK *to Liz and get back to you.*

"I CAN SEE by the look on your face that something's wrong. What is it?"

"The text is from Steve Carson. He's flying home tomorrow, instead of Thursday. He wants to know if we want him to stop and pick us up."

"Why tomorrow?"

"The anarchists are threatening to burn down Seattle on Wednesday. Mike wants everyone back in case they try. We have a lot of clients in Seattle."

As they started trying to digest the information, the waiter arrived with their orders.

Nothing needed to be said and they started eating. If they were needed in Seattle, their short vacation just got even shorter.

Drake poured maple syrup over his pancakes and put his fork down. "How did we get to this point in America, where a mob of discontents can threaten to burn down a city and we take them seriously?"

"It's not just here. Europe is experiencing the same thing. The young think capitalism is the enemy and want the return of socialism. *Das Kapital,* Marx's treatise, is very popular, if you can believe it."

"But why here and why now? I don't understand it."

"Neither do I."

The French toast and pancakes were delicious, but they both left food on their plates and sat quietly drinking coffee.

"Is there anything left on our list that you would like to do today?"

"I would like to go back to the villa. There are a couple of things on my list that we still haven't done."

He saw her shining eyes and signaled for the check. "We better hit the road then. I want to make sure everything on your list is checked off."

"Don't worry, it will be."

While he waited for his credit card and copy of the check to be returned, he sent a text message back to Steve Carson.

Pick us up tomorrow. Let me know your ETA.

Chapter Fifteen

AFTER ARRIVING in Seattle Tuesday evening in the PSS Gulfstream, Drake and Liz checked into the Woodmark Hotel for the night. With the three-hour time difference between Hawaii and the mainland, it was nine o'clock Pacific Time when they got to their room and called it a night.

Mike Casey had asked them to meet him at PSS headquarters the next morning and promised to have a light breakfast for them when they arrived. When their cabbie dropped them off and they made their way to the top floor, they found the light breakfast was a meeting of the PSS management team. A sidebar of pastries, coffee and a selection of fresh fruit and juices was provided, as promised.

Casey greeted them at the door of the conference room. "You two rested and finally ready to go to work?"

"We are," Liz answered for them both. "Thank you for a wonderful vacation."

"The vacation was all Adam's idea. I just supplied the transportation."

Liz walked to the sidebar to get some fruit and juice, leaving Drake with Casey.

"Are we expecting any of our clients to be in danger?"

Casey shook his head. "No way to tell. Most of them are located between here and the Microsoft Campus in Redmond. When Antifa says 'the city,' it could mean anywhere. We have armed security at our clients' offices in the area. If two hundred anarchists clad in black storm one of them, there's not a lot we can do."

"That doesn't mean there isn't anything we can do. I imagine you have a couple of things in mind."

"That's what we need to talk about, counselor. Grab something to eat and let's get to it."

Drake loaded a small plate, poured a cup of coffee into a blue PSS mug and sat down next to Liz. She was nibbling on a scone of some kind and making a face when she looked at his plate with two peach fritters.

"What? It's an old army thing; eat when you can. You never know when you'll be able to eat again."

"I think that applies when you're on a battlefield. But go ahead and enjoy them. We'll go for a long run later."

"Do you get this at home, Mike?" Drake asked his friend sitting across the table.

"Megan doesn't care what I eat because I never gain weight. You, on the other hand…"

"All right you two, let me enjoy my fritters. What are you thinking of doing to protect our clients?"

"I bought a dozen long range acoustic devices (LRADs) from LRAD Corporation this summer after the Antifa activity in Portland. Eight of them are with security personnel at the offices of clients we think could be possible targets. The other four are on standby and ready to be deployed, if we need them."

LRADS were developed by the military as an acoustic weapon and used by law enforcement around the world for crowd dispersal.

"You know the NYPD was sued by some protesters and a couple of journalists who complained of headaches and hearing loss after a portable LRAD was used to break up a demonstration," Drake cautioned.

"I do. That's why we're discussing it."

"Do our clients know we're using LRADs? They'll be liable for any damage, same as us."

"They've all agreed to share the risk with us."

Liz raised her juice glass. "Are there other nonlethal ways to protect our clients?"

"There are. Our security guards have tear gas and Tasers, if they need them. But that means the anarchists get closer to our people than I want them to be when they use them."

Drake considered the variables and then provided his opinion. "The police are easy targets that juries love to punish. A private company that jurors know is local will be different. If we make sure the anarchists are warned in advance, and at a distance, and they proceed anyway, then it's on them. I say let's do it."

Casey's assistant knocked on the conference door and stuck his head in. "There's breaking news you need to see. The anarchists are rioting in downtown Seattle."

Casey stood up and walked to the cabinet beneath the TV flat screen and used the remote to turn on the news.

Cars were on fire in the downtown streets.

A breathless young female reporter was holding a microphone and looking into the camera. Over her shoulder, a line of cars was stopped in the middle of the street. People were abandoning them and fleeing to the sidewalks and into buildings.

"At the intersection of Pine and Fifth Avenue, a stalled car was set on fire. Four black clad protestors got out and started running back down the line of cars breaking windows with crowbars. There's

another burning car a block away blocking a way out. There's nowhere for these people to go. You can hear passengers trapped in their cars screaming for help," she reported.

Casey changed the channel. A reporter was describing a similar scene on First Avenue near the Pike Place Market.

"When people saw the protestors coming down the line of stalled cars toward them, smashing windows, they left their cars to run for safety. When the protestors reached those cars, they set them on fire as well. It looks like they're tossing Molotov cocktails into them. I count six cars burning on First Avenue," he reported.

The network switched to another of its reporters at a similar scene at Sixth Avenue and University. Cars stopped in the street, people running with burning cars at either end of the block; there was no way out of the trap.

"The police are cordoning off downtown Seattle wearing riot gear, but so far they're not advancing on the rioters. A spokesman at SPD headquarters has just announced that, as long as it's just property that's being destroyed, there's no need for any loss of life today."

Drake pounded the conference table with his fist and pushed his chair back. "That's just great. It's no wonder they act like this. They know they're not going to get hurt. It's people in their cars, getting their windows smashed, that might get hurt. What good's a police department if it won't take these bums on?"

Casey was still standing watching the live coverage of the riot. "This was coordinated and well planned. They've effectively locked up downtown and scared a lot of people. But what's the point? These aren't white supremacists they're terrorizing. They're just people. I don't get it."

Liz stood and carried her plate to the sidebar and poured herself another cup of coffee. "Maybe they just want to provoke a reaction. After you watch something like this, the other side will want to hit back."

Chapter Sixteen

ZAL NAZIR WAS STANDING at a window in the small upper bedroom in a secluded mountain chalet in Rhododendron, Oregon. He preferred the smaller bedroom upstairs because it provided a commanding view of the only road with ingress and egress to the property.

Technically, the chalet near Mount Hood belonged to the father of his number two, Bijan Jahandar. Bijan, or BJ as Nazir called him, was a commando in the Islamic Republic of Iran Army before leaving to enter America on a student visa. He was currently enrolled at Oregon State University, but his real role was to provide Nazir and the Council a military capability to the tech-savvy group.

BJ's uncle in Iran was Nazir's contact and the sponsor of the Council's terror activities.

Nazir's spotter had followed the FBI agent from the farm back to his apartment in Portland Sunday night. It hadn't taken him long to learn that Wayne Williams was the counterterrorist expert in the Portland Field Office of the FBI.

When the spotter had returned to his duties at the farm this morning, he found it swarming with FBI agents searching the place. They wouldn't find anything because it had been sanitized as soon as Umara and her fighters left on their disastrous mission to Portland. But now the FBI had found a link to him.

Now it was up to him, as leader of the Council, to derail the FBI investigation, if they were to continue their mission in America. The only way he could think of doing that was by killing the bulldog FBI agent who wouldn't let it go. The FBI had Professor Ahmadi in custody awaiting trial, and still Williams was continuing his investigation.

The problem was how to kill the man and not make things worse. His spotter had found that Williams lived in an apartment close to the FBI office, and it took less than five minutes to drive there every morning and every night. But the route was too short to effectively stage an accident that would guarantee a kill.

And to kill him outright while he was investigating the farm and its ownership would only expand the investigation to explain his death. There had to be a way to get rid of him in a way that could be blamed on someone with no ties to the Council or to himself.

That's why he was now thinking about calling Mason Bradley. He was planning to instigate a police raid on a Black Panther headquarters to provoke retaliation against law enforcement. There might just be a way to use the raid itself to eliminate FBI Special Agent Williams.

But his last meeting with Bradley had made him nervous about working too closely with him or his anarchist hooligans. He had to be careful, but he also had to move quickly. Bradley wanted to set up the raid to follow the rioting in Seattle.

The only way Nazir could think of to get the FBI involved was to convince Bradley the police in Portland were too concerned about overreacting and making things worse for the city. Portland and its mayor had recently told the police not to engage the anarchists. That hadn't stopped the killing in San Francisco, but in uber liberal Portland that didn't seem to matter. Antifa was defending the country from the Nazis, white supremacists, Jew hating KKKs and were justified in their anger and rage the liberals thought.

Bradley was in Portland for a series of lectures he was giving. Nazir had his number for a burner phone they used to communicate and called him.

"Do you have a minute?"

"There's someone here with me. Can this wait?"

"No, we need to talk."

Nazir heard Bradley tell someone to wait in the bedroom, he wouldn't be long.

"Make it quick. This hour is costing me plenty."

"I've been thinking about what you have planned for Wednesday. With the politics in Portland, I'm not sure we can count on the police to overreact the way we want. Their order not to engage the anarchists will make them be especially careful when they raid a Black Panther headquarters."

"I know that. What are you saying?"

"To get the result we want, we need a very aggressive raid in Portland."

"And you think the police won't go in hot. What's the alternative?"

"The FBI. I know just the hothead in the Portland field office to lead the charge."

"How do you know that?"

"I've been a Muslim informant for the FBI for the last year."

When Bradley didn't say anything, Nazir was afraid his second-guessing of Bradley's plan had gone too far.

"Fine. I'll give you the details tomorrow night. You can tip off the FBI the next morning."

"Consider it done. Enjoy your evening."

"I will, if I'm not interrupted again."

Chapter Seventeen

FBI SPECIAL AGENT WAYNE WILLIAMS had just returned to his desk from the FBI's Portland Field Office breakroom when his phone pinged with the arrival of a message.

At first, he thought it was a hoax. He had never received an anonymous tip during his career in the FBI and didn't have any idea why he would be receiving one now.

I saw you on TV with that terrorist guy at Hillsboro

Airport when he was arrested. Are you FBI counterterrorism?

I have information for you.

HOW DID **you get this number?**

THAT'S NOT IMPORTANT. **Do you handle terrorist things?**

WHAT'S THIS ABOUT?

. . .

PLEASE ANSWER ME.

YES, **I am. Now, why did you text me?**

I SUPPORT NONVIOLENT PROTEST, **but my group is going**
     somewhere I don't want to go. We're getting a bunch of
     AK-47s from some jihadist group around here tonight
     and sharing them with the Portland Black Panthers.

HOW DO YOU KNOW THIS?

I'M LEADERSHIP, **but I'm pulling out while I can. I can find**
     out where and when the weapons will be deliv-ered, if you
     promise me you'll be there to take them away.

WHY ME?

I WAS IN ST. **Patrick's when the terrorists came to attack**
     the church. I saw you outside afterwards. From what the

media reported, you're responsible for protecting me. I
    know you can handle this.

HOW DO **I know you're telling me the truth?**

YOU WON'T. **But I'll put you where you can witness the**
    delivery for yourself.

I'LL TALK **with the special agent in charge and get back to you.**

I'LL BE WAITING.

WILLIAMS SAT BACK and read the message again. He couldn't ignore it, but without a way to confirm any of it, he knew his SAC could, especially with the friction in the office he caused by working with Adam Drake to protect the Catholic churches after the field office had announced the case was closed.

What he did know was that Antifa was becoming more violent. In San Francisco they used knives to attack the Free Speech rally. In Seattle they were using Molotov cocktails to burn cars and crowbars to smash windows. If Antifa was taking the next step and arming itself and in some alliance with the Black Panthers, a lot of people were going to die.

Williams forwarded the text to his email account and printed out two copies. There wasn't anything he could add to the message itself. He would just have to trust the good judgement of the agent in charge of the office. He'd point out all the publicity the office would receive if they were able to keep a cache of AK-47s off the streets.

To his surprise, he returned to his desk an hour later in charge of organizing the office's Special Weapons and Tactics Team (SWAT) to determine if the AK-47 assault rifles were illegally being transported or sold in the country. If they were, the weapons would be seized and all those involved arrested.

A text message to the anonymous tipper confirmed that he would be waiting for information regarding the when and where of the weapons delivery.

———

ZAL NAZIR READ the text from the FBI agent and thanked Allah for the American's willingness to be deceived.

The meeting between Antifa in Portland and the Black Panthers had been arranged so that the two groups could unite to work together against their common enemy, the cops. Both groups wanted revenge, the Black Panthers for the unarmed blacks the cops kept killing and Antifa because cops enforced the laws of the "one percenters" and their oppressive government. It was a marriage of convenience and shared goals.

The meeting place had been carefully chosen. It would take place in the historic Albina district of Portland, home to the majority of Portland's African American population for most of the twentieth century.

In 1962, eighty percent of Portland's black populations lived in the area. In the seventies and eighties, the Crips and the Bloods began operating out of the area and families who could afford to moved out to escape the violence. In the nineties, Portland tried to revitalize the area with urban renewal, the resulting gentrification of the area tripling and quadrupling the values of the remaining old Victorian homes. Even more of the black population was forced to leave.

Now the black population hovered around twenty percent. But Albina was still the heart and soul of Portland's African American community.

A police raid against young black men there, even if they were Black Panthers who were unarmed when they were massacred, would demand that they be avenged. Nazir would make sure of that.

Add to that a few dead anarchists and you might get the spark that would ignite an uprising. At least that was the hope of Mason Bradley; anger in the hearts of the antifascist forces and the African American community would be the fuel for a raging civil war.

All of that was good, if it helped tear apart American civil society. All Nazir wanted was one dead FBI agent.

He called his number two, BJ. "The FBI agent is waiting for me to call him. Find a place to take your shot so that it looks like it's coming from the old house the Black Panthers are renting. When you've found a place, call me with the location of somewhere within range where the FBI can see everything.

"A van is going to pull up and stop in front of the house. When it does, kill the FBI agent first and take out a couple more of them if you want. I want them going in with guns blazing."

"Understood."

"Then come to the chalet and we'll watch it on TV. This will be fun, watching the FBI explain why they were there and why they killed innocent people. No one's going to pay much attention to one dead FBI agent who died in the raid."

Chapter Eighteen

THE FBI DROVE to northeast Portland at nine in the evening in two unmarked, dark blue Freightliner Sprinter cargo vans. Each van was driven by an agent in civilian clothes and carried eight FBI SWAT team agents wearing tactical gear.

The assistant special agent in charge rode shotgun in the first van and served as the on-scene commander. Special Agent Williams rode shotgun in the second van, waiting for his anonymous caller to make contact and give him the address where the weapons exchange would take place.

Williams had tried to get the address earlier, but the caller had warned that any police presence in the neighborhood, too much before the arrival of the weapons, would prevent the exchange from happening. The earliest he would be given the address would be just ten minutes before a white painting company van was scheduled to arrive. A good assembly location would be provided that was promised to be minutes away from the Black Panthers' house.

The hastily assembled plan would put the second van, with Williams in it, at the spot where he would be able to see the exchange take place. An agent from the Photographic Operations Unit would be with him to video the event. The

SWAT team would remain in the back of the cargo van until the weapons were unloaded and in the possession of the anarchists and Black Panthers.

The other cargo van would converge on the address and park close enough to remain out of sight but close enough to get a drone in the air to see how many of the anarchists and Black Panthers they might be dealing with. The surveillance drone was equipped with a thermal imaging camera. It would be able to identify the number of people in the house and tell if any of them were armed.

Without advance knowledge of the location of the house, the Photographic Operations Unit couldn't make an operational site survey that would have provided detailed venue information for a pre-surveyed and mapped scene of operation. With the site survey and more time, they could have planned and rehearsed a run-through for the raid. As it was, they were prepared to go in blind. Keeping the weapons off the street was worth the risk.

At nine fifty, Williams received a text message directing him to a street corner that was supposed to be half a block from the Black Panther house. With little time to spare, the second cargo van hurried to the spot while the other van drove around the block and approached from the other end of the street.

A rundown, dirty-white post-depression minimal tradition house sat in the middle of the block. An old brown Oldsmobile Tornado was parked in the driveway in front of its attached single-car garage. A late model baby-blue Honda Civic was parked at the curb in front of the house. Window shades were drawn, but there were lights on in the house.

Williams' position at the corner south of the house gave him an unobstructed view of the front and south-side exposures. The on-site commander would have a similar view from the corner north of the house.

"Thermal imaging from the drone shows ten people

inside," the on-site commander relayed over the tactical radios they were using. "They keep moving around, but it looks like most of them are armed."

The driver of the second cargo van saw a white van turn the corner a block away in his rearview mirror. "Looks like the delivery is right on schedule. White van headed our way."

Williams didn't turn his head to look. Ten seconds later, a white commercial van with Snyder Commercial Painting lettering down its side drove by and turned left toward the Black Panthers' house.

When it stopped, Williams raised his binoculars and watched the driver get out and walk to the rear of the van. He stood there without opening the rear panel doors, waiting for something.

"Come on," Williams said under his breath. "Let us see what you have in there."

The information they had was that AK-47s were being delivered, but they had no way of knowing if the assault rifles would be crated, wrapped in blankets or concealed in some other manner.

Two men came out the front door; a tall African American and a shorter man wearing a black hoodie walked to the curb. After a brief exchange with the driver, the African American walked around the driver and opened the two rear doors wide to look inside.

Williams could see boxes stacked inside, but he wasn't able to estimate the dimensions of any of them.

The tall black man at the rear of the van turned toward the house and signaled for someone inside to come out. Four men filed out and stood in line as boxes were handed out to them by the first two men.

The on-site commander gave the command, "Execute."

Eight FBI SWAT agents piled out of the cargo vans and ran down the street shouting, "FBI, get on the ground, get on the ground."

Williams followed the SWAT team from his cargo van. He wore the same tactical gear they did minus the helmet and the MP5s and M4A1s they carried. His 1911 .45 was held low in both hands.

He ran to keep up with the others but never got that far. A 168-gram .308 caliber bullet, traveling at 2,716 feet per second, hit him between the eyes, knocking him onto his back in the middle of the street.

When the crack of the shot that killed FBI Special Agent Williams was heard, the men unloading boxes from the van panicked. Drawing their guns, they fired wildly at the shouting men in tactical gear. When they did, pursuant to their rules of engagement, the SWAT team returned fire, killing all seven men at the rear of the white painting company van.

The four men, still inside the Black Panther's house, wisely marched out when ordered to do so with their hands above their heads.

It was only when the seven men were checked to see if an ambulance was needed, and the four others were restrained and face down on the front lawn, that the FBI agents had time to open the boxes from the van.

There were no weapons in any of them.

Chapter Nineteen

DRAKE RETURNED to their PSS suite at the Woodmark Hotel Thursday morning after a five-mile run along the shore of Lake Washington. Liz was standing at the foot of the bed watching the news.

She turned when she saw him and nodded in the direction of the TV screen. "All hell is breaking loose. The FBI raided a Black Panther house in Portland last night and killed seven men. Three men were unnamed Panthers, three were unnamed Portland Antifa and one was an innocent delivery driver. One FBI agent was killed. If you listen to these announcers, they all should be tried and hung for murder. They're saying this is just the type of fascist oppression Antifa is protesting against."

"It didn't take them long to come up with that narrative. Why did the FBI raid the Black Panthers?"

"It's not clear. The FBI hasn't released a statement yet."

"Well, I'm going to go take a shower. Order breakfast from room service if you want or we'll go downstairs when I finish."

Standing under the rain shower as the hot water relaxed his muscles, Drake thought about what a coalition of antifascist anarchists and new Black Panthers might mean for the country. Working together, as the darlings of the media that they were, law enforcement would be damned if they acted forcefully against them. Conversely, they would be called incompetent if they failed to push back against a storm surge of new violence.

With the FBI raid coming on the same day as the rioting in Seattle, he knew things were only going to get worse.

Drake had decided to stay in Seattle for the rest of the week before returning to Portland. He considered the time an extension of their short vacation and dressed casually; khaki pants, a dark blue polo and brown Sperry boat shoes.

He was delighted to see that Liz felt the same way and had on shorts, a lavender polo and sandals.

"I called down and reserved a table outside at the Beach Café. Let's go eat. Thinking of you running along the lake made me hungry."

Drake started to ask why that made her hungry but, instead, opened the door with a flourish. "Lead the way, my lady."

When they were seated on the deck of the Café with the morning sun shimmering off the surface of Lake Washington, he thought about the decision he would ultimately have to make about where he was going to live. His law practice was in Portland, but his expanding responsibilities for PSS required him to spend more of his time in Seattle each month. And that didn't factor in Liz, her new position at PSS and the condo she wanted to buy in Seattle.

After they both had ordered the market omelet, juice and coffee, Drake told Liz he needed to call Margo and see how she was getting along without him.

The sweet smile from Liz suggested that she already knew. Margo was doing just fine with him out of her hair.

He walked to the far end of the deck to make the call. "Good morning, Margo. Miss me?"

"Just a minute. Paul wants to talk to you."

Margo had been curt and a little cold since Paul started working out of the office as a private detective, but this was a new level of curtness.

"Morning, Adam. Liz and Margo have been in touch and I know you're in Seattle, so you might not have heard. Wayne Williams was the FBI agent killed last night."

Drake was stunned. "What in the world was he doing on a SWAT raid?"

"My friend in the Sheriff's Office talked with an FBI agent he knows. Wayne got an anonymous tip that AK-47s were to be delivered to a Black Panther house in Albina. The person said he'd seen Wayne on TV when you turned Ahmadi over to the FBI at the airport. Wayne was the only person the guy would talk with. He said he wouldn't provide the address of the exchange until ten minutes before it was going down. Wayne had to ride along with SWAT to direct them when he got the call."

"Someone wanted to make sure Wayne was on scene."

"That's what I'm thinking."

"Does the FBI think Wayne was set up?"

"They're not saying, but they have to have reached the same conclusion. There were no AK-47s, and the bullet that killed Wayne was a .308. The guns the dead guys had were all handguns, all nine millimeters."

"Do they have any leads?"

"Not that I've heard. I'm not sure how hard they're going to work this. They're throwing Wayne under the bus. They're blaming him for acting on a tip that got people killed."

"Yeah, including Wayne. The SAIC had to approve this. If he didn't think the tip was credible, why did he authorize the raid?"

"Great question, one that will never be answered. When are you coming home?"

"We were thinking of staying until the weekend. This changes the plan for me. I don't know what I can do there that

I can't do here, but this isn't right. Someone's responsible for Wayne's death. I'd like to know who it is."

"Let me know when you're headed back. I'll call if I hear anything new."

Drake put his phone in his pocket and took a minute, looking out over the lake, before returning to Liz. He knew she would tell him to go back to Portland if he thought he needed to. He also knew if he stayed in Seattle it wasn't going to be an extended vacation. He was already thinking of how he was going to find out who set his friend up.

He would let Liz decide if they stayed or not. She was a part of his life now, and he needed to stop making all the decisions on his own.

Chapter Twenty

NAZIR WATCHED the news on the morning shows to gauge the impact of the FBI raid and the narrative the media had generated. He was satisfied to see that several of the networks had adopted the phrase "Blue Revenge", a tagline that members of his Council had used on Facebook and Twitter the night before.

The Antifa groups were furious, of course, and claimed the fascist government had declared war. They pleaded with freedom loving Americans to take up arms and join the fight before it was too late.

The message wasn't new, but the level of anger was. In and of itself, it might not produce a civil war, but he knew how to fan the fire until it did.

He had decided it was time to leave the safety of the secluded chalet and return to work in Portland. With the FBI agent out of the way and the battering the FBI office was receiving from the media, he wasn't concerned about another FBI agent taking over the discredited Agent Williams' investigation anytime soon.

While he waited for BJ to drive from Portland to pick him up, he went online to give the order to launch the next wave of his planned media campaign. Council members, scattered around the country, were waiting to take down all the websites on the list of hate groups he had compiled. Local Antifa groups would claim responsibility. Then, to enrage the hate groups that lost their online presence, social media would be flooded with all manner of violent and fake revenge threats. If more was needed after that, Mason Bradley had promised to provoke a few more violent confrontations between the two sides.

Smart war, as he liked to think of it, was the antithesis of the bloody war being waged by ISIS. Instead of lifting a sword yourself, you caused the enemy to fight amongst itself and do it for you. The tactic was no different than that used by politicians, to divide the society into classes and promote the grievance of one class against another. Marx and Lenin did it, national socialists in Germany did it and progressive socialists in America were doing it too.

It was why he slowly put together a network of Muslim hackers and social media gurus he met at hacker conferences like DEF CON in Las Vegas, ShmooCon in Washington, D.C. and ToorCon in San Diego. After carefully vetting each of the twenty members of his "Council", to determine their Islamist leanings and if they had clean records, he had obliquely mentioned and sometimes praised the courage of the jihadists in conversation. When he felt a person was of a kindred spirit, he carefully explained his vision of a smarter way to defeat the West and asked if they wanted to join him.

There were now Council members in nine major cities across America, working with him completely under the radar. They all had good jobs and were loyal appearing young Americans. They had no known associations with radical mosques, imams or Muslim organizations with ties to jihadist groups.

They were the perfect twenty-first century cyber guerillas

with the skills to wage a clandestine war against the leader of the West, America.

Nazir's phone chirped to announce the arrival of a new message.

PASSING THROUGH RHODODENDRON, **arriving in ten. Dagger**

Nazir responded.

Ready and waiting. Wrath

Wrath was his online handle and he felt it suited him perfectly. BJ wasn't technically a member of the Council because of his limited hacking skill. But he'd been given a handle that fit him, as well; there was a dagger in the patch Iranian Marine commandos wore.

Nazir carried his duffel bag down to the front door and returned to the bedroom upstairs to watch for BJ. Before he started down the driveway from the road, BJ flashed the head-lights three times to show that he wasn't being followed. It was a little cloak and dagger, but BJ insisted on being careful.

Nazir opened and closed the curtains to signal for BJ to approach and went downstairs to open the door to greet him.

"Would you like something to eat or a cup of coffee before we head back?"

BJ rolled his shoulders and rotated his head to relieve muscle tension as he entered. "Coffee would be fine, if it's made. We need to leave as soon as you are ready."

"What's the rush? I want to hear all about last night."

"I would like to get back before dark. I need to take care of something."

Nazir led him into the kitchen and poured them both a cup of coffee from a Yeti thermos he'd prepared for the drive to Portland.

"What is it you need to take care of? You've earned the night off, BJ."

"I wish that was true. I think a neighbor of the Black Panthers' house may have seen me when I returned to my car. My Siyavash rifle was in its carrying case and he wouldn't have been able to tell what it was. But he saw me. I stole the car I drove, so that's not an issue. I need to make sure he doesn't have a chance to tell the police he saw me."

Nazir leaned back against the counter and considered the opportunity. "Is the man black?"

"Black, forty maybe and heavy. He lives two streets over from the Black Panthers' house.

I took the shot from the second floor of an abandoned house that was boarded up and directly behind the Panthers' house. I left by an alley at the rear of the house. He saw me later when I crossed the street to my car that was parked in front of his house."

"How do you plan on keeping him from talking to the police?"

"I don't know yet. I don't know where or if he works, when he comes and goes or what's the best way to get to him without being seen again in that neighborhood. I just know I don't have a lot of time to figure it out."

"Then I suggest we get moving."

Chapter Twenty-One

BY FRIDAY MORNING IN SEATTLE, it was back to business as usual for most residents. The chaos and confusion seen on television two days before, of cars burning and people running for safety, were ugly images best forgotten and remembered as an unfortunate anomaly that happened from time to time in places like the Emerald City.

For the city's Black Panthers, the only ugly image they remembered was the sight of the dead bodies of their black Portland brothers on the ground. The camera crews had been on the scene so early that the FBI hadn't even had time to cover the bloody evidence of its raid.

Isaac Newton's third law says that for every action there is an equal and opposite reaction. Huey Newton, the co-founder of the original Black Panthers, would have stated the law differently; for every black man killed by a cop there will be a cop killed by a black man. It was a right of nature to defend yourself, and they had cowered for too long under the jackboot of the police.

Seattle Police Department's East Precinct was located in the old Central District of the city. It was formerly the center of the city's black community and culture. But now many black families couldn't afford to live there and had moved away. The hood wasn't what it used to be, but it was the right place to raise a fist and strike back.

At shift change that morning, when the cops were coming and going, two jacked-up SUVs drove past the precinct at Fifteen Thirty Twelfth Avenue and fired at every cop in sight with blazing AK-47s. A third SUV followed and lobbed Molotov cocktails under police cruisers on the street, setting four of them on fire.

Three police officers were killed in the drive-by shooting, several more were wounded, and the burning cruisers prevented police from chasing the SUVs in time to apprehend the perpetrators.

———

IN PORTLAND, Police Sergeant Martin Neely and his partner, Officer Richard Watson, were on patrol in Kings Heights when a man with a rifle was reported walking toward Lincoln High school. The high school was quickly put on lockdown and Neely and Watson were dispatched to investigate, along with every other available unit in west Portland.

Lincoln High School was established in 1869 as Portland High School and had more National Merit scholarship semifinalists than any other high school in the state. The enrollment was seventy-four percent white, nine percent Asian, seven percent Latino and five percent African American.

Sergeant Neely approached the high school from the west on SW Salmon Street and pulled to the curb at the intersection with SW Fifteenth Avenue. Another cruiser was stopped a half a block away at the corner of SW Salmon and SW Fourteenth Avenue.

Neely and Watson stepped out and searched the area for the man with the rifle.

With their backs turned to traffic coming south down SW

Fifteenth Avenue, they didn't hear the speeding pickup approaching from the north until it slid to a stop behind them. When they turned to wave the pickup back up the street, they were surprised to see the barrels of two rifles thrust out the open windows on each side, pointed at them.

Before they had a chance to react, both men were cut down by bullets from two AK-47s. The pickup then turned right, going the wrong way on SW Salmon until it turned right again on SW Fourteenth Avenue and sped away.

———

IN OAKLAND, California, Assistant Chief of Police Anthony Brooks was one step away from the job he'd coveted since joining the Oakland Police Department twenty-eight years ago. His career had been a slow and steady climb to the top but was blocked at the moment by a woman. She didn't have his experience or his reputation as a no-nonsense tough cop.

He understood the politics of being appointed assistant chief of police in a large metropolitan police department. He'd honed his skills over the years to become an eloquent public speaker as well as a recognized leader and crafty politician in the Oakland black community.

He lived in the wealthy neighborhood of Seqouyah Hills and belonged to the prestigious Seqouyah Country Club, with other wealthy black businessmen, entertainers and professional athletes. His nineteen seventies ranch-style home had a market value of a million three, and his personal ride was a black Mercedes AMG GLE S, with a biturbo V8, that would outrun any cruiser in the department.

At the moment, that black beauty was parked safely in his garage. He was driving a new Ford Taurus Police Interceptor from the motor pool on his way to speak to a Rotary Club about the rising crime rate in the city.

Assistant Chief Brooks was met at the front door and

escorted to the banquet room, where two hundred and thirty concerned Rotarians were waiting for him to speak. They were mostly white, and friendly, judging by the smiles and waves he received on the way to the head table. Friendly or not, they were not going to like hearing the latest crime statistics in Oakland and what the city council and the chief of police were preventing the department from doing about it.

Brooks sat down and asked for a glass of water while the club's president finished giving the announcements. When he felt a tap on his shoulder and turned, it wasn't a hotel attendant with a glass of water standing behind him.

It was an Oakland Police Department detective telling him to excuse himself and come with him.

They left the banquet room through a side door where Assistant Chief of Police Brooks learned that his home in Seqouyah Hills had been fire bombed fifteen minutes ago and was a total loss.

Neighbors had reported seeing a car roaring up the driveway and seeing three black men jump out to lob Molotov cocktails through the front windows of the house.

Chapter Twenty-Two

DRAKE BORROWED a PSS Yukon to drive back to Portland after breakfast. He had declined Casey's offer to fly them home in the PSS Gulfstream and decided they could use the three-hour drive to make plans for the coming weeks. The moving van bringing Liz's belongings, after she had cleaned out her condo in Washington, was scheduled to arrive next week. Drake had offered to let her use the building behind his farmhouse to store her things for as long as she wanted.

The building had been designed to serve as the vineyard's tasting room and small-production winery. The previous owner had lost interest in growing grapes on the old and established vineyard after a year and moved back to the East Coast. The tasting room and winery had never been finished, and the building was only used now to shelter Drake's old Porsche, his old pickup and tractor.

The real estate market in Seattle was red hot at the time and Liz wasn't in a hurry to buy another condo when she didn't know for sure what the future held for the two of them.

He knew they would work things out when it was time.

But now all he could think about doing was finding out who was responsible for the death of Wayne Williams.

"Liz, is there anyone else in the Portland Field Office you know well enough to ask for a copy of Wayne's notes about this anonymous tip?"

"Even if I did, and I don't, that's not something that anyone who wants to keep their job would give me. There will be an internal investigation, but whatever it discovers isn't likely to be made public."

"What do you think? Was Wayne the kind of agent who would ask for a SWAT raid without a good reason?"

"I worked with Wayne on a couple of terrorist things at DHS, but he was never directly involved in the planning or execution of the operations. He was a thinker and a by-the-book agent who was one of the best counterterrorism experts in the FBI.

"A kid brother of his was killed in Afghanistan three years ago. He vehemently opposed the plan to withdraw troops from the region. He let his opposition be known, a little too publicly, and was called to testify before a senate committee questioning the president's withdrawal plan. That's why he was transferred to Portland."

"But why would he be involved in something out of his area of expertise? He wasn't investigating Antifa or the Black Panthers, as far as I know. When I talked with him when we were in Hawaii, he was trying to identify the owner of the farm where he thought Umara and her terrorists had camped out. He didn't mention that he was working on anything else."

Liz turned and looked at Drake for a long moment as she evaluated a thought she'd just had. "Is it possible Wayne thought there might a connection between the AK-47s to be delivered that night and the AK-47s Umara and the women got their hands on?"

Drake shrugged his shoulders. "If he did, it might explain why he wanted to be involved in the raid. But it doesn't explain why he was the one to receive the anonymous tip. Unless … unless someone thought he was getting close to identifying the owner of the farm and used the tip about AK-47s to set him up."

"That's a theory that will be hard to sell. The FBI office would like to bury its lack of involvement in the whole Umara affair."

"Who said anything about trying to sell the theory to the FBI?"

"We can't do this ourselves, Adam. We don't know if Wayne was getting close to finding out who owns that farm. Where would we start?"

"With Wayne's notes. You said there would be an internal investigation into the raid and his death. Who gets to see the investigation report? Anyone outside the FBI?"

"DHS might get a copy, if it requested one. Domestic terrorism is its biggest concern and the Black Panthers are on its domestic terrorist list."

"Do you still have friends at DHS?"

"I do, but if I can't get a copy that way your father-in-law could probably get us one."

Drake leaned over and squeezed her knee. "We make a pretty good team, Ms. Strobel."

"I thought you knew that a long time ago, Mr. Drake."

He saw that they were approaching the outskirts of Olympia, Washington's state capital, and knew they had another hour and a half before they reached Portland. They might be cutting their vacation short, but it didn't mean they had to miss all the sights along the way.

"Have you been to Olympia? I know it's not Washington, D.C., but it has a nice capital building. There's a great seafood restaurant on the waterfront with a fantastic wine list. Care to take a side trip with me?"

"You've shown me around Seattle, so why not Olympia? I'd love to see the capital of my new home state."

For the next three hours they walked around the State Capitol Campus. They strolled along the boardwalk at Percival Landing Park while they waited for the table they reserved at the Dockside Bistro and Wine Bar.

They were squeezing every last ounce of pleasure out of the time left in their vacation. Despite everything going on, it didn't mean they had to stop smelling every rose they encountered.

Chapter Twenty-Three

WHILE DRAKE WORKED on the files his secretary had stacked up on his desk while he was vacationing, Liz spent the morning at Senator Hazelton's Portland office saying goodbye to his staff. On his behalf, she had also requested that the FBI's file on the Black Panthers' house raid be sent over, complete with all the notes from Special Agent Williams about the anonymous tip and anything else the agent was investigating.

The special agent in charge of the Portland field office acquiesced in the request, only after receiving a terse phone call from the director of national intelligence himself, ordering the file to be delivered to Senator Hazelton's office immediately. The DNI oversaw all of the FBI's intelligence gathering activities. After a call from Senator Hazelton, who chaired the Senate Select Committee on Intelligence and suggested there might be a foreign intelligence angle involved, the SAIC had done the prudent thing.

Liz arrived at Drake's office just before lunch with the FBI file. She offered to take him to lunch but only if Margo and her husband, Paul, could come along. Drake suspected that the invitation was just a ploy to get a chance to talk with

Margo while he was occupied talking with Paul about Agent Williams' death.

He didn't mind. It was going to happen one way or another, and he was better off knowing what they were talking about. Liz had mentioned that she was concerned that Margo was going to resent being alone so much of the time when he was in Seattle.

With the men in tow, Liz and Margo led the way on the short walk to the restaurant at the Kimpton RiverPlace Hotel where she'd made a reservation for lunch.

"Did you see the news this morning?" Benning asked.

"I watched it for a bit in the loft, after Margo told me about the cops being killed."

"The assistant chief of police in Oakland just had his home fire bombed. No one was hurt, but the house is destroyed."

"What are you hearing from your friends in the Sheriff's Office?"

"The new Black Panthers are claiming responsibility, saying it's retaliation for the FBI raid here."

Drake looked across the river toward the Albina district in northeast Portland, where the raid took place, and shook his head. "Black Panthers might have pulled the triggers and thrown the fire bombs, but someone else is stirring things up, if we're right about Williams being set up. What I can't fathom is why. What does anyone gain by turning the Panthers loose on the police?"

"Have you read about the original Black Panthers in the seventies?" Benning asked. "Back then, they were working with the Weatherman to start a Marxist-style revolution in America. When the Weatherman started fading away and became the Weather Underground, a splinter cell of the East Coast Panthers in New York started killing cops, trying to start a black revolution to overthrow the government."

"So you think Antifa and the new Black Panthers could be teaming up to start a revolution?"

"That's what a couple Antifa websites are promoting."

"It's not going to happen, Paul. There's no public support for overthrowing the government."

Benning patted Drake's shoulder. "Depends on whose government you're talking about. Half the country seems to be prepared to do just about anything to get rid of the new president."

"But that half isn't going to take up arms to do it."

"Maybe they won't have to. Black Matter protestors are being paid to show up whenever a black man is killed by a cop. Maybe Antifa and these anarchist groups are being funded as well. Get enough people feeling that they have a fascist and oppressive government and who knows what could happen."

Liz and Margo were standing on the veranda, waiting to be shown to their table, when the two stragglers caught up to them.

"Paul, have you ever noticed how fast women walk when they don't want to be overheard?" Drake said, loudly enough to make sure both women heard him.

"It was for your own good," Margo said, turning round. "We had some catching up to do and wanted to talk about some new ground rules for you men. There was no need for you to be a part of the conversation."

Drake just smiled and said, "Rules are made to be broken."

Margo stuck her finger in her husband's chest. "Don't listen to him, sugar, 'cause you better not even think about breaking these rules."

The hostess stood waiting with their menus when Drake bowed his head and motioned for Liz to lead the way. When the women walked on ahead, he whispered to Benning, "Do you know what your wife's talking about?"

"Why do you think it's my wife? Liz set this up. What do you think she's talking about?"

"Not a clue, but I think we'll find out shortly."

When they were seated on the veranda, with an excellent view of the city's waterfront, and had ordered lunch, they found out.

Margo took the lead. "You're both precious to us and we only want what's best for you. With that in mind, and wanting to keep you happy and healthy, here are the new rules. Cases that might be dangerous, for either or both of you, will require a majority vote, since you're both working out of the same office and usually on the same case. We each have one vote after we've had time to evaluate the new case. To make sure that you're fit and rested enough to take on said possibly dangerous cases, you'll be taking each of us on a two-week vacation every three months."

Drake tried to read Liz's mind. He knew Margo well enough to know Paul didn't have a choice. He also remembered thinking maybe it was time to stop winging it alone, if he wanted to make it work with Liz. It wasn't like she was going to be his partner or anything. She'd just be there to make sure he didn't act too impulsively and get involved in things that were better left to others.

"Sounds all right to me, Margo, if you think you can clear the calendar for two weeks every three months."

As the women high-fived, Drake winked at Paul. "It could have been worse."

Paul leaned close and whispered, "But you don't know all the places she wants to see. I just lost the boat I was going to buy to go salmon fishing."

Chapter Twenty-Four

AFTER A FINE LUNCH and sending Liz and Margo shopping for clothes suitable for working in the vineyard, Drake got down to business and started through the FBI's file on the raid.

The report about the raid was carefully crafted to demonstrate that the Portland Field Office had been suspicious about the anonymous tip from the get-go. Voice recordings from the calls made to Agent Williams' phone in his office and his cell phone, when he was at the scene of the raid, were compared to recordings of known Antifa members. The few informants the FBI had within the anarchist and Antifa movements were hastily contacted and asked about anyone in leadership of Antifa having had second thoughts about some delivery of AK-47s for the revolution. Nothing supporting the tip that there was going to be a weapons delivery was ever discovered.

In the end, the special agent in charge was left with the unfortunate choice of believing his experienced counterterrorist expert. The FBI could attempt to keep the weapons out of the hands of Antifa and the Black Panthers or ignore the tip and risk the lives of countless residents of the city.

There was nothing in the report that attempted to explain

why the autopsy found that Williams had been killed by a .308 bullet when none of the guns carried by any of the seven killed, nor any that were found in the Black Panthers' house, was a .308 caliber rifle.

If anyone in the Portland Field Office suspected that Agent Williams had been set up, they were not identified or mentioned in the report. Further investigation of Agent Williams' murder was, of course, ongoing, but nothing had been found that suggested his death was anything other than an unfortunate fatal agent shooting.

Because the investigation of the terrorist attacks on the Catholic churches was closed, there was nothing that referenced the finding that both Umara, the lead terrorist, and Agent Williams were killed by a .308 caliber bullet. It was the round commonly used by snipers the world over.

Agent Williams' notes regarding the anonymous tip and the raid didn't provide any information that wasn't included in the Field Office report. He hadn't expected that there would be. The Field Office report was prepared after the raid to minimize culpability for the deaths of seven innocent civilians.

Drake was looking for something else, though; a reason for Williams being set up. He thought he would find it in the agent's ongoing investigation of the ownership of the farm, but Williams hadn't made much progress by the time he was killed. The last entry, though, made the day before he was killed, recommended investigating local used car dealers suspected of selling stolen vehicles with altered vehicle identification numbers. Examination of the VINs on the three terrorists' vans had revealed all the VINs were cloned. It was something Williams had never mentioned.

Beginning his career in the District's Attorney's Office, Drake had prosecuted Class C felony cases for the unauthorized use of a vehicle. Several of them had involved VIN cloning, where the car thief had either taken a VIN from a recently salvaged vehicle in a junk yard or counterfeited a

VIN using a computer, typewriter and a barcode label printer.

The victims of these low-level felonies involved not only the owners of the stolen vehicles but the buyers who bought the vehicles and that included used car dealers. From the police reports in a couple of the cases, he knew there were used car dealers suspected of knowingly buying vehicles with cloned VINs and bogus certificates of title obtained from the DMV.

Drake called down to Benning, who was using Margo's desk to finish a report while she was out shopping with Liz. "Detective Benning, got a minute? I need your help with something."

Benning came upstairs to the loft with a quizzical look on his face. "I don't remember you ever calling me Detective Benning. What's up?"

"The day before Wayne was killed, he was investigating the identity of the owner of the farm where one of the terrorists took a selfie. He made a note to investigate local used car dealers because the VINs on the vans the three terrorists drove were cloned. How would you go about finding the used car dealers who sold these vehicles?"

Benning sat down and thought for a moment. "You clone a VIN to conceal that the vehicle is stolen or has damage you don't want the buyer to know about. Used car dealers can buy a car and not know the VIN was cloned or they can buy the car knowing or suspecting that it's stolen and has a cloned VIN. Those two categories include a lot of local used car dealers. I'm not sure where you would start unless you just canvassed them all, and who has the manpower for that?"

"What if you narrowed the search to just used car dealers suspected of selling stolen vehicles with cloned VINs?"

"What are you thinking?"

"Someone bought three old vans that were used to get the terrorists to the Catholic churches for the attacks. Maybe the vans were purchased from the same used car dealer and maybe that used car dealer can tell us who he sold them to. It's possible, but not probable, that someone bought three vans from different dealers and they all just happened to have cloned VINs."

"I agree, but how are you going to get the police or the Sheriff's Office to question suspected used car dealers? The FBI isn't going to help, it closed the case."

"We're not going to ask them to question anyone. We're going to do it ourselves. Ask someone you know in the Sheriff's Office, Detective Benning, to identify local used car dealers suspected of selling stolen vehicles with cloned VINs. Wayne had a hunch and I want to see if he was right."

Chapter Twenty-Five

ZAL NAZIR WAS on the balcony of his apartment, resting his forearms on the railing and watching two women sunbathing down at the pool below. There might never be a time when he could ever allow a woman to know him very well, but, for now, the lush offerings for casual mating were more than enough to keep him satisfied.

He was waiting for members of the Council to report in. Over the weekend, every fascist website he could identify would be hit with a cyberattack that would lock up the site and demand a ransom to unlock it. The ransom would never be paid because it was set ridiculously high and would be offensive to any red-blooded American patriot group. The ransom that would be demanded was ten million dollars from each group, to be paid to a specific and well-known liberal organization—The LGBT Alliance, Black Power, the American Communist Party, the American Green Party or the Jewish Anti-Defamation League.

If the websites were quickly replaced by similar websites, they would be just as quickly locked up and the ransom doubled. With no way to communicate with its members, the only recourse the groups would have would be to retaliate against the obvious parties they felt were responsible for the cyberattacks.

To make sure they went after the right "obvious" parties, the Council's hackers and skilled social engineers had developed fake social media postings that were designed to press each ransomed group's hot button.

What a sweet way to fight a war, Nazir thought as he went inside to wait for BJ to arrive. His commando assistant had wanted to fire bomb the Black Panthers' neighbor's home while he was sleeping to make sure he didn't identify him to the FBI.

Nazir had suggested something a little different but with the same result. He still had the drone used to bomb the mosque and more of the PE8 plastic explosive. If the neighbor hadn't talked with the police, it wouldn't make any difference if he accidentally died in a house fire or was intentionally murdered by a bomb dropped on his house. If he had talked to the police, he wouldn't be around to testify at trial.

Nazir checked his laptop and saw the other members of the Council were all reporting they had successfully shut down each of the websites assigned to them.

He thought about letting Mason Bradley know, but he knew it was smarter to keep the communication with him to a minimum. Bradley was brilliant, in his own way, and effective in dealing with Antifa and the protesters. But Nazir wasn't convinced that he was as careful as he should be. Bradley was more interested in drinking and womanizing than being a disciplined revolutionary.

BJ arrived on time and declined the beer he was offered. He'd been out practicing with the drone all afternoon and was anxious to learn how to attach the bomb and release it on the neighbor's roof.

Nazir told him to sit at the kitchen table and went to his bedroom to get another of the bombs he'd had the bomb maker in Los Angeles make after the successful bombing of the mosque. He came back carrying it in a shoebox.

When he set it down on the table, BJ sat back and stared at the shoebox. "Is that it?"

Nazir nodded and opened the shoebox. He took out a black polymer box the size of an old-fashioned cigar box. "This is much nicer than the one I was provided. Have you worked with explosives?"

"Just breeching charges, not heavier ordinance."

"This plastic explosive is very stable and very powerful. There's just enough PE8 in this to level the neighbor's house without taking out the houses around it. You attach the polymer box to the mount under the drone the same way you fix a laser under the barrel of an AK-47. You'll feel it snap into place when it's secure. Hit the release button on your controls and the mount will open and release the bomb. It's really very simple."

BJ picked up the polymer box gently and inspected it. "What if the bomb doesn't release?"

"Fly it back and we'll find out why it didn't. Until you use the burner phone to detonate the bomb, it's harmless."

BJ put the bomb back in the shoebox. "Is there anything else I need to know?"

"No, that's it. Where will you launch the drone?"

"From the abandoned house I used to shoot the FBI agent."

"Afterward, take the drone to our safehouse here. We'll keep it there until the next time we use it."

BJ stood and picked up the shoebox.

"Go with Allah's protection, BJ."

"Insha`Allah, Nazir."

Nazir prayed that Allah did indeed will the success of BJ's mission and eliminate the only person they knew who could provide the FBI with evidence that led back to them.

Chapter Twenty-Six

IT BEGAN where some say it started.

Portland, Oregon had a well-earned reputation as the most politically violent city in the nation. On November 10, 2016, three days after the election of the new president, anarchists split off from a group of peaceful anti-Trump protesters and started a riot. Damage resulting from the rioters' baseball bats and thrown rocks was estimated to exceed one million dollars. One hundred twenty anarchists were arrested; fewer than ten of them were from Portland and only thirty-one claimed to have voted in the election.

In April of 2017, the famous annual Rose Festival parade down 82nd Avenue was canceled. Two Antifa groups had pledged to protest and disrupt the parade because the Multnomah County Republican Party would be in the parade. An anonymous email had been sent to the parade organizers demanding that the Republican Party's participation be canceled or else. The demand was said to be nonnegotiable.

The Grand Floral Parade had proceeded down the 82nd Avenue parade route as part of the city's Rose Festival every year since 1907.

Patriot groups and militias in the Northwest had refrained,

for the most part, from taking on the black-clad anarchists head on. But when the ransomware cyberattacks that took down their websites and social media posts taunted them, they'd had enough.

While the anarchists hid behind black hoodies and masks and withheld their last names from reporters, arrest records provided enough information and verified addresses that identified over two hundred of them in the Northwest alone.

Four-men teams were dispatched to the homes and apartments of identified anarchists in Portland, and later in Seattle, Friday night. They wore white balaclava ski masks and hunting jackets and carried baseball bats that they used when they broke doors down and beat anarchists until they were unconscious. Witnesses, who were not called out by name, were told to watch and learn. One witness reported a fascist said to her, "You want a war, you got one."

Eighty-five anarchists were beaten and rushed to the nearest emergency rooms. Four of them died there. Those who were able to talk could only report the number of the attackers involved in each beating and what they were wearing. The only words spoken by the bat-waving fascists were when they asked the anarchists what their names were. If it was the person they were looking for, not another word was said and the beating began.

The next morning, the media threw gasoline on the fire when it accused the president and his followers of being responsible for the reprehensible violence. One talking head was so incensed that, in a spit-laden on-air tirade, he shouted, "You people elected a fascist, what did you expect would happen?"

There were calls for all patriot and white nationalist groups to be disbanded and declared to be domestic terrorist groups. Vocal politicians, shocked by the violent response to the anarchists who had rioted in their cities, wanted every member of the so-called hate groups arrested on suspicion of being involved in the beatings and a conspiracy to commit murder.

While those who were sympathetic and supported the anarchists and protesters screamed for something to be done, there was no mention in the media of the ransomware cyber-attacks and the fake and inflammatory social media postings. Drake and Liz watched the news coverage Saturday morning after a morning run while they had breakfast on the farm in Dundee.

Drake got up to refill their coffee cups, shaking his head. "This is the way a civil war starts, a divided nation that can't agree on anything. And politicians, who curry favor with one side or the other to get reelected, do nothing and the good of the nation be damned."

Liz held her cup up for Drake to refill. "I'm interested in seeing what DHS does to deal with this. When I was there, as the director's executive assistant, we published a report just after the previous president was elected on "Rightwing Extremism". It was widely criticized as an attack on conservative ideologies because it included opponents of abortion groups and uncontrolled immigration. We elected to quiet the uproar by cutting back our staff that dealt with the militias and antigovernment groups. In hindsight, that was probably a mistake."

Drake sat down across from her. "Was there any attention paid to the anarchist groups or was it just about rightwing extremists? Because this anarchist violence isn't new, the protests and riots in Seattle at the World Trade Organization meeting were way back in 1999. There were forty thousand protesters then, and the governor had to call in the National Guard to restore order. It'd be nice to know the government's prepared because the numbers could be a lot bigger this time."

Liz just shook her head. "Since the disaster in Waco, local

law enforcement has had to deal with it. No administration wants to have something like that happen again."

Drake finished his pancake and got up to clear the table. "Let's hope it doesn't have to. Since I see you're wearing your new work clothes, why don't I show you what it's like to be a grape farmer after I clean the kitchen? You may find that it's not your cup of tea."

Liz stood and pushed up the sleeves of her new plaid shirt. "Lead the way, Farmer Drake. I'm anxious to see if it's as hard as you grape farmers make it out to be."

Drake turned around to put their dishes in the dishwasher with a smile on his face. He was just as anxious to see how his city girl handled getting her hands dirty. If he kept the farm and stayed in Oregon, there would always be hard work to do. It would be nice if they could do some of it together.

Chapter Twenty-Seven

TWENTY-FIVE MILES north of Drake's farm outside Dundee, Oregon, Zal Nazir was watching the news in his condo. He was satisfied with the coverage of the attacks on the anarchists in the Northwest. The ransomware cyberattacks and social media provocations had worked exactly as planned.

The next phase was being handled by Mason Bradley. Patriot and fascist groups around the country were heading to the Northwest for rallies in Oregon and Washington and marches to the capitols in both states. The events were being called "Patriots United 2017" and they were asking freedom-loving Americans, who wanted their country back, to march and stand with them.

Antifa and the anarchists would be waiting for them and they wouldn't be carrying just baseball bats any longer. Bradley was spreading enough of the Russian's money around for the groups to arm themselves with the favorite weapons of revolutionaries the world over, AK-47s. They were weapons you could learn to use quickly and they didn't require sniper accuracy to be effective. Just the sight of them being carried by the anarchists would probably be enough to start the gunfight.

There wasn't much he could do to help at this point, but he was determined to help Bradley in any way he could.

Nazir called the number that only he and Bradley used. "How can I help?"

"I have it handled."

"Would it help to have aerial surveillance? You know the police will."

"You mean with a drone like you used in LA?"

"Or one like it."

"If the police don't recognize it as one of theirs, won't they shoot it down?"

It was his turn to say, "I've got it handled. The drones used by law enforcement are vulnerable and there are several ways they can be hacked. We can force any drone the police put up to crash or land."

"It will help to have eyes in the sky. Do you need money to accomplish that?"

"If you want to share some of the money you're getting, I'll take it."

"Tell me where to send it and it's yours."

"On the way. We'll need to figure out how to get the surveillance intel to your protest leaders."

"They'll have radios. I'll supply you with one to use. Anything else?"

"No."

"I'll be in touch."

When the call ended, Nazir returned to watching the news. Reporters were interviewing members of Congress and asking what they expected, if they expected anything at all, to be done by the president about the escalating violence.

One outspoken Congressman, who repeatedly criticized the president, was happy to answer. "We're not hopeful, to tell you the truth. He's been heard to say cities that coddled the anarchists have themselves to blame. He fails to recognize the anti-fascist protests as legitimate free speech."

It just couldn't be any better than this, he thought. *Both sides refusing to acknowledge their roles in the unrest made the job so easy. Tear yourself apart, America. The world is watching to see you fall.*

When the channel switched to local news, a young reporter was standing across the street in front of the smoldering remains of a house.

"Police believe the explosion that occurred last night
was caused by a bomb. Arson investigators tell us they've
ruled out a natural gas explosion. Fifty-eight-year old
Leroy Evans lived alone and died in an explosion that
happened just two blocks away from the Black Panthers'
house that was raided by the FBI. Neighbors of his say he
didn't have any involvement with the Black Panthers, but
the police are investigating the possibility. This is Alicia Cook
for KGW Portland."

"Well done, BJ, well done," Nazir said out loud. "You deserve a reward and I have just the thing for you, my friend."

The fascist rallies were planned for the Labor Day weekend and it would give BJ a whole week to keep practicing with the drone.

Nazir grabbed a Red Bull out of the refrigerator and took his laptop to the small desk in his bedroom. He would need two or three more drones to monitor the marches and brothers to operate them. And he would need people to hack the police drones and keep them out of the air. He'd have to estimate the number of police drones on the high side, to be safe, and then buy the devices he needed. They were readily available and would allow them to exploit the radio signal protocol that remotely controlled the consumer drones used. With that, they could take control of the police drones and put them on the ground.

Nazir made a list of the needed Council members, selecting those in the closest states, and sent them an encrypted invitation to join him for the Labor Day festivities. He didn't need to spell out the reason for the invitation, they would come without question. They were the new generation of jihadists and they were as eager to join the battle as any jihadist in Iraq or Afghanistan.

They were just doing it in a new and smarter way, using the cyber weapons at their disposal just like the big boys.

With the neighbor who saw BJ the night of the FBI raid and the FBI agent both dead, he didn't to need worry any longer. Getting involved with the ISIS plan to hit churches had been a mistake, but it was a lesson learned. The old tactics ISIS used were not going to bring down America.

But letting America tear itself apart, the crippled giant of the West would have to leave Muslims alone in the world and focus on rebuilding itself.

They still had a way to go, but America was lending a helping hand.

Chapter Twenty-Eight

PAUL BENNING RETURNED from the Multnomah County Sheriff's Office Saturday morning with a list of used car dealers who were suspected of selling stolen cars. He also had a confusing bit of information a fellow detective had mentioned when he stuck his head into his office to say hello.

Captain Michael McCluskey was a twenty-year veteran officer in the department. In his career, he'd attended a ten-week FBI Academy training program at Quantico, Virginia, designed to promote professionalism in law enforcement departments around the country. With the contacts he'd made in the FBI while attending the Academy, he became the officer that coordinated joint operations with the FBI and kept the peace between the rival agencies.

When he was asked how things were going with the FBI's Portland Field Office, McCluskey had told him to shut the door.

"Did you hear about the guy over in Albina who was killed when his house was bombed?"

"Just what was in the news."

"The FBI said they were looking into any connection the guy may have had with the Black Panthers. That's BS and they know it. What they're trying to figure out is how the plastic explosive that was used turns out to be the same plastic explosive used to bomb that mosque in Los Angeles a week or so ago."

"So why mention that he might be connected to the Black Panthers?"

"Because, in a way, he might be, just not in a way they want the public to know about.

"I don't understand."

"The neighbor lived two blocks away from the Black Panther house. He saw someone on his street he thought looked suspicious when he came out to see what was going on. He reported it to the FBI the next morning."

"Why was he suspicious of the guy he saw?"

"He was a Marine. He said the guy was carrying a case that might have had a rifle in it."

"Like a rifle that could have been used to kill FBI Agent Williams."

"Exactly. It gets better, depending on how you look at it. They've matched the bullet they took out of Williams to the bullet that killed that terrorist at St. Patrick's."

"What? How can those two things be connected?"

McCluskey shrugged his shoulders. "They don't have a clue. That's why they're running around like chickens with their heads cut off this morning. That's why I'm here on a Saturday morning when I should be fishing. They asked me to see if we have old or pending homicides where a .308 caliber bullet was used that they can look at."

Benning had asked Captain McCluskey to keep him apprised of any new developments as he searched for .308 caliber bullets, or rifles, that were used in cases he found in the MCSO data base.

Before he started going over the list of suspected used car dealers, he called Drake.

"Are you at the vineyard?"

"We are. Where are you?"

"In the office. I just got back from the Sheriff's Department. Your hunch that Williams was set up might be right. The FBI matched the bullet that killed him to the bullet that killed Umara. Both are .308 calibers, fired from the same rifle."

"Someone went to a lot of trouble to make his death look like it didn't have anything to do with his investigation."

"Whoever they are, they've got connections. Staging a fake weapons exchange between Antifa and the Black Panthers that got people killed on both sides is complicated. What connects jihadists, who want to kill Catholics, with anarchists and Black Panthers?"

"The 'what' is easy enough; they all hate America for one reason or another. It's the 'who' that's important and connects these groups to the owners of that farm registered in Panama that Williams was trying to identify. Did you get anything on the used car dealers who might be selling vehicles with cloned VINs? That's where we start because it's all we have."

"I have the list of dealers the department's been keeping an eye on. I'll go through it today."

"That can wait until Monday, Paul. Go have fun with Margo. It's too nice a weekend to be in the office."

"All right, you do the same. I'll see you Monday."

Benning checked his watch and saw that it was only eleven o'clock. If he took Drake's advice, they had plenty of time to drive to Cannon Beach, go for a walk on the beach and have a late lunch at Margo's favorite eatery, the oceanfront Wayfarer Restaurant, and be back by dark.

If they hurried, there might even be enough time to check out the farm in Helvetia that Williams found by analyzing the selfie on one of the terrorist's phones. If he timed it right, they might even be able to see a sunset reflected off Mount Hood.

Benning took the back stairs that connected the condo

above the office they leased from Drake to invite Margo for a walk on the beach and a crab Louis salad for lunch. He'd stick with his favorite meal, Northwest steamer clams, and a nice glass of wine.

Great idea, Drake. Thanks for making me enjoy my day.

Chapter Twenty-Nine

TWO MEN ARRIVED SEPARATELY Sunday afternoon at Senator Hazelton's home in Georgetown. The first man was Michael Montgomery, the former Director of National Intelligence. The second man was Senator Martin Montez (D-NM), the former chairman of the Senate Select Committee on Intelligence during the eight years of the last administration. Both were members of the five-member committee for safety.

Senator Hazelton had convened the meeting to discuss a list of wealthy donors who could be the source of the funds the anti-fascist movement was receiving. The committee had to decide the best way to investigate the names on the list without them or the government finding out. There were too many career bureaucrats they couldn't trust in agencies they would normally ask for the information.

The three men of the committee had met many times before in the senator's study and skipped the usual perfunctory small talk to get down to business.

"Mike, why don't you tell us what Mark Holland was able to find out and then give us your thoughts on how we should proceed?" Senator Hazelton suggested.

"Right. Mark met with a friend in the Intelligence Division at NYPD and asked if they were investigating Antifa and the anarchist groups, to determine where they were getting the money to move around the country and show up for all these rallies. Since New York would sooner or later have to deal with the expected violence, the NYPD was already on it.

"The list of names Mark was provided was shorter than I thought it would be. There are a lot of elites that donate to nonprofit organizations known to support activist groups. Martin probably knows most of them because they support his party and keep the coffers full. The NYPD is familiar with them because a lot of them live in New York. They narrowed the focus of their investigation to consider whether any of them were likely to go beyond funding activist groups and donate to groups openly calling for revolution.

"There are six names on this list the NYPD believes are giving money directly to these groups," Montgomery said and handed a copy of the list to the two senators.

Senator Montez scanned the list. "I know all of them, but I don't believe three of them would risk their reputations by getting involved with Antifa or any of the anarchist groups. Sam Orenstein, the Hollywood producer, likes to host fundraisers for people running for president, but you can't get him interested in state races. He is seen with some odd characters occasionally, but I can't see him wanting to fund a revolution.

"The two on the list from New York inherited their fortunes and seem to want to give it all away before they die. They give to everyone and talk openly about socialism to anyone who will listen, but no one takes them seriously. The closest they will ever get to a revolution is the trip they took to Cuba to shake hands with Fidel.

"I don't know much about the Silicon Valley billionaire, other than he's a big donor, and I don't think I've heard of the real estate billionaire in Seattle. Mikhail Volkov is the one on the list I'm worried about."

"You would focus on Volkov and the other two then?" Senator Hazelton asked.

"Yes, especially Volkov."

"Mike, what do you think?"

"I agree with Martin. The two dilettantes in New York don't worry me. Orenstein's a maybe, but the other three are definite possibilities, especially Volkov. He claims to be an enemy of Putin, but there's too much evidence that says they were close when Volkov was building his natural gas empire, and they probably still are. They were both KGB and who's to say they aren't working on something together for the Motherland? The problem is proving it."

"How did you handle something like this when you were in the DNI?"

"My friends in the NSA would have the information for me within twenty-four hours. With all the leaks coming from the CIA and NSA these days, I wouldn't trust anything they come up with now."

"How would you do it now without the CIA or the NSA?"

The former DNI smiled. "I'd hire the best hacker I could find."

Senator Hazelton turned to Senator Montez. "Would you be comfortable with that, Martin?"

"I don't think we have a choice with what's going on. But even if we stop the flow of money to these groups, we can't be sure that will stop the violence."

"What do you think, Mike?"

"If we know where the money is going and who's receiving it, you could arrest the leaders for inciting a riot. It's is a federal crime with a maximum penalty of five years in prison and a fine. When the next leaders take their place, you repeat the process until all the people who would risk going to jail are in jail, and the movement dies."

"Do we have a hacker in mind we can trust?" Senator Montez asked.

"I do, actually," Senator Hazelton said. "My son-in-law is special counsel for a security firm that has one of the best white hat hackers in the world. I'll ask him if his company and its hacker are willing to work with us on this. If they are, we might even have the information we need by then.

"Are we agreed, then, that we'll investigate the names on the list that we've discussed? If so, I'll let Mark Holland and Secretary Rallings know what we've decided this evening."

Montgomery and Montez both said yes and the Sunday committee meeting was adjourned.

After a light dinner on the patio at the rear of the townhouse with his wife, Senator Hazelton called his son-in-law to see if Kevin McRoberts, the white hat hacker employed by Puget Sound Security, would undertake the covert investigation into three of the richest men in the world.

Chapter Thirty

NAZIR WAS ENTERTAINING a neighbor that he'd admired sunbathing down at the pool and was annoyed when his phone vibrated in his pocket. The phone was only used for Council business and was always with him.

He excused himself and ducked into the guest bathroom. When the door was shut, he took a deep breath to slow down his hammering heart before answering.

"What is it?"

"You've had another visitor snooping around the farm."

"The police?"

"I don't think so. A man and a woman in a Ford F-150 stopped and took pictures of Mount Hood at sunset. Then the man got out, took more pictures of the farmhouse, barn and fence lines, turned around and they drove back the way they came."

"I need to know who he is."

"I got his license number. I'll make a call."

"Call me as soon as you know. I need to put an end to this."

Nazir took a moment then washed his hands. They started sweating the moment his spotter said someone else was snooping around the farm. Damn it all. Killing the FBI agent should have ended any interest the FBI had in the place. With only a week left to prep for the Labor Day fascist rallies, he didn't need this distraction.

He needed to make another call, but he couldn't stay in the bathroom any longer. He would just have to apologize to the girl, send her home early and hope she would come back another time.

When he came out of the guest bathroom next to the entertainment room, she wasn't on the red leather sofa where he'd left her. She wasn't in the kitchen either, but the door to his bedroom, which he always kept closed, was open.

Thinking she probably had to use the master bathroom while he was in the guest bathroom, Nazir entered the bedroom and saw that she wasn't in the bathroom. She was lying on his bed wearing nothing but a coy smile of invitation.

Maybe the evening didn't have to end just yet.

At one in the morning, Nazir's phone vibrated on the night stand. His lovely and naked neighbor was sleeping soundly on the other side of the bed with the sheet draped across her lower body.

He slipped out of bed and went to the kitchen without stopping to put anything on.

"Did you find out who he is?"

"Yes, but you're not going to like it. He's a retired detective from the Sheriff's Office and now a private investigator named Paul Benning. He works out of the office of that attorney who shot one of Umara's girls at that cabin near the coast, Adam Drake."

Nazir was silent. Without knowing how the private investigator or the attorney were involved, he didn't know what to do. Worse yet, he couldn't think of a way to find out.

"Do you know where they live?"

"The attorney lives on a farm outside Dundee. The

private investigator lives in a condo at RiverPlace near the marina."

If you knew where to look, there really wasn't any such thing as privacy anymore, a fact Nazir and his group of hackers knew better than anyone else. But he needed more than names and addresses.

"Let me think about the best way to deal with these two. I'll call if I need your help."

He took a can of Red Bull out of the refrigerator and sat on a stool at the kitchen counter. He needed to know more about both men. It took him an hour.

The attorney had played football at the University of Oregon, graduated law school, but didn't practice law right away. His first job as a lawyer appeared to be as a prosecutor in the District Attorney's Office. He married the daughter of the state's senior U.S. senator, but she had died three years later from cancer. He was now in private practice and was listed as special counsel for Puget Sound Security in Seattle.

There was an unexplained number of years following his admission to the Oregon State Bar, shortly after 9/11. It could be explained by military service, but there was nothing in the records of any of the U.S. branches of the military that confirmed it.

The private investigator had been an intelligence officer in the army before joining the Sheriff's Office. He worked there as a senior detective until he retired earlier in the year and started working as a P.I. shortly thereafter. He was married to the attorney's secretary. There were no records of the couple having children, which was unfortunate. Children provided such great leverage when you needed to know something from a parent who didn't want to cooperate with you.

He was on his second can of Red Bull when he decided what he was going to do. He needed to provoke a reaction from the duo that would tell him if they had any idea who he was. He didn't need to kill them right away until he knew what they had learned and if they were working with anyone else.

He would bomb the attorney's office using the same plastic explosive he used on the mosque in Los Angeles and the nosy neighbor's house. If they knew of his involvement in either of those bombings, they would come straight for him. If that happened, he would know it was time to go underground and stay there.

If they didn't come for him, he would just have to ride it out and be careful. He didn't know how long the Russian would keep supplying him funds, but as long as he did, he'd keep taking them.

The risk he was most concerned about was being identified as a co-conspirator in the attacks on the Catholic churches and the massacre of the gays on the Steel Bridge. He didn't fear death at the hands of the enemy after a trial, but he would never let them put him in jail for the rest of his life. He would martyr himself first.

Chapter Thirty-One

PAUL BENNING WAS eager to get started Monday morning. He was already in the breakroom making coffee when Drake came down the backstairs from the parking garage to the office at eight o'clock.

"Good morning, Adam," Benning said cheerfully from the breakroom.

Drake stopped at the door and heard him whistling while he poured water into the coffee maker.

"Pretty chipper for a Monday morning. You must have taken my advice and had fun with Margo this weekend."

"I did indeed. We drove to the coast, walked on the beach and had a great meal. Margo seemed to enjoy it. What did you and Liz do?"

"Nothing much. Showed her around the vineyard with Lancer and told her about the kinds of root stock we're planting. Then we visited a couple tasting rooms that used the same root stocks and had breakfast yesterday at the Black Walnut Inn. Pretty quiet weekend all around."

Drake headed up to his loft and said on the way, "Bring some coffee when you come up and tell me what you're doing this sunny morning."

One of the files he'd brought with him from PSS to review was for Caelus Research, Inc., a DARPA contractor. It was working on a grant to make the military's Unmanned Aerial Vehicles (UAVs) safe from hackers.

Someone was trying to hack Caelus and it appeared to be one of its competitors, not ISIS or a foreign power like Russia or the Chinese. Caelus was a PSS client and wanted advice on how to deal with the suspected competitor, and they wanted it now.

He opened the file and was scanning the summary on the first couple of pages when Benning came up the stairs with a cup of coffee in each hand.

Benning handed him a cup of coffee and sat down in a chair in front of his desk.

"I'm heading out to visit the used car dealers that we suspect of moving vehicles with cloned VINs. Want to come?"

"I can't this morning. Besides, you're better at dealing with criminal types than I am. I could never get them to talk when I was in the D.A.'s Office unless there was a plea deal on the table."

"I remember seeing that 'rot in jail for the rest of your life' look on your face more than once. It was effective, but you're right, I'll do better without you."

"How many used car dealers are on the list?"

"Eleven and they're located all over the metro area. I'll start with the ones closest to the farm in Helvetia and work from there."

"It shouldn't be too hard for someone to remember selling three old vans a couple of weeks ago, if you can get them to talk."

"I think they will when I mention that the FBI analysts discovered the vans the terrorists used all had cloned VINs. I'll ask to see the sales records for the last month that they're required to keep. I can't represent myself as someone I'm not any longer, but I can't help it if someone assumes that I am."

"Good luck and be careful."

"As always. I'll check in later today and let you know what I find out."

When Benning left, Adam decided to call his friend and boss, Mike Casey, the CEO of PSS, before he got back to working on the Caelus Research file.

"Good morning, Mike. Am I interrupting anything?"

"Just my enjoyment from eating a nice bagel I brought back from a staff meeting. Is Liz any closer to getting up here to start work?"

"She'll be there after Labor Day. She hasn't found a condo she wants. Her real estate agent is looking for a short-term lease on an apartment close to headquarters."

"What is she doing with all her stuff? We have a storage facility she can use until she finds something."

"She had stuff shipped here to the vineyard. I've got the old winery and tasting room building that's got plenty of empty space."

There was a pregnant pause before Casey asked, "Does that mean what I think it might mean?"

Drake had to laugh at his best friend's careful wording. "No, Mike, she's not moving in with me. She's out there right now, unpacking what she'll need for a temporary apartment until she finds something she wants to buy. This is only temporary here with me."

"If you say so. Why did you call and interrupt me eating my morning snack?"

"Senator Hazelton called last night. He has a project for Kevin he wants me to talk to you about."

"Is it something we should discuss when you come up Wednesday?"

"Yes. I just wanted to know if Kevin is available to use his special skills between now and Labor Day weekend. I'm meeting the senator and some of his friends at his cabin at Crosswater."

"What's that about? Sounds important if some of his friends will be there too. Do you know who they are?"

"Not a clue, but I get the feeling it is something important. The project for Kevin involves a couple of the wealthiest people in the world."

"In that case, I'll have Kevin clear the deck for the senator's project. Do you want him to get started before you come up day after tomorrow?"

"If he's available, sure."

"He will be. Use the encrypted messaging on your company phone and he'll get started today."

"Thanks, Mike. See you Wednesday."

Drake knew Kevin McRoberts spent longs nights in his office drinking his favorite energy drink when he got his teeth into a matter. He decided to wait a couple of hours to give the kid a break, in case last night happened to be one of those nights.

He had his own project he needed to get his own teeth into. The competitor suspected of the hacking had used a server that was located in a software division of Intel in Hillsboro.

Chapter Thirty-Two

PAUL BENNING DROVE onto the lot of Action Auto Sales ten minutes after nine o'clock. It was the first used car dealer on his list and, from the looks of the place, one of the more profitable lots around. At a glance, there were thirty to forty cars and trucks and they were still glistening in the morning sun from an early morning washing.

Some of the cars were late-model Lexus and Mercedes luxury cars in decent shape and they were parked closest to the street. Parked in a row along one side of the lot were jacked-up pickups that looked like they'd seen a lot of off-roading, the kind of truck a young man would buy after graduating high school and getting his first job. Toward the back of the lot the cars were older and cheaper, but he didn't see vans of any vintage.

A man in his forties, with a shaved head and a coal-black moustache and goatee, came out of the raised sales office and down the stairs to greet him.

"See anything you like?"

"I'm looking for an older van, something I can use to deliver things to Saturday market that won't cost me an arm and a leg. I see that you don't have any on the lot."

"There's not a lot of money to be made selling old vans, sorry," the dealer said and turned to walk back to his office.

"Unless they're stolen with cloned VINs."

That stopped the man, who turned around with a sneer on his face. "You a cop?"

"Let's just say I'm someone who knows you sell hot cars from time to time. I'm looking for a man who bought three old vans a couple of weeks ago. That's all that I'm looking for right now."

"I can't help you. I don't buy or sell old vans."

"Is that what your sales record will show?"

The used car dealer flashed a deadpan smile. "Of course that's what they will show. If that's all you wanted to know, it's time for you to leave and for me to get back to work."

The next used car dealer on the list was a block away on SW Oak Street, Mike's Auto Wholesale. When he pulled onto the lot, a man in his early twenties was changing the price on the window of a used Camry.

Benning got out of his truck and walked over. "Are you Mike?"

"Mike owns the lot, but he's never around. I just work here."

"You sell many old vans? I'm looking for one to haul things I make to Saturday market."

"I sold one a couple of weeks ago, but that's the only one we've had on the lot in a long time."

"Do you remember who you sold it to?"

"Sure, Ray over at Ray's Auto Sales in Beaverton. He had a buyer and needed one more to go along with three others some guy was buying."

"Where did you get the one you sold Ray?"

The man took a step back and looked at him suspiciously. "Why do you want to know that?"

"Maybe the guy you bought it from has another one."

It was a pretty lame answer and he knew it. He didn't expect it would be answered.

"Mike buys all of his cars at auto auctions in Portland. You might try there."

Benning thanked the man and got in his truck to drive to Ray's Auto Sales. The salesman watched him from beside the Camry until he turned the corner and was out of sight.

He was sure the man knew more than he was saying. Taking vehicles to auction was a way car thieves moved cars with cloned VINs or fraudulent certificates of title that were all too easy to get. Oregon's DMV used the honor system and relied on the information it was provided by the person requesting a replacement title for one that was claimed to be lost. Finding the buyer of three vans with cloned VINs, with all the auto auction wholesalers in Portland, would be nearly impossible.

But Ray's Auto Sales was going to be it, he could feel it. A man buying four old vans at one time would be remembered, even if all of them were bought at auction.

Wait a minute. Four vans? The terrorist only used three vans. Two at the Catholic churches and one for the attack on the Steel Bridge. Where was the fourth?

Ray's Auto Sales was more like what he'd been expecting. A sales office that towered over the lot where the dealer could watch over his inventory without leaving his office. Rows of metallic red, white and blue streamers strung overhead and Beach Boy music was playing over an outdoor sound system.

Even Ray met his expectation for a dirty used car dealer. Fifty plus with a pot belly and wearing a garish orange and black Hawaiian shirt.

Benning saw something else that fit the image. The bulge under Ray's long shirt concealed but didn't hide the presence of a gun on his belt.

Ray held out a beefy hand in greeting. "Welcome to Ray's Auto Sales. What ya looking for, friend?"

"An old van like the one you bought from Mike's Auto Wholesale a couple of weeks back."

Ray's eyes squinted slightly, enough for a trained detective to know he'd hit a nerve. Ray remembered all right.

"A couple of weeks ago, you say. I don't remember buying anything from Mike's Auto Sales this month."

"It was to go along with three others with cloned VINs you were selling some guy."

"Who are you?"

"Your worst nightmare if you don't answer my question."

"You a cop? DMV?"

"I'm just a guy looking for some answers. I'm a former detective with the Sheriff's Office helping out on an FBI investigation."

Ray's right hand drifted down to brush against the gun under his shirt. "So, you're just a citizen like me, huh. Well, I think you've overstayed your welcome here. It's time for you to get off my property."

"Be smart, Ray, and listen to me. I don't care about the possibility my friends at the Sheriff's Office are right in thinking that you move stolen cars off this lot. I'm looking for the man who bought four vans. Three of them had cloned VINs that were driven by the terrorists who attacked two Catholic churches and slaughtered people on the Steel Bridge. If you're involved with him and cooperating with a terrorist, you're in big trouble. If you can help me and demonstrate that you're not a terrorist by telling me what I want to know, I'll leave. You'll never see me again."

"I may be a lot of things, mister, but I'm not a terrorist. I don't know the man's name. He paid cash for the four vans, twenty-five hundred for each of them, and told me to keep the titles, that he didn't need them. For ten grand in cash, I didn't ask a lot of questions."

Benning had noticed the security cameras pointing down on the lot from the sales office.

"Do your security cameras work or are they just up there for show?"

"They work. You can't be too careful with the people I see here."

"Make me a copy of what your security cameras captured over the last month and I'm out of here."

Ray looked at him for several seconds before turning around and walking toward the sales office. Benning followed behind him.

Chapter Thirty-Three

DRAKE WAS STILL WORKING on the Caelus Research file when Margo buzzed him and asked if he had a minute. She needed to talk with him before her husband returned.

"Come on up."

Margo came up the stairs a minute later carrying a stainless-steel coffee carafe. "I thought you could use a refill."

"I can, thanks."

She refilled his coffee cup and remained standing. "Are you going to Seattle Wednesday?"

"Margo, have a seat. Is this about Paul?"

"It's not what you think. I was angry at you at first, when you said it was okay for him to work out of the office, doing his PI thing. I wished you had talked with me before telling him it was okay. But that's yesterday's grievance and I've forgiven you. I would like to take the day off Wednesday when you go to Seattle."

"You don't need to ask me when you want to take a day off, or a week, for that matter. You run the office, I should be asking you when I can take a day off."

"Paul's birthday is Wednesday. I want to surprise him with something."

"I know it's his birthday. I already have his gift. Do you want me to help with something?"

"I want to know if you think taking him dory fishing at Pacific City is something he would like. He wants to buy a boat to go fishing but he keeps putting it off. A friend of mine went out with her husband and she's still raving about it. I thought going dory fishing might encourage him to go ahead and buy one."

"Margo, that's a great idea. I know Paul will love it. Have you made a reservation with anyone yet? These guides are usually booked for months in advance."

"I just came up with the idea yesterday. I didn't think about needing a reservation."

"Let me see if I can help. I've used Grant Rilette Fishing a couple of times and he's the top guide out of Pacific City. I'll give him a call and see if he has an opening Wednesday."

"That would be great."

"You'll go, too, right?"

"If there's room."

Lucky Paul. Launching a dory from the beach and then running it up on the sand when you return to clean your fish and eat fresh crab your guide is cooking. What a birthday present.

Drake made a note to call the guide as soon as he finished reading the Caelus Research file.

If the client's information was correct, and someone at Intel was hacking its system about a DARPA project, he would have to be very careful about the advice he gave the company. Accusing a giant like Intel of corporate espionage would swiftly bring out the big legal guns and land Caelus in court for the next ten years. If Kevin verified the client's information, he had a decision to make; a frontal assault or a flanking action.

He closed the file and picked up his phone to call Grant

Rilette Fishing when he heard Benning greet his wife and then bound up the stairs to the loft. Drake put his phone down before he got there.

"I found the used car dealer who sold the vans."

Drake motioned for him to have a seat and catch his breath. "Did he identify the buyer?"

"He only gave his first name, 'John'. He paid ten thousand dollars for four vans and said he didn't need the certificates of title. There's no paperwork, nothing to trace back to him."

"So, this dealer knew the transaction wasn't legit all the way around. He's on the list of suspected used car dealers selling stolen vehicles for a good reason. Did you say he sold four vans? We only know about three vans."

"Four vans, twenty-five hundred for each. The good news is I have a copy of the security camera's DVR recording of the used car lot for the last month." Benning held up a black memory stick. "Ray, the dealer, is big on security and it makes me think he might be selling something other than used cars."

"Can we identify the buyer?"

"Clear shots of the buyer and the four vans. I'm going to take this over to the Sheriff's Office and see if I can get someone to run the recording through their facial recognition database."

"Great work, Paul. What does our buyer look like?"

"The four security cameras are mounted on the sales office, pointing down on the lot, so it's hard to eyeball height. Our guy looks to be about five eight or nine, slender build like someone who runs to keep in shape, in his mid-thirties. He wore a red and black Trail Blazer hat, but you can see his face."

"You're a detective, does he look like a terrorist?"

"How do you spot a terrorist these days? But I will say his skin coloring suggests that he might be of Arab or Indian descent."

"How long will it take to run this through the facial recognition database?"

"Shouldn't take too long, if I can talk someone into doing it for me."

"Use the office credit card if you have to. Dinner for two or something, you decide. I want to know who this guy is."

"I think they call that a bribe."

"Technically, yes, but for a good purpose. Which reminds me, I'll be in Seattle on your birthday, Wednesday. Don't feel like you have to be in the office."

"I appreciate it, but it will depend on how soon I can get someone to run this through the database."

"Well, if you get the opportunity to celebrate your birthday, take it."

Benning left, and as soon as he did, Drake called his guide to beg for two seats in his dory for the day after next. As far out as the guide was usually booked, he knew it would take a miracle to have someone cancel their reservation and allow Margo to surprise her husband.

Chapter Thirty-Four

IT WASN'T A MIRACLE, he learned, that made two seats available on Rilette's dory. It was a simple case of the flu. The guide had been hit with it over the weekend and rebooked his customers for the week to keep from giving them what he had. When Drake called, he said he was feeling better and thought he'd be fine by Wednesday. He would be happy to take Margo and her husband fishing, on one condition; Drake had to make a reservation to go fishing with him for winter steelhead.

He quickly agreed. He'd never fished for the fighting anadromous trout that spent two or three years in the ocean before returning to spawn in the cold-water tributaries of the Pacific Ocean.

The next thing on his list for the morning was calling Kevin McRoberts at PSS for an update on the two things he'd asked him to do and then brief him on a third request.

"Kevin, how are things in Seattle?"

"Couldn't be better, Mr. Drake. Mr. Casey has increased the budget for my division and we're getting the latest Razer Blade laptops for everyone. I'm also collaborating with the developer of our Linux operating system on a couple of improvements."

"Sounds like you're keeping busy. Have you had time to work on those two projects I called about?"

"Oh sure, Mr. Drake. I work on the collaboration with the OS developer in my spare time. Which one do you want to talk about first?"

"How about the farm registered in Panama? Were you able to identify the owners?"

"I'm still working on that. I've worked through a string of twelve shell companies and I'm not to the end yet. Someone went to a lot of trouble to set this up."

"All right, keep working on it. What about the wealthy donors I asked you about?"

"That was easier. Their tax returns list plenty of donations to nonprofit organizations. Most of those were made to tax-exempt nonprofits. I followed the donations made to nonprofits that weren't tax exempt, thinking the nonprofits you're interested in wouldn't want the scrutiny the tax-exempt nonprofits get.

"Then I tracked the money spent by those nonprofits to see who they were giving money to. I'll send you a list of the groups and individuals who are getting the money. I didn't investigate those groups or individuals. I thought you might know them or have someone who does."

"Good work, Kevin. Now, do you have time for one more project? It's for Caelus Research, one of our clients."

"I'll make time, Mr. Drake. What is it?"

"Caelus Research is working on a DARPA project to eliminate the vulnerabilities of our military drones. Someone has tried to hack their system and they believe they've traced it to a competitor. I'd like you to get in touch with their IT head and see if you can confirm what they have."

"Can do, Mr. Drake. Who does Caelus think it is?"

"They say they've traced it to a server in the software division of Intel in Hillsboro."

"Wow, that doesn't sound like something Intel would do."

"I agree, so be extra careful. Our job is to advise our client how they should handle the hack while making sure we don't accuse Intel of something without having ironclad proof that it was responsible."

"Copy that, Mr. Drake. I'll get right on it."

Drake had to smile. The kid was picking up the lingo of the former military men he was around at PSS.

When he looked down at the Omega Speedmaster chronograph on his left wrist that Liz had given him at Christmas, he saw it was almost noon and time to see how she was doing with her unpacking.

"How are you doing?"

"Wishing you were here to help me. I have way too much stuff. I can't believe all of this was in my condo."

"There's no rush if you want to wait to unpack things until we find you a place in Seattle."

"I know. I'm trying to get rid of things I really don't need. When are you coming home?"

It was comfortable hearing her call his place home. "I'll leave a little early and be there by five to take you to dinner."

"Sounds wonderful. See you at five."

He'd wanted to take her for dinner at the Joel Palmer House in Dayton ever since they got back from Hawaii and had made a reservation that morning. It was a restaurant in an 1859 farmhouse that specialized in offerings using mushrooms and truffles, like its famous wild mushroom risotto. It also had a world-class wine list.

He was about to call down to Margo and ask if she would call the Little River Café and have them deliver a turkey sandwich and whatever she wanted when she buzzed him.

"Look out your window. There's a man taking pictures of the office. He's been out there for the last ten or fifteen minutes."

Drake got up and went to the window and looked down to the boardwalk. A man wearing a black polo shirt, jeans and a red and black Trail Blazer hat was using his phone to take pictures of every inch of the office and the Benning's condo above, judging from the way he was pointing the camera.

He leaned over his desk and used the intercom to call Margo. "Are you getting a good look at him on the security camera monitor?"

"His hat is pulled down and he's not looking up much, but he studied the camera above the door for several seconds. We should have a good look at his face. Do you want me to call security?"

"No, I'm going down to have a word with him. He's doing surveillance. He's not someone stopping to admire the beauty of our building because it's not that special."

Drake took the stairs three at a time and ran to the front door. When he opened it, the man put his phone away and started walking away south on the esplanade.

Chapter Thirty-Five

THE MAN WAS ten yards ahead of Drake and turned to see if he was being followed. When they locked eyes for a moment, it was like two fighters measuring an opponent before the start of a fifteen-round championship fight. There was no fear or anxiety, just the calm recognition of a worthy opponent.

Drake quickened his pace as they approached the turn-around at the end of SW Montgomery Street next to McCormick and Schmick's Harborside at the Marina. A black Mustang was idling at the curb and the man pulled open the door and jumped in before Drake got there.

As the Mustang sped away, there was no mistaking the look in the man's eyes. It was cold and dismissive. Drake recognized the look of someone accustomed to killing.

He whipped out his phone, but by the time he had it in camera mode, the Mustang was turning the corner onto SW Harbor Drive.

He jogged back to the office, trying to think of a reason someone would send a killer to scope out his office. His immediate thought was that it had to be something to do with what

FBI Agent Williams was working on when he was ambushed and killed.

He was trying to determine the ownership of the farm where the terrorist took her selfie, just like Williams had been. If trying to find out who owned the goat farm got an FBI agent killed, whoever owned the place wouldn't hesitate to come after him if they knew he was trying to find out the same thing.

Margo was on her phone when he got back to the office.

"Is that Paul? If it is, tell him to get back here as soon as he can."

"Who was that?"

"Someone I don't think wants to retain our services. Play back the DVR footage, I want to take a closer look at this guy."

The office had been a rare book store. When the owner died, it came on the market just as Drake was about to leave the D.A.'s Office. It had a state-of-the-art security system at the time and he had updated the office security since then. The front door was a forced entrance resistant security door capable of withstanding skilled attackers using axes, crowbars, hammers, saws and power drills. It could only be opened when Margo recognized the person on the security monitor on her desk and buzzed them in.

Margo reversed the DVR to the time when the man first appeared outside. Drake leaned over her shoulder and studied the man he followed. Medium height, with dark brown eyes and an aquiline nose. He had broad shoulders, muscular forearms and moved from place to place with the deliberate grace of a cat.

"He looks like some of the cartel members you prosecuted," Margo said.

"I bet he is or has been an elite soldier somewhere. I saw it in his eyes when he turned around to see if I was still following him."

Paul came down the back stairs from the parking garage and asked, "Who's an elite soldier?"

"The man out on the esplanade taking a lot of pictures of the office," Margo said. "Adam went out to talk to him and he walked away as soon as the front door opened."

Benning came to stand behind his wife and watched as she reversed the DVR. "I don't like the looks of this."

Drake agreed. "That makes two of us. If this has something to do with that farm we're investigating, I don't want to take any chances. If they're bold enough to kill an FBI agent, they won't hesitate to come after us to keep us from finding out who they are."

Benning pointed. "There's a glimpse of his face when he looks up. Do you want me to go back to the Sheriff's Office and run it through their facial recognition database?"

"It can't hurt, but I doubt this guy is in any database."

"Why wouldn't he be?" Margo asked.

"For the same reason I'm not in any database because I was with Delta Force. Countries protect the identity of elite soldiers so they can get them in and out of places without setting off alarms. Paul, did you find the guy who bought the vans in the MCSO database?"

"He wasn't in our database, but they're trying the FBI's NGI facial recognition database. The NCIC criminal database doesn't include facial images, but the FBI's Next Generation Identification (NGI) database does. Oregon cooperated with the FBI and shared DMV license photos and mug shots, but that still leaves a lot of people out of the database.

"The FBI did a study of the facial images in the Oregon's database called the 'Face Report Card' when I was working in the MCSO. They found significant problems with the quality of the images in the database. The median resolution of the images was well below the recommended resolution of .75 megapixels. Newer iPhone cameras are capable of 8 megapixels resolution, for example. But even if a person's facial image is in the state's database, half the time the image is not good enough to be recognized by the FBI's NGI facial recognition database."

"Well, let me know if they get a match anywhere," Drake said. "I'm going to take some files home and work there today and tomorrow to help Liz before we drive to Seattle, Wednesday. When I get back, we'll go see that used car dealer. He may know more than he was willing to tell you."

Chapter Thirty-Six

ZAL NAZIR WAITED for BJ at the Copper River Restaurant and Bar in Hillsboro. The message from the Iranian commando reporting his recon of the attorney's office said it presented a problem they needed to discuss.

BJ walked through the restaurant to the bar right on time and sat down across the small table from Nazir.

"I waited to order. Are you hungry?"

BJ pulled the menu across the table and turned it around. "I could eat, thanks."

"What's the problem that we need to discuss?"

BJ continued scanning the menu until he tapped it with his finger. "I'll have the steak tacos and a beer."

"What's the problem, BJ?"

"The only way to deliver the package is to fly it through a window. You won't get your drone back."

"Expensive, but if that's the only way, do it! Can you do it without being seen?"

"The only way would be to do it from across the river. I haven't been over there yet, but I'll find a place. Another possibility would be to fly it from a boat on the river. The boat would need a cabin where I could be inside."

"Which way is best?"

"Using a boat would get me closer and give me the best chance of not being seen."

"Do you know how to operate a boat?"

BJ leaned over the table and said, "I wouldn't suggest using a boat if I didn't know how to operate one. This is what I'm good at. Don't question my judgment, just let me do my job."

"Okay, okay, a boat it is. Where will you get one?"

"There are marinas all along the river. I'll steal one."

Nazir waved to the waitress to signal they were ready to order. "Steak tacos for two and my friend will have a beer."

"What beer would you like, sir?"

"Let me try the Dead Guy Ale."

When she left, BJ laughed. "Appropriate, don't you think? Speaking of dead guys, I saw the attorney. He came out of his office and followed me. He must have seen me taking pictures in front of his office."

"Will that complicate things?"

"No, there was a security camera above the door, but there's no way for them to identify me. I'm not in anyone's database."

"You'd better not be. This can't be traced back to me."

"Relax, it won't be. Is there anyone else you're worried about, other than the attorney and his PI?"

"There is one other person. The used car dealer I bought the vans from. He doesn't know my name and I paid cash. But he could describe me to the police."

"Do you want me to take care of him?"

"We should tie up all the loose ends. His name is Ray at Ray's Auto Sales in Hillsboro."

Their steak tacos were delivered and both men ate without talking until Nazir finished his first taco. "Tell your uncle we're still working on that other matter for him. Their security is better than we expected, but I have the best group of hackers in the world working on it. He'll know the vulnerabilities of American drones very soon."

BJ wiped his mouth with a napkin and took a drink of his beer. "That's why I'm here, to make sure that he does. He's concerned that your involvement with the anarchists will jeopardize what you agreed to do in exchange for his support of the Council. He thinks you're serving two masters. He worries you might be putting their interests ahead of his. Are you?"

"I am Persian first, BJ, just like you. I work with them because I was told to."

"He needs the ability to down the American drones at will or take control of them and turn them back against their soldiers. With that, the Americans can be driven from our lands and the Middle East will be ours. You understand that, right?"

"We're working on it, BJ."

"He wants you to work harder. What you're doing isn't getting the job done. Have you tried everything?"

"Not everything. There are two cyber weapons that were stolen from the NSA called EternalBlue and DoublePulsar. They were made available by a group calling itself the Shadow Brokers. One will lock up a company's data and demand a ransom to unlock it. But the ransomware hides a more invasive cyberattack that steals employee credentials. With those credentials, you have access to the company's computer network and can take confidential information or destroy machines if you want.

"The problem is the company knows about the ransomware attack and may or may not discover the more invasive attack. My understanding is that your uncle wants the ability to take control of military drones but doesn't want the military to know about the vulnerability before he chooses to exploit it."

"Do you have these stolen NSA cyberweapons?"

"Of course."

"If the ransomware cyberattack is successful, do you get the employee credentials right away?"

"You would have until the company pays the ransom and unlocks its data."

"I will ask my uncle if he wants you to do this."

Nazir checked the time. "I've got to get back to work. Let me know what your uncle says."

He paid the tab on his way out of the restaurant and left with the uncomfortable feeling that he was just a tool of the Iranian Army and no longer the leader of a force that wanted to conduct jihad its own way. He might not have two masters, but it was clear he had one.

Chapter Thirty-Seven

AFTER BREAKFAST THE NEXT MORNING, Drake helped Liz for an hour pack the things she needed for one or the other of the two furnished apartments her real estate agent had found. When she told him that she wanted to go over her list just one more time, he returned to his study to review the recommendations for a new PSS office in Honolulu. Property was ridiculously expensive, but that was the price you paid for a presence in Hawaii.

Benning called at eleven from the Sheriff's Office to report they had identified the man taking pictures of the office.

"Hope you're sitting down because this is really getting crazy. His name is Badar Jamali, a Pakistani, here on a student visa to study engineering at Oregon State University. He attended classes spring term but isn't enrolled for the summer term. When my friend at the Sheriff's Office ran his facial image through the FBI's NGI facial recognition data, he got a match.

"The guy's real name is Bijan Jahandar, an Iranian. The CIA have of picture of him standing with his uncle, Masoud Jihandar, at some military parade. Masoud Jihandar is a high-ranking officer in the Iranian Ministry of Intelligence and

Security or MOIS. The CIA believes Bijan Jahandar is an officer and commando in Iran's army."

Drake was stunned. It took him a minute to process the information.

"You still there?"

"I'm here, just having a hard time making any sense of all this."

"I said it was crazy."

"There are too many things that don't connect, starting with Umara being killed by a .308 bullet, presumably from a sniper, before she could be captured. Then Wayne Williams was lured to an ambush and was also killed by a .308 bullet from the same rifle that killed Umara. Williams wouldn't stop looking for someone he believed had helped Umara and he was silenced. We're trying to identify the owner of the goat farm and now some Iranian commando is taking pictures of the office. That all connects, I suppose.

"But then there's the plastic explosive used to bomb the mosque in Los Angeles, from the same batch of PE8 as the explosive used to bomb the neighbor's house two blocks away from the Black Panthers' pad. How does that connect to Umara, Williams and me?"

"It doesn't, unless there's one person or group behind all of it."

"The outlier is the mosque bombing. Everything else could be an attempt to keep us from identifying the owner of the goat farm. But the mosque bombing is thought to have been done by some fascist group unhappy with all the Muslim refugees the government's bringing in."

"Maybe we're not seeing the big picture just yet. What do you want to do with the information about Badar Jamali and Bijan Jahandar being the same person?"

"It should go to the FBI, but the Portland Field Office would like to keep the Umara file closed and might not pay much attention to it. What's your friend in the Sheriff's Office going to do with it?"

"He'll file a report about Jahandar being in the country on a student visa, but I didn't tell him how we think all of this is connected."

"Let me talk with Liz and see what she thinks. Whatever we decide to do, keep your eyes open. This guy is dangerous."

"You do the same."

Drake sat back and let his mind work on the puzzle for twenty minutes then went out to talk with Liz.

The unfinished tasting room and winery were located across a small paved parking area from the rear of the farmhouse. The section that was to have been the winery occupied three quarters of the building and had a large commercial overhead door at the far end for shipping and receiving.

The overhead door was up, and Liz was sitting in a blue canvas folding chair staring at the Atlas Van Lines boxes scattered all over the floor.

Drake walked up behind her and said, "If you forget something, I can always bring it with me the next time I come to Seattle."

"Look at all this! How in the world does a single woman living in a two-bedroom condo wind up with this much stuff?"

Liz wasn't a hoarder by any means, but it was a question that was better left unanswered.

"Seventy-two boxes aren't all that much. Some of them aren't even full."

Liz got up slowly and turned around to face him. He was grinning.

"Wise guy. Did you quit working so you could come out here and make fun of me?"

Drake moved closer and put his arms around her waist. "I would never do that. I came out to see what you think about the call I just received."

He pulled another folding chair over and sat beside her.

When he was finished telling her about his conversation with Benning, she got up and started walking slowly in a circle around their chairs.

"You left out something. Your father-in-law asked you to find out if those two donors were contributing money to the anarchists causing all the trouble. Terrorists like Umara and Antifa have similar goals. One wants to destroy America and the other wants to eliminate the government, which would do the same thing.

"What if someone is providing money so they're both successful? Antifa says it wants a revolution. After every revolution, someone new comes to power. Why not the people behind the curtain that's funding the whole thing? Remember that Volkov's a Russian oligarch. Russia interfered in the last election, maybe it's behind this as well."

"Let's assume you're right. I have a list of nonprofits that may have been used to distribute money to Antifa and anarchist groups. But they can just say they didn't know how the money was going to be used."

"Then we'll figure out a way to prove that they did."

Chapter Thirty-Eight

BIJAN JAHANDAR PARKED down the street a block away from Ray's Auto Sales and waited for the used car dealer to arrive.

The first time he'd driven by earlier in the morning, the used car lot boy was washing cars in the row closest to the street. He didn't see anyone else on the lot. An hour later, the cars were washed and the lot boy was gone.

It was now ten minutes to ten. BJ thought he was wasting his time when a red Cadillac El Dorado with a white vinyl top pulled into the lot and parked at the bottom of the stairs to the sales office.

The man who got out of the car was the man Nazir described; thinning blond hair, mid-fifties with a big gut and wearing a Hawaiian shirt. He watched him lock the Cadillac and walk up the stairs carrying a thermos in one hand and briefcase in the other.

BJ waited five minutes before he got out of his car and crossed the street at the corner to approach the car lot on foot. He was wearing khaki pants, a long-sleeved white shirt with the cuffs rolled up and a tie loose at the collar, trying to look like one of the thousands of young men working for tech companies in the area.

When he entered the lot, he walked directly to the red Cadillac Eldorado and stood admiring it, with his chin cupped in his right hand and his left hand across his stomach supporting his right elbow.

He heard Ray open the door of the sales office and come onto the deck that ran along the front. "She's a beauty, isn't she?"

BJ looked up and saw Ray leaning over the railing looking down at him. "It's a classic. What year is it?"

"Nineteen fifty-seven, but it's not for sale."

"I couldn't afford it even if it was. I've been riding a bike to work. I need something reliable that gets good gas mileage. I'm taking my girlfriend to the coast next weekend."

Ray started down the stairs. "I think I have just the car for you."

BJ kicked tires and got in and out of a dozen cars before he agreed that a ten-year-old Honda Accord with only forty-seven thousand miles was the car he wanted. From the condition of the fabric seats, he knew the odometer had been turned back, but he wasn't there to buy a car.

"Let's go inside, take care of the paperwork and get you on your way. You made a great buy, that's a good little car," Ray boasted.

BJ followed behind him to the sales office, where Ray sat down at a cluttered desk and started filling out the sales agreement. His desk faced the wall and his back was turned to BJ, who was standing across the room looking at a wall of five-by-seven photos of cars Ray had sold. The used car dealer was so engrossed in the killing he was making on the sale of the Honda that he wasn't paying any attention to the man behind him.

At the sound of the blade of a folding knife locking into place behind him, Ray dropped his pen and reached for the

Glock in his paddle holster. His hand didn't get there before BJ grabbed a handful of his blond hair with his left hand and pulled a razor sharp SOG Twitch folding knife across his throat.

BJ stepped back and waited for the used car salesman to die. When his body fell forward and Ray's head was down on the top of his desk, he ran down the stairs. There were two red five-gallon gas cans under the stairs he'd spotted using binoculars when he surveilled the dealership earlier. He grabbed both cans and carried them back to the sales office.

The first gas can was emptied over Ray and his desk and the second was sloshed around the office. When both cans were empty, he unrolled ten feet of pyro-coasted firework cannon fuse he'd bought at Walmart that morning for twelve dollars and ninety-eight cents after he'd spotted the red gas cans. Leaving one end of the fuse a foot inside the door, he trailed the fuse down the stairs and lit the other end with a Bic lighter. The fuse burned at a rate of one foot every thirty seconds, giving him plenty of time to walk casually to his car and drive away.

Pyromaniacs might like to stay around to admire their work, but BJ had no intention of being captured on someone's cell phone taking pictures of the fire.

When he was safely out of the city and driving north on NW Glencoe Road, he called Nazir. "It's done. I don't know if you spotted the security cameras he had, but the DVR's toast. No one will be able to identify you from it."

"What about the fourth van Umara didn't use? Did you take care of that too?"

"It's a burned-out hulk at a boat ramp on a nearby lake. The only loose ends now are the attorney and his PI."

"I'll bring the package for the drone to your house tonight. Did you find a boat to borrow?"

"There's one at a marina just south of his office that will do. I'll get it at sunrise then motor down river to the Columbia like I'm going fishing. Then I'll turn back in time to move past his office before noon."

"Good. I'll see you tonight at nine o'clock and we'll prepare the drone. I want this to be the last we hear of this meddling attorney."

Chapter Thirty-Nine

DRAKE AND LIZ left for Seattle Wednesday morning at sunrise. They were driving the gray metallic Porsche Cayman GTS Casey used as a bribe to get him to serve as special counsel for PSS.

Lancer had been fed and his automatic dog feeder and watering system filled to last for the thirty hours they would be away. With the locking pet door Drake had installed, Lancer could go in and out of the farmhouse as he pleased and guard the vineyard from unwanted visitors.

After stopping at a Dutch Brothers Coffee stand in Tigard, they were ahead of the morning traffic and clear of Portland an hour later. Liz was looking at an apartment listing on her iPad her realtor sent her, while Drake listened to the news on the radio.

"Violence is spreading across the country like wildfire," a dramatic announcer proclaimed. "Black Panthers bombed police stations in six cities last night, while Antifa anarchists were rioting in downtown Denver, St. Louis and Chicago to protest the Labor Day marches by fascist groups planned for Portland and Seattle. More black-clad Antifa riots will take place in the days leading up to the weekend, an Antifa spokesman named John has promised, if the police don't do more to stop the fascist violence that's happening around the country."

The other all-day news channels were repeating the same narrative and Drake changed the channel to an FM station that played classic rock and roll.

Liz laid her iPad down and turned to him. "The violence being reported is all coming from the left. What fascist violence has occurred that we're not hearing about?"

"You noticed that. If it's as bad as they're saying, it should be the lead story everywhere. This kind of one-sided inflammatory reporting isn't helping the situation."

Liz poked him in the ribs. "Come on, Adam, you're not seriously saying the media has a bias?"

"Sounds like it to me. Find anything your realtor sent you that looks interesting?"

"Two of the listings are appealing. They're both in Kirkland and very expensive. As soon as I stop in and say hello to Mike, I'd like to borrow your company car and meet my realtor to see them."

Drake smiled and said, "Sure, I'll be busy. Take some pictures for me."

Company car? Is this how it starts? Will she want to drive the 993 next? If she does, I'd better get over being possessive about a car. It's just a car. Okay, the Cayman might just be a car, but my 993? I forgot that sharing a life with a woman means sharing everything. But my 993?

"Did you say something?"

"What?"

"You said, 'My 993.' Were you thinking about your other Porsche?"

"I must have been."

"I've been thinking about cars too. I sold the Cadillac CTS-V to a friend in Washington. I'll need to buy something here, unless I get a company car too."

Okay, time to change the subject before I say something I'll regret.

"Did Margo tell you what she was doing for Paul's birthday?"

"She said she was taking him dory fishing or something. She made it sound like fun."

"It is. I'm glad they're out of the office. Paul can handle himself, but I didn't want Margo left alone until we know why the Iranian was hanging around our office."

Liz's phone pinged with a message for her. "It's my realtor inviting me to lunch. Want to come?"

"Thanks, but I need to get with Mike and figure out what we're going to do about Caelus and Intel."

While Liz responded to the lunch invitation and looked at more of the listings her realtor just sent her, Drake drove on thinking about something she'd said earlier. Could there be a single sponsor behind all the crazy things going on in the country?

What enemy had the ability to stir up such a diverse group of players? The only enemy he could imagine being able to do it would be a nation state, like Iran or North Korea or even Russia. And if that was true, this was the start of something bigger than just violent protests and street riots.

Chapter Forty

BADAR JAMALI, aka Bijan Jahandar or BJ for short, followed a member of the Waverly Marina through the gate without having to use the marina key in his pocket.

He wore a pair of overalls and carried two toolboxes down the dock to slip 47, where a twenty-six-foot Bayliner Discovery 266 was docked. He chose the boat for its small cockpit and fully enclosed cabin that would allow him to stay inside when he was flying the drone.

Without looking around or hesitating, he stepped on the swim platform and opened the starboard transom door to set the toolboxes on the floor of the cockpit. He wasn't worried about the owner coming down the dock screaming for him to get away from his boat because the man was lying on the floor of his kitchen having had his throat cut the night before, when he'd followed him home.

BJ used the key on the owner's miniature buoy key chain to start the engine and jumped out to cast off the bow lines. He unhooked the bumpers and left them on the side of the slip before returning to the cockpit and casting off the stern lines. With the toolboxes safely sitting on the floor in the cabin, he backed the boat out of its slip and motored slowly out of the marina into the river.

The Waverly Marina was upstream from the RiverPlace Marina on the east bank of the Willamette River. The attorney's office was on the other side of the river above the River-Place esplanade. He kept the boat throttled back to minimize its wake and set the largest toolbox on the seat to his left. His right hand was on the steering wheel, keeping to the right side of the river while he got the drone out and unfolded it on the floor.

It was ten minutes to eleven and he was in no hurry. The attorney wouldn't have left for lunch yet. He didn't need to arm the drone until he crossed over to the other side of the river further downstream from the RiverPlace Marina.

There wasn't much traffic on the river midweek and BJ had the luxury of being on the water on a sunny day with an unsuspecting adversary close by. While he savored a kill that allowed him to see the defeat in an enemy's eyes as he died, this would still provide some satisfaction.

When the attorney had chased after him down the esplanade, he'd turned around and seen the eyes of a warrior looking at him. The ultimate outcome would have been the same if they'd fought hand-to-hand there and then, the man would still have died. For now, death at a distance would have to do if they wanted to put a quick end to the investigation the FBI agent had started.

BJ drove slowly down the river passing under one bridge after another, five in all, until he approached the I-5 Marquam Bridge and needed to cross to the other side of the river. He put the boat in neutral and let it float under the bridge. From there, he could arm the drone without being seen from above.

The molded case for the plastic explosive slotted in easily under the drone and he checked the remote-control trans-mitter to make sure everything was ready. The green light came on, telling him the drone was ready to fly.

BJ stood behind the steering wheel and checked for river traffic ahead and behind him. A sleek ski boat was speeding toward him from astern with its loudspeakers blaring. He let it pass before he started to cross the river.

The wake from the boat rocked the Bayliner from side to side, but he kept a smile on his face as he waved to the three near-naked girls at the rear of the boat.

He waited until the boat stopped rocking and then turned across the river, bringing the big boat up on plane quickly to cross to the other side. When he got there, he throttled back and kept the Bayliner nosing ahead at five miles an hour. He hugged the shore along Poet's Beach until he had to turn back out into the river to drive around the RiverPlace Marina on the west bank.

BJ let the boat drift downstream and studied the marina to see if there were moorages available there. When he reached the point directly across from the attorney's office, he put the boat in neutral and carried the drone back to the open cockpit. Stepping back inside the cabin, he started the rotors spinning. He watched the drone as it lifted off and soared up until it was level with the window above and to the left of the door of the attorney's office.

Before he flew the drone forward to crash through the window, he took the burner phone from his pocket and held it in his left hand. The bomb would be detonated when the drone was through the window, producing maximum destruction to the office and the condo above it.

BJ looked around to see if anyone was watching the drone hover above and then sent it forward as fast as it would fly.

He was concentrating so hard on hitting the attorney's window dead center that he didn't pay any attention to the siren of the Sheriff's Office green river patrol boat speeding upstream past him. The wake from the jet boat rocked the Bayliner so severely that BJ was thrown into the window and then back across the boat onto the floor.

He didn't see the drone bounce off the window to the right and ricochet upward, where it exploded a hundred feet in the air.

Chapter Forty-One

DRAKE WAS READING KEVIN MCROBERTS' report on the Caelus Research hacking attempt when Casey's assistant ran down the hall to his office and grabbed the remote for the flat screen TV on the wall.

"This just happened in Portland near your office."

A news reporter in a KOIN helicopter was describing the destruction believed to have been caused by an explosion of some sort.

"We were returning from the scene of a boating accident when
the first reports came in of an explosion at the RiverPlace on
the Willamette. When we arrived, first responders from the
fire department were already on scene, going from store to store
along the esplanade, searching for casualties. Windows are
blown in along at least half of the store fronts and offices on
the north end of the esplanade.

"Off to the right, we see a dozen or more bodies on the ground
along the way from the esplanade to the Kimpton RiverPlace
Hotel. EMTs are rushing to help them and, from our vantage point
hovering over the river, we can see ambulances coming from
every direction.
"We'll stay here for as long as we can, but KOIN reporters are
arriving now to report to you from the ground. For now, this is
Charles Cooper for KOIN News."

Drake saw that the window in his loft was blown in and the picture window in the Bennings' condo above it was as well. The front of the office and the condo didn't appear to be damaged, but several store fronts north of the office had doors hanging crookedly.

From what he could see, the damage was likely from an air burst explosion, like the ones he'd seen produced by an antipersonnel artillery round. Whatever it was that caused the explosion, he couldn't see anything that suggested it was caused by a gas leak somewhere. There was no cratering or obvious sign of an explosion originating on the ground.

Drake turned off the TV and called Liz. "Have you seen the news about an explosion in Portland?"

"No, why?"

"It was just outside my office. There are casualties and the windows along the esplanade are blown in. I need to get back to Portland."

"Wait for me. I'll be there in fifteen minutes."

Casey was watching the continuing coverage on the Portland explosion in his office when Drake walked in.

"Lucky you weren't sitting at your desk when your loft window blew in."

"Tell me about it. Margo took Paul fishing for his birthday, so they weren't there either."

"Are you driving back?"

"As soon as Liz gets here. I need to get the windows covered and clean up the mess."

"Any idea what happened?"

Drake sat down and looked across the desk at his friend. "I didn't have time to tell you about the guy outside my office taking pictures the other day. Turns out he's an Iranian, here on a student visa using a false name. His real name is Badar Jamali, an Iranian Army commando and nephew of a high-ranking Iranian intelligence officer."

Casey's eyebrows shot up. "You were the target of the explosion?"

"It's possible. I have a theory but nothing to support it yet. Wayne Williams was trying to find out if Umara had someone helping her to attack the Catholic churches when he was killed. Paul Benning is following up on his investigation because the FBI consider that case closed. If someone did help Umara, and that's why Williams was killed, they can't be happy we're trying to find them too."

"What does Iran, or at least an Iranian commando, have to do with Umara? She and Professor Ahmadi attended a Sunni mosque in Portland. Iran is Shia."

"I don't know, but I intend to find out."

"Does the FBI know about this commando?"

"The Sheriff's Office does. A friend of Paul's identified him using a facial recognition database and filed a report. I don't know if the FBI has seen the report."

"You might want to make sure they do. This isn't something you should handle on your own."

"It's starting to look that way."

"Before you leave, how are you doing on the Caelus Research matter?"

"Kevin's confirmed the attempt to hack their system can be traced to a server in a software division of Intel. I thought Kevin and I should pay Intel a visit and see if they'll assist us in our investigation."

"Do you think they will?"

"I do. Kevin doesn't believe Intel is behind this, but someone within Intel might be. He thinks Intel will be interested in proving they're above corporate espionage. Caelus isn't a competitor of Intel."

"Let me know how that meeting goes. Is there anything you need from here to deal with this explosion or this Iranian commando?"

"I can't think of anything, Mike. I'll know more when I see how bad the office is. I can always work from home, if necessary. Which reminds me, Liz met with her realtor to view two furnished apartments in Kirkland. If she likes one of them, she'll be here the first of the month, reporting for work as promised."

Casey leaned back in his chair before asking, "How's that going to work out for you two, with her living in Seattle and you living in Portland?"

"I don't know. We'll make it work somehow."

"For both your sakes, I hope you do. You seem happier than I've seen you since Kay died."

Drake nodded in agreement and got up. "I'd better hit the road and get my windows boarded up before it gets dark. I'll call you tomorrow with a damage report."

"Watch your back, Adam. If this commando tried to bomb your office and failed to kill you, he'll be back."

"I'm counting on it."

Chapter Forty-Two

PAUL AND MARGO BENNING were cleaning up the living room of their condo when Drake and Liz got back to the office.

Liz hugged Margo and then held the dustpan for her as she swept up broken glass on the floor.

Benning motioned for Drake to follow him to the bedroom. "I called a contractor I know to board up the window here and in your loft. He'll order new windows for us. I hope that's all right."

"Thanks. Were you still at the coast when this happened?"

"Fortunately. We were eating crab your guide cooked for us after fishing when I got a call from a friend at the Sheriff's Office. We drove right back."

"How bad is it?"

"Five dead over by the Kimpton. They were the closest to the explosion. Maybe another fifty were seriously injured by flying glass. Half a dozen people have been reported to be in critical condition. I expect there are a lot of people with ringing ears and headaches, if not full-blown TBIs."

"Did anyone see what happened?"

"That's why I wanted to talk in here. An eyewitness on a

boat in the marina said he saw a drone bounce off the window of your loft and then explode in the air. He didn't see who was flying the drone."

"We both know who it was."

"Our Iranian commando?"

"Has to be. That's why he was here taking pictures of the office. What he couldn't know was the loft window was made to withstand flying debris in a hurricane. That's why the drone bounced off."

"But not strong enough to withstand an airburst from the same plastic explosive that killed the guy in Albina over by the Black Panthers' place. They've found traces of it on a couple of tiny pieces from the drone."

"Does Margo know this?"

"I haven't told her all of it."

"Hold off, if you can, until we figure out where we go from here. In the meantime, pack a bag and check into a hotel. Put it on the office. I'll stick around until the windows are boarded up and take Liz to the vineyard."

"Are you concerned that he may know where you live?"

Drake put a hand on Benning's shoulder and flashed a tight grin before mimicking a version of Clint Eastwood's famous line, "Let him come and make my day. I'll meet him sooner or later, might as well be on my turf."

———

ZAL NAZIR WAS WAITING in his apartment after work, finishing his second beer, when BJ used his key and let himself in.

"What happened? I thought you said you knew how to fly that thing."

"The unexpected happened. The wake from a passing boat I didn't see coming knocked me off my feet just as the drone was about to smash through the window."

"Couldn't you have flown it around and tried again?"

BJ glared at Nazir before admitting that he had detonated the bomb accidentally when he fell.

"What do you intend to do now? I can't have this attorney, or his investigator, identify me. There's still too much to do."

"I'm aware of that. So is my uncle. You said you wanted to know if they had any idea who you are. If they do, they'll come after you. Then you'll know."

"I can't let them get that close."

"Don't worry, I'll be watching you. If they come, I'll be there to handle it. If I were you, I'd worry less about this attorney and more about getting the research from Caelus my uncle wants. He's not someone you want to disappoint."

"Did you ask him about using a ransomware cyberattack?"

"He doesn't like the idea, but he said if you continue to fail with everything else, go ahead and do it."

"All right, I'll do it as a last resort. Do you want a beer?"

"No, I have work to do. You do too."

———

BJ LEFT NAZIR'S APARTMENT, angry with himself and angrier yet that Nazir thought that he was in a position to criticize or question him. The man was a computer nerd who thought he was a mighty jihadist. Hackers were useful, and Nazir's band of hackers were among the best around, that's why his uncle was willing to support their grand ambitions.

But at the end of the day, the war would be won the old-fashioned way, with bullets and bombs and men who knew how to use the old weapons of war.

He knew he needed to calm down. Once they had the research that would allow Iran to control America's military drones, Nazir was expendable. His uncle had granted him his wish to make sure the pompous hacker was silenced if it looked like his involvement would implicate Iran. He relished the thought of being the one to do it.

For the present, his task was a simple one—put an end to the investigation of the ownership of Nazir's goat farm. The attorney and his investigator were proving to be harder to kill than anticipated, but no man was safe from a sniper's bullet forever. He'd just have to find the right place and the right time to take the shots if the two men got close to finding Nazir before Nazir got the research his uncle needed.

Chapter Forty-Three

MASON BRADLEY STOOD with his arms folded across his chest, watching twenty-five selected anarchists firing new Serbian AK-47s at targets fifty yards away. It was a greater distance away than he expected them to be when they opened up on the fascists, but it was good practice. They had to be prepared to shoot at more distant marchers, if they were given the opportunity.

When the range master beside him in the tower called, "Cease fire," he slid his hearing protection down around his neck and walked down the stairs to talk with his five captains.

"They aren't hitting many of the targets at this distance," he told his lead captain. "Give them a fifteen-minute break and pull the targets back to twenty-five yards."

The Antifa captain from Portland took his shooting glasses off and put them up on the bill of his black hat. "Do we have enough ammunition for another session on full auto?"

"That's what we'll finish up with today."

"Did the raincoats get here?"

"You'll get them when you leave, along with the radios, five police scanners and body armor for everyone."

"After the Labor Day marches, will there be more training?"

Bradley thought back to his training in Cuba as Weatherman. Mikhail Volkov was a young KGB officer then, in charge of the training camp for revolutionary fighters. The training had been extensive, not only in tactics and warfare but also in Marxist philosophy. He wondered what the young man beside him believed in, other than wanting to kick ass and kill fascists.

For what he wanted to accomplish, however, that was enough.

"We'll see how effective you are this weekend. If you're successful, we'll consider setting up training camps to grow the number of fighters in your movement."

When the fifteen-minute break was over and the targets had been reset at twenty-five yards, Bradley walked a distance away from the firing line and called Volkov in New York.

"I'm at the ranch, watching men learn how to shoot. It reminds me of how you taught me the same thing."

"Those were good times, weren't they?"

"Do you miss them?"

"Sometimes, but I enjoy what I'm doing now."

"Looking down on Central Park from your condo and eating caviar?"

"There's no need to be sarcastic. I did my time in the field. Now there are better ways for me to contribute, just as there are for you."

"One of my wild-eyed young men just asked me if there would be further training."

"There will be within the year."

"How will you select people to attend?"

"I won't, you will."

"Who will cover the cost?"

"I will. Why do you think I've been allowed to become a billionaire? Is there anything else you need before the weekend?"

"No. I'll leave here tonight and fly home. I've done as much as I can. The rest is up to them."

"Call me if anything changes."

Bradley's second call was to Nazir in Portland. "Are you at work?"

"I am."

"Take a break and call me back."

He lit a cigarette and waited for Nazir to call him back.

"Go ahead."

"I'm flying home tonight. Are you prepared to keep an eye on things this weekend?"

"Yes. Friends are giving me a hand."

"How many?"

"Four."

"I'll text you the numbers of the men you need to coordinate with. Call me if there's a problem."

"I will. Enjoy your weekend."

Bradley field stripped his cigarette and put the filter in his pocket. If anyone here was arrested and mentioned him or the ranch, he didn't want to leave anything behind that could be traced to him, not even a cigarette butt.

The Antifa captains only knew him by a first name, just as he only knew them by their first names. That's why they wore black bloc clothing and masks at protests; they fiercely guarded their identity. Autonomy was their watchword and it was his as well.

He returned to the tower and watched the instructors move along the line of twenty-five men, correcting stance and aim where necessary. More of the targets were now being hit, he saw through his binoculars, but it didn't really matter that much. There would be a lot of dead fascists and innocents, too, with the way these men were shooting. But it was the shock value, from a new level of violence, that he was after.

Antifa and the anarchists would later say they were only defending themselves against the weapons they expected the fascists to have. The media would agree with them because he'd already planted the seeds for that reporting. With city after city begging the fascist groups not to come to their city, how could the media report otherwise?

In the end, it would all be blamed on the new administration and its anti-immigration, anti-progressive and racist policies.

Politicians would pile on, just as they had during the fifties and sixties, when someone was accused of being an anti-communist. Lenin had called people who wittingly, or unwittingly, allowed themselves to become propagandists, "useful idiots." They'd been "useful dupes" then, ideologues so bent on defending their beliefs they didn't care to find out what was really going on as the U.S.S.R. manipulated public opinion.

Just like the media was allowing itself to be propagandists for Antifa.

Bradley smiled and walked back to watch his recruits empty their magazines on full auto. The communist agenda hadn't changed all that much since his college years. It still sought world domination, just like the Islamists. But its methods were subtler and more deceptive. Conflict was necessary, of course, but you didn't have to be the one doing the fighting.

As he was demonstrating with his manipulation of the current situation in America. The time was right to increase the divisions in the country and start a new civil war, one that would be bloodier than the last.

Chapter Forty-Four

DRAKE GOT UP EARLY Friday morning, after suffering a second frustrating night thinking of a way to find the Iranian commando. His mind had continued working on a solution through the night, without success. He finally gave up on getting any sleep and got up to make a pot of coffee and watch the sunrise turn the eastern sky pink.

The window in the office was boarded up and the replacement window wouldn't be installed until Tuesday, so they'd decided to drive to the senator's cabin south of Bend, Oregon. The area outside the office was still an active crime scene and the reporters and news camera crews still flocking there were a huge distraction. He knew it was unlikely that he'd accomplish anything if he showed up at his office.

But he was glad for an opportunity to get out of Dodge. He was looking forward to the drive over the mountains with Liz and meeting the senator's "friends".

Senator Hazelton had many friends, some of them long-time personal friends in Oregon and some of them friends from his long years as an elected official and politician. Drake had met some of them on occasion, but the senator had never extended an invitation to him for the sole purpose of meeting any of them. He knew it could be the senator's way of introducing him to potential new clients or it could be just a chance to see Liz again. Either way, he was glad they were going to spend time with his in-laws.

Liz came out onto the front porch wearing one of his long-sleeved white shirts and carrying two cups of coffee. She sat down in the Adirondack chair beside him and handed him his cup. "I smelled the coffee and saw you out here. You were so deep in thought you didn't even hear me ask if you wanted a cup. You okay?"

"Absolutely. I couldn't sleep and wanted to watch the sunrise. How about you?"

"I slept well. The smells on the breeze coming up from the valley over the vineyards are heavenly. They put me right to sleep."

"Is oatmeal with all the toppings and juice okay for breakfast? I thought I'd go light this morning and save room for lunch in Bend. I have a treat for you there."

"Oatmeal sounds great. How soon do you want to leave?"

"We're in no rush. Whenever we're ready. Why don't you go shower and I'll finish packing and fix breakfast?"

She ruffled his hair and went inside, taking her coffee with her.

Funny how something as simple as a gentle brush through his hair made him feel so good. He was going to miss the mornings when she was in Seattle.

He followed her into the bedroom and heard her singing softly in the shower. His old leather duffel bag in the closet was packed, except for his shave kit and a few last-minute things, like his Kimber, his tactical folder and his Surefire Defender flashlight. With everything that was happening in the country, there were some things you didn't leave home without.

Drake set his duffel bag on the bed and went to the kitchen to put on a pot of water to boil. Then he set out his favorite toppings for oatmeal; slices of apple and bananas, blueberries and walnuts.

When the water was boiling, he reduced the heat to simmer and gently stirred in the oats. He let it cook for four minutes, stirring occasionally, added a pinch of salt and filled two bowls with stovetop oatmeal, the same way his mother had made it for him.

When Liz joined him at the breakfast table, a bowl of steaming oatmeal was waiting for her, along with a pitcher of milk, small bowls of the toppings and a glass of orange juice.

Drake pulled out her chair and sat down across from her. "My mother used to make oatmeal for me this way. She was a nurse and very health-conscious."

Liz poured milk over the top of the oatmeal and added a spoon of each of the toppings before trying his creation. "Best oatmeal I've ever had. You have to show me how to make it."

"Can you boil water?"

"Very funny. You've never told me about your mom."

"She was special. Dad was a Green Beret and gone most of the time before he was killed. Mom was essentially a single parent. She helped me with my homework, never missed one of my games and taught me how to be a gentleman. That was my dad's thing, too, but she was the one who made sure I remembered my manners. And she coached me on how to get along with girls."

"She did a great job, from what I've seen. When did she die?"

"The summer before I started college. A drunk driver hit her head-on one morning on her way home from work. She was working a friend's night shift for the week. He'd been partying all night. I found out at his trial that he'd had two prior drunk driving convictions. It's why I wanted to be a prosecutor after law school."

"I'm so sorry about your mom. She sounds like the mother every boy should have."

"Yeah, I really miss her. You'll have to tell me more about your family on the way to Bend."

"There's not much to tell really. Dad was a real estate developer in San Diego and Mom was the belle of the country club. I'm the only child of a wealthy businessman who wanted a boy and a woman whose happiest moment was when she was mentioned in the paper for some social event she was involved with. They've been divorced for years. I rarely see either of them."

Drake got up to refill their coffee cups. "Is that why you joined the FBI, because your dad wanted a boy?"

"Oh, he got one. I was a tomboy that had to prove I was equal to or better than the boys. That's exactly why I joined the FBI after law school. It didn't make a difference if I was better than most of them, and I stopped caring. Which reminds me, I saw your Kimber in your open duffel bag. Should I bring my Glock with me to Bend?"

"It might be a good idea. Who knows what this weekend will turn out to be."

Chapter Forty-Five

THEY SAID goodbye to Lancer at eight o'clock with instructions to guard the house over the weekend. The vineyard manager and Drake's neighbor was bringing a crew in to make final preparations for the fall planting and said he'd check on Lancer throughout the weekend.

The temperature was seventy-seven when they left and eighty-eight by the time they turned off I-5 and headed east on OR-22 an hour later. The Labor Day weather reports were forecasting temperatures in the high nineties and it looked like they might have underestimated the high temperatures a little.

Drake liked to drive through the mountains with the windows down. He enjoyed the changing scents as they drove through Sublimity and then along Detroit Lake before climbing higher into the northern reaches of the Willamette National Forest and then the Cascade Mountain Range before crossing over into Central Oregon.

The forests along the way were home to a variety of trees, from Douglas Fir and Ponderosa Pine to Quaking Aspen along the highway at Black Butte Ranch and Western Juniper by the time they reached Sisters and turned south toward

Bend. To his nose, they all had a distinct scent and he pointed each of them out to Liz as they drove along.

When they reached the outskirts of Bend, it was almost noon. Traffic funneling into the city from OR-20 and US-97 filled the streets as people searched for parking close to their favorite restaurants, brew pubs or shops.

"I have a place I think you might like for lunch, if you're hungry."

"Your oatmeal was wonderful, but I am hungry. Where are you taking me?"

Drake was driving south on NW Wall Street and pointed to the next corner where the street intersected with NW Franklin Avenue.

Liz leaned forward to get a better look and started laughing. "The Drake? With a name like that, it has to be good."

"Trust me, it is."

He turned right at the corner and found a parking place half a block away.

The outside table he'd reserved before they left the vineyard turned out to be the closest one to the entrance of the restaurant, at the iconic corner in the old town.

After savoring a salad of apples and pears, a grilled Red Snapper sandwich and glasses of King Estates Pinot Gris that Liz said was "beyond wonderful," they drove south again, fifteen more miles on US-97 to the Crosswater Resort.

Drake gave the gate guard their names, which were checked off the visitor's list, and then drove to a secluded area of the resort where the Hazeltons had a two-story log cabin.

When the cabin came into sight, Liz whistled softly. "This brings back memories."

"Good or bad?"

"Both. I remember how gentle you were when you were taking care of me."

A sniper had shot at Drake from across the river and missed. The bullet had passed through a glass of red wine Liz was holding, shattering the glass and peppering her neck and face with slivers of glass. The red wine had looked like blood and he had rushed to her, fearing the worst.

"If that's the good memory, what's the bad one?"

She reached over and squeezed his knee. "Having to return to my job in Washington after you killed the terrorists before they blew up that dam."

"That seems like eons ago."

"What seems like eons ago?" Senator Hazelton asked, standing three feet from the door of Drake's Porsche.

"Where did you come from?"

"Just coming back from a walk. Snuck up on you from behind. Are you two coming in or do you need a minute?"

"Hi, Senator," Liz said. "I was remembering the last time I was here."

Liz and Drake got out and greeted the senator, Drake with a handshake and Liz with a hug.

"You two head in," Drake said, "I'll follow with our luggage."

When he stepped through the front door with their bags and set them on the floor, Meredith Hazelton was hugging Liz just inside the great room.

"I'm so glad you and Drake could come for the weekend. We miss seeing both of you."

Drake walked over and gave his mother-in-law a hug as well. "You need to come to Oregon more often, Mom."

"I know. When we rebuild our home in Lake Oswego, we will."

"Drake, you and Liz have your choice of rooms upstairs. The Carters, next door, couldn't come this Labor Day and the others will be staying there. There wasn't enough room for all of us here."

"How many of 'us' are there?" Drake asked.

"Four, in addition to the four of us. You'll meet them all as soon as they finish their round of golf. Why don't you take your bags upstairs then come meet me out on the deck?"

Drake grabbed their two bags and took them upstairs, pausing at the top. They hadn't talked about whether they should sleep in different rooms and he didn't know how Meredith or the senator would feel about it if they didn't.

He made the safer choice and put Liz's carry-on in one bedroom and his duffel in another.

Meredith led Liz into the kitchen. "It's early, but would you to like to join me and have a glass of wine?"

"I'd like that a lot."

"You may not have noticed, but Drake got to the top of the stairs and didn't know what to do with your bags. I'll bet he put them in different rooms. We'll let him wonder whether I'll approve of you two sharing a room a little longer before I let him off the hook."

Liz laughed softly and said, "Thank you. We didn't talk about it, but I know he wouldn't do anything you didn't approve of. Neither would I."

"Liz, we love you both and you deserve to be happy. We're delighted to see you two together."

"I'm sorry about Kay. I know Adam loved her deeply."

"He did, but I can see he loves you as well. I know you make him happy. That's all we want for both of you. The Chardonnay is chilled, let's take a glass and go sit down by the river."

Drake came downstairs and saw his mother-in-law leading Liz down to the river. The senator was waiting for him out on the deck with his arms folded across his chest, watching them.

"What do you think they're talking about, Adam?"

"I don't have a clue."

"Oh, I think you do. My wife is telling her it's okay for you two to sleep in the same room. She's going to let you worry about it until you bring it up. She's devious that way, so don't bring it up. It'll be more fun to see how she forces the issue."

Chapter Forty-Six

AT FIVE THIRTY in the afternoon, two golf carts rolled to a stop in the driveway of Senator Hazelton's summer home. Four men climbed out and came up the walkway, laughing at a joke Senator Montez had just told.

Senator Hazelton heard them coming from in the kitchen where he was seasoning steaks for dinner and greeted them at the front door.

"We skipped the nineteenth hole to come and enjoy your hospitality instead," said Mark Holland, the former head of the counterterrorist division of the New York Police Department.

"He means your free booze," Michael Montgomery, the former director of national intelligence injected. "The cheapskate wins the round at four dollars a hole and still wouldn't buy drinks at the clubhouse."

Senator Hazelton waved them all in. "I thought it might be something like that when the club called and asked if I wanted to close my tab when you guys didn't show up. The bar's set up, help yourself."

Secretary Rallings, the former director of the Department of Homeland Security, was the last in line and stopped beside

Senator Hazelton. "I see Drake's here. Did Liz come with him?"

"They're out back. Go say hello."

Secretary Rallings walked through the great room and stepped out onto the deck behind Drake and Liz who were sitting in two rocking patio chairs watching ducks float down the river.

"That wouldn't be the best executive assistant I ever had sitting there, would it?"

Liz jumped up with a big smile on her face. "It's good to see you, Mr. Secretary. I had no idea you were going to be here."

Secretary Rallings reached over the rocking chair and shook hands with Drake. "Adam, thank you for coming and bringing this lovely lady with you."

"Mr. Secretary, it's been a while. Have you enjoyed being home in Montana on your ranch?"

"I have, and it was the right place to be after my heart attack. But I'll confess, I miss my old job at DHS."

"And DHS misses you, Mr. Secretary. It got so political in the department after you left that I went to work for Senator Hazelton."

"When I heard you were unhappy, I called Bob and told him to reach out to you. Now he's going to miss you, too, I hear."

She glanced to her right and smiled at Drake before saying that she would miss the senator and the work they were doing.

"We might be able to do something about that, but we'll discuss that later. Have you met the others?"

"Not yet," Drake said.

"Let me introduce you."

Secretary Rallings walked back inside and led them over to a group of three men, standing together around the black granite bar in the great room.

"Gentlemen, let me introduce you to our guests. Liz

Strobel and Adam Drake. Liz and Adam, this is Senator Montez, Michael Montgomery and Mark Holland."

After shaking their hands, Drake said to Secretary Rallings, "The former DNI, former chair of the Senate Intelligence Committee and former counterterrorist head of the NYPD. I suspect it's no coincidence you gentlemen are here together this weekend."

Senator Hazelton came in from the kitchen and joined the group at the bar. "I said I wanted to introduce you to some of my friends and that's what I've done. But you're right, this is more than just a gathering of friends. For lack of a better name, we just refer to ourselves as "the committee". We all have intelligence and counterterrorist experience and share a concern for the future safety of the country. After dinner, we'll tell you about our current concerns and how you and Liz might help us."

Drake looked at the men standing before him and thought back to the time Secretary Rallings and his father-in-law had asked him to act as a trouble shooter for the government from time to time. He didn't know what he and Liz could do about their concerns, but he was willing to listen.

"Speaking of dinner, Bob," Secretary Rallings said, "who gets to grill those steaks I brought you?"

"I thought I'd ask you to do the honors," Senator Hazelton said. "Clearly, you don't trust any of us with the Wagyu beef you raise."

"No offense, it's just something I love to do."

"It's settled then. I'm going to see if my wife needs any help. Adam, try a glass of the Blanton's Single Barrel Bourbon while I'm gone. I think you'll like it."

Liz excused herself and left with the senator to see if Meredith needed any help. Drake poured himself a glass of the bourbon.

"Adam, your father-in-law told us about your involvement

in the terrorist attacks in Portland," Mark Holland said. "That was good work. How did you figure it out?"

"Just lucky, I guess."

"I doubt that luck had anything to do with it. In New York, when we prevented a terrorist attack, it was based on good intelligence, hard work and sometimes a hunch I was willing to trust."

Drake remembered being in the house the terrorist women had rented and seeing a calendar in the leader's bedroom with a date circled. It was the date of a holy mass of obligation, guaranteeing the Catholic parish churches would be full. He'd had a hunch that was when they would attack, and they had.

"It was a combination of things, but there was a hunch involved."

"Secretary Rallings told me you were also instrumental in preventing his assassination at the chemical weapon depot," Senator Montez said. "It sounded like you had a good hunch about that too."

He knew he was being interviewed and was curious about what they wanted from him. "That was just putting the pieces together, like I'm trying to do with these questions. What can I tell you about myself that you might not already know?"

Secretary Rallings smiled at his two compatriots. "I've seen you in action, they haven't. They're just trying to make sure you're someone they can trust. We're considering a course of action that could be dangerous for all of us."

Chapter Forty-Seven

AFTER THE DINNER table was cleared, and Secretary Rallings was complimented for the last time for his perfectly grilled T-bone steaks, they all moved into the great room. Senator Hazelton stood in front of the massive river rock fireplace and waited for everyone to get comfortable before he began.

"A year before the last election, I met with Senator Montez to get his thoughts on the state of the union. We agreed that the partisan divide in Congress was getting worse, that our enemies were emboldened by our confusing foreign policy and the economy wasn't growing as it should. Things any honest politician would agree on. But we also talked about the feeling we both had, that elected leaders of our republic weren't in control anymore. Bureaucrats ran the government and outside interests were funding campaigns, and even projects, that Congress had never approved. We had become a nation that was too divided to agree on the things that needed to be done. We decided we could no longer leave it to the bureaucrats to manage things unchecked.

"It was time to find a way to deal with the problem outside, and independent of, the government we used to direct and trust. Over the course of this last year, I shared our concerns with Secretary Rallings, Mark Holland and Michael Montgomery, men who had the experience and the love of country and were willing to explore ways to deal with the problem.

"The only tool we have at our disposal is our collective intelligence experience, based on the positions we've held and the contacts we've made. But we recognize that isn't going to be enough. We need someone to work with us without appearing to be an agent of ours.

"To prepare for this meeting, Secretary Rallings reached out to a couple of sources he trusts and has some information to share."

Rallings got up from one end of the leather couch and took the senator's place in front of the fireplace.

"You may have seen the 1976 FBI report that the *New York Times* obtained, with a Freedom of Information request, about the Weatherman being trained in Cuba by KGB officers. We also have records the CIA recovered in the fall of the U.S.S.R. that go beyond identifying Bill Ayers and Mark Rudd, the more famous members of the Weatherman. One of the KGB trainers in Cuba was Mikhail Volkov, billionaire oligarch and contributor to just about every liberal, progressive and socialist cause he can find.

"One of his trainees in Cuba was Mason Bradley, a radical professor and university lecturer here in America. Bradley recently organized, just before the last election, a radical student group along the lines of the old SDS, the Students for a Democratic Society. He calls the group the Students for Social Justice or SJS. Digging into Bradley's past, we learned that he was a professor at the University of Oregon in the 1990s. Berkeley Antifa traces its lineage back to that university at the time Bradley was there."

Drake looked at Liz and then back to the Secretary before saying, "My young friend at PSS has traced the money Volkov

SCOTT MATTHEWS

donates to over a hundred nonprofit organizations. Millions more have been passed on to four organizations that are not nonprofits and don't have to report to the government how they spend their money. The one that's been getting the most money is the SJS."

Rallings looked around to the other members of the committee for approval before he continued. "It's possible the Russian government, using Volkov as a front, is encouraging or organizing the Antifa violence and its call for civil war. We know they meddled in our last election. We think this could be a continuation of Russia's effort to meddle in our internal affairs."

"Why isn't the FBI or DHS investigating this?" Liz asked.

"Because Volkov is the single biggest donor to my party," Senator Montez said. "Not only that, but Antifa is the darling of the media for standing up to our new president and anyone they label as haters or fascists. The bureaucrats run the government. Those bureaucrats with a more progressive ideology, I'm afraid, aren't going to investigate one of their own."

Mark Holland got up to freshen his drink. "I'm a Marine and military history buff. I have to say, I've been impressed with Antifa's tactics. They're straight out of the writings of Clausewitz and Sun Tzu. Antifa had allies before all of this got started, with the media calling the president a racist and Hitler. Then its social media wing started attacking statues, as racist icons of the slave-owning Confederates. They knew if they threatened to tear the statues down, it would draw out the opposition they'd been calling racists and fascists. Now you have even more of the media, and even some prominent conservatives, defending Antifa for standing up against hate and bigotry. It's been brilliant."

"Is it your conclusion that Volkov is behind this call for civil war because of his KGB background and the work he did in Cuba training the Weatherman?" Drake asked Holland.

"It is. The goals of the old Weatherman and Antifa are

the same; spark an uprising that leads to civil war and a new form of government."

"Adam, we invited you and Liz to meet with us because we need you to help us investigate Volkov and Bradley. We can't go through the usual channels to see if we're right."

"What exactly are you asking us to do?"

"Find out if Volkov and Bradley are working with Antifa and the anarchists."

Chapter Forty-Eight

SENATOR HAZELTON SUGGESTED they all get a good night's sleep and meet again after breakfast, to give Drake and Liz a chance to think about the committee's proposal.

When the other members of the committee left to walk to the neighbor's house where they were staying, the Hazeltons said goodnight and left Drake and Liz alone.

"Let's go for a walk," Drake suggested.

The temperature had hit a high of ninety-nine that day. It was still in the sixties when they walked outside and looked up at the spectacular night sky above the high desert of Central Oregon.

Liz put her arm around Drake's waist and pulled him close. "I'm always in awe of the night sky here."

"It's one of the reasons I love this place, that and the mountains. We'll have to come back and go skiing this winter."

"Can we stay here?"

"We can use it whenever we want. I have an open invitation. I imagine you do, too, the way you're getting along with my mother-in-law."

He walked with her to the end of the driveway and

crossed over to the cart path that ran along the fourteenth hole and headed north.

"Do you think they invited me because they want my help or so we could be here together? Meredith made a point of letting me know how happy they are that we're seeing each other."

He chuckled and put his arm around her shoulders. "Did she also tell you that we're all adults and she wasn't concerned with whatever sleeping arrangements we decide on?"

"She was just being kind. You haven't answered my question. Do they really want me helping you investigate Volkov?"

Drake knew the committee probably did, but he wasn't sure that he did. If the idea was for her to assist him from an office at PSS, he was okay with that. If they wanted her to operate beside him and put herself at risk, he'd have to think about it.

She was a trained FBI agent and could take care of herself, he knew. But he didn't want to worry about her safety. If he told her that, he would sound like the misogynistic men in the FBI she'd worked so hard to outperform.

"Senator Hazelton and Secretary Rallings both know you and what you're capable of doing. I'd say yes, they want both of us to help them. What are you thinking?"

Liz stopped and turned to face him. "I'm wondering what you're thinking. Do you want me helping them?"

"Of course I do. But when you call me 'cowboy,' I think part of it's because you think I'm taking too many risks. Do you really want to saddle up and take the kind of risks I'm used to taking?"

"If it means being there to make sure you come back to me, absolutely. But I don't see how helping the committee investigate Volkov means we're going to be dodging bullets together."

"But what if it does?"

"Then I'll be right where I want to be." She slipped her

arm through his and walked on. "The bigger question is do we want to get involved in what the committee is proposing? They not only want to take on one of the richest men in the world, who may or may not be fronting for Russia, they want to take on the entrenched bureaucracy of the federal government. Elected presidents have tried, and all of them have failed."

"I don't think we have a choice. If they're right, the escalating violence has to stop before there is a civil war. We have to find who's behind this. If it is Russia, or Volkov acting on behalf of Russia, that has to be exposed."

"How do we do that?"

Drake stopped and looked up at the Big Dipper low in the evening sky. "Kevin gave me a list of four organizations that receive money from nonprofits Volkov supports. If we trace the money from one of them to Antifa, we'll know where to look for the evidence to unravel this whole thing."

"And then what?"

He faced her and clasped his hands behind her neck. "Then we find a way to force the government to do its job without years of congressional hearings and endless FBI investigations and put the bad guys away."

"And how do we do that?"

"We don't. The committee members know where the bodies are buried. They'll find a way to do it for us."

They turned around when they reached the fourteenth green and headed back to the Hazeltons' cabin, walking arm in arm. The night was so still they could hear the whisper of the river and music and laughter floating across the river from a nearby vacation home.

They agreed they would help the committee investigate Mikhail Volkov and Mason Bradley and trust the instincts of two men they knew and admired, Senator Hazelton and Secretary Rallings. If those two, and the other members of the committee, were willing to put their reputations on the line, they really couldn't say no. And if helping the committee required risking more than their reputations or their livelihood, they would at least be taking the risk together.

For now, they had a long holiday weekend to enjoy, with the threat of civil unrest hundreds of miles away.

When they got back to the Hazeltons' cabin, the lights in the great room were dimmed and a black bottle of Remy Martin V.S.O.P. cognac and two snifters were sitting on the kitchen counter.

Drake picked up the bottle with one hand and the two snifters in the other and nodded his head toward the French doors leading out onto the deck. "Let's do some more star gazing. Grab a couple of the throw blankets and we'll sit down by the river," he whispered.

The quarter moon provided enough light for them to see a pair of ducks floating by on the Little Deschutes, while Liz spread the throws on the ground and Drake poured the amber cognac into their snifters.

When they sat down, he put his arm around her and kissed her lightly on the cheek. "Great way to begin a weekend."

With her head tilted back to look at the stars, the soft moon glow provided a cameo of her that was stunningly beautiful. The serene look on her face told him that she was enjoying the night.

"Penny for your thoughts," he said.

"I was thinking about how my life has changed since I met you."

"For better or worse?"

"What do you think? I'm sitting here with the first man I've ever really loved, drinking cognac under these incredible stars. Could it get any better than this?"

Drake looked at the stars with her and said, "Finish your cognac and let's find out."

Chapter Forty-Nine

SATURDAY MORNING IN PORTLAND, Oregon, five hundred men and women from all over the west assembled at the north end of Waterfront Park. The permit issued to the patriot group sponsoring the "Day of Unity and Prayer" allowed them to march down the park trail along the river to the Tom McCall Waterfront Park for a rally at noon.

Some of them carried signs defending the Constitution and the right of free speech. Others had U.S. flags draped over their shoulders. They were dressed casually in jeans, T-shirts and hats, and most of them had small backpacks on. The average age appeared to be forty, but a number were older. A few were young children who marched with their parents.

They milled about, greeting those they knew and picking up copies of a flyer to read that had been prepared by the organizer. It reminded them that the march was to be peaceful and not to be provoked by the anarchists. Armed security was being provided, so they had nothing to be worried about.

Judging by the obvious tension and nervousness the marchers were displaying, the flyer wasn't reassuring them. They all knew the black clad and masked anarchists would be waiting for them at the other end of the park. The violence they had experienced in the past had consisted of being punched by anarchists wearing brass knuckles or being hit with signs the anarchists carried. Armed security wasn't going to protect them from the in-your-face confrontation they expected.

At eleven o'clock, the organizer raised a megaphone and thanked everyone for coming and refusing to be silenced by the tactics of those who sought to destroy the country.

"The tactics of our black clad, black bloc opponents aren't new. The violent tactics they use against us are the same tactics used in Germany by Hitler, and Mussolini in Italy, to gain power and silence the opposition.

"This isn't about the last election. It's about shouting down anyone who opposes them and wanting to make this country something our Founding Fathers never intended it to be. We have the right to be heard, and we will be heard today.

"We are not white supremacists, Nazis or the KKK. We are citizens of the greatest nation the world has ever known and we intend to keep it that way. So be brave, be respectful and let's go show them we won't ever let them take our freedoms away."

The organizer led the way south on the park trail that bordered the Willamette River, surrounded by a dozen men armed for their security. The rest of the marchers followed behind, talking among themselves and keeping an eye out for any black clad protesters headed their way.

No one noticed the anarchists moving into the north end of the park behind them on the trail when they were a hundred yards south of their assembling place.

By the time they marched under the Burnside Bridge, a scattering of hecklers had formed along the trail, whistling and jeering and shaking signs with black swastikas and red lettering proclaiming, "Fascists aren't wanted here!" and demanding, "Take your hate someplace else!"

Air horns blared and mixed with the jeers of the hecklers along the trail. Most of them were in their twenties, and a few wore bandanas tied across their faces to hide their identity. A few wore black clothing in support of Antifa.

As they marched past the Saturday market off to their right, a limited police presence was forming up thirty yards behind the jeering hecklers. The police stood stoically, dressed in riot gear, and made no effort to get involved in the developing confrontation between the two groups.

The crowd of hecklers and protesters continued to grow as the marchers continued walking toward their ultimate destination, the Salmon Street Fountain. With the fountain in sight, as they passed under the Morrison Street Bridge, the size of the jeering crowd had swelled to over a thousand people.

They were outnumbered four to one, but they didn't stop their forward progress. In past marches, that was when marchers and protesters broke into small groups and began arguing about immigration, capitalism, global warming, gender equality and white privilege, the usual talking points the left and right loved to debate.

At the Salmon Street Fountain, the marchers crowded around the organizer and started chanting, "USA, USA, USA," before the designated speakers used a megaphone to explain the reason they were marching.

A hundred air horns drowned out the first speaker, and the pushing and shoving began. Punches were thrown, and several marchers and protesters were knocked to the ground, but it was the noise and shouting that dominated the chaotic scene initially.

The small formation of riot police was now standing along the Naito Parkway, watching from a distance. Their backs were turned to three groups of Antifa running down SW Salmon, SW Madison and SW Yamhill, toward the Salmon Street Fountain. Two more groups of Antifa were running on the Waterfront Park Trail approaching from the north and south, cutting off the escape routes along the river.

Among the members of the five Antifa groups running toward those assembled around the fountain were fifteen anarchists Mason Bradley had trained. They were wearing long, black raincoats that concealed their AK-47s with folding stocks and their body armor.

Chapter Fifty

THE SIGNAL for the five Antifa groups to move in came at twelve fifteen, when a local Republican running for the state legislature was handed the megaphone to speak. That was all the spark the protesters seemed to need to ignite the incendiary confrontation and start pepper spraying the marchers. But it wasn't the sound of the young politician's voice. It was the signal from the five Antifa captains.

The marchers who had been pepper sprayed before came prepared and pulled gas masks out of their backpacks and retaliated by pepper spraying the protesters closest to them. Those who didn't have gas masks, on both sides, blindly fought their way out of the melee and stumbled into the crowd of onlookers gathered at the edge of the fountain.

The five black-clad Antifa groups used the confusion of the moment to pull on their masks and black bandanas. They moved around the line of riot police to make their way through the onlookers. They were confronted by the armed security of the marchers, who had moved to the front and were now trying to break up the fighting.

Mason Bradley's armed captains among the Antifa anarchists surrounded the patriot marchers. On command from the lead captain, they threw open their black raincoats to bring out their stubby AK-47s with folding stocks slung at their sides and began firing on full auto into the crowd of marchers.

At the sound of gunfire, people began screaming and running in all directions, falling over each other in the panic to escape the killing. The marchers' armed security, who survived the initial onslaught and were still standing, responded as they had been trained in the military and drew their own weapons to return fire. They, too, were cut down and fell beside their compatriots.

Before the police could move in, the armed Antifa anarchists dispersed into the fleeing crowd and ran toward three extraction sites.

Overhead, three DJI Inspire 1 surveillance drones, operated by three brothers of Zal Nazir's Council, monitored the police response to the massacre to make sure the shooters escaped capture. The surveillance proved to be unnecessary. The police had no way of singling out the shooters, who had concealed their weapons back under their black raincoats and ran away with the rest of the protesters and anarchists running from the fountain.

In three minutes, from the time the last round was fired, the Antifa killers had reached the vans waiting for them at the Portland Saturday Market, in the underground parking lot of the World Trade Center, across the Naito Parkway from the Tom McCall Waterfront Park and the parking lot of the nearby Kimpton RiverPlace Hotel.

Forty-seven people died in the massacre at the Salmon Street Fountain. Thirty-nine were patriot marchers, including three mothers and two children. Five of the dead were innocent bystanders and three were photo journalists filming the march.

None of the Antifa anarchists died in the shooting at the fountain.

———

MASON BRADLEY WAS WATCHING the coverage of the Portland violence on his houseboat in Berkeley when he received a text from Volkov.

IT BEGINS.

Bradley got out of his reading chair with his glass of Scotch in his hand and walked out onto the rear deck of his houseboat. A light haze hung over the bay to the west, but the afternoon was warm and pleasant.

He thought about the years he'd devoted to the revolution and the resilience of the nation he despised; the mindless people who voted for empty suits with no ideology to guide them other than the ideology of expediency and the greedy fundraising for their reelection. The wealthiest nation on Earth was controlled by one percent of the population, who didn't give a damn about the workers who made them rich or the world they plundered for their own benefit.

Well, that had to change. The winds of rebellion and revolt were blowing strong in Europe and were picking up in America as well. He responded to Volkov's text.

IT'S TIME.

Zal Nazir was waiting in his condo for his three Council brothers in Portland to check in when the first message arrived.

WE WEREN'T NEEDED. ALL OK.

He slapped his leg and walked to the refrigerator to get a beer. Bradley had pulled it off. According to the news reports, no arrests had been made. The police had secured the area but mainly to clear access for the first responders and ambulances.

Camera crews from the local television channels were on site within minutes to broadcast the carnage to the world, each of them trying to outdo the other with streaming news banners describing the horror of the massacre with the narrative they were committed to.

BLOODY HATE IN PORTLAND!

MARCHERS PROVOKE DEADLY VIOLENCE IN THE CITY OF ROSES.

47 DEAD AT FASCIST MARCH IN PORTLAND.

He wondered what the talking heads were going to do when the first few videos appeared on YouTube, showing the black clad shooters firing into the crowd of patriot marchers with their AK-47s. They had agreed with the anarchists when they said it was okay to punch a fascist. Would they find a way to exonerate their darlings for killing as well?

What a messed-up country. If America was Muslim and Sharia ruled the land, violence like this would not be tolerated. Allah's justice would have silenced both the infidels and the godless Marxists.

This was working out as well. Volkov and Bradley were playing America like a Stradivarius, and he got to sit back and enjoy the music.

Chapter Fifty-One

AFTER AN EARLY MORNING run on the cart paths winding around the championship golf course at Crosswater and kayaking on the Deschutes, Drake and Liz were having lunch with Meredith Hazelton on the deck at Hola's Trout House in Sunriver.

"I've been to the Trout House many times, but this is the first time since it changed hands and became a Peruvian and Mexican restaurant," Meredith said. "What's good?"

"I've only eaten here once," Liz said, "but the shrimp enchilada I had was excellent."

Meredith decided on the enchilada.

They were watching a young family float by in a canoe on the river when Drake's phone vibrated in his pocket. He excused himself and walked to the railing of the deck to take the call.

It was from Senator Hazelton. "Have you seen the news from Portland?"

"No sir, I haven't."

"Forty-seven marchers were gunned down at a Free Speech march half an hour ago. We're cutting our round short and heading back to the cabin. Is Meredith with you?"

"She is."

"Go ahead and have lunch, but come to the cabin when you finish. We need to get ahead of this."

Drake walked back to their table shaking his head.

"What is it?" Liz asked when he sat down.

"There's been a shooting at a Free Speech march in Portland. Forty-seven people were killed."

"Oh no," Meredith said and covered her mouth.

"They're cutting their golf round short and heading back to the cabin. I think we should join them."

"That's fine with me. I just lost my appetite," Liz said.

"I'll go pay for lunch, if they've already prepared it. Liz, why don't you and Mom go get the car? I'll meet you out front."

Twenty minutes later, Liz parked the senator's black Lincoln Navigator behind three golf carts in the driveway of the cabin. The five men were in the kitchen making sandwiches and watching the news on the small television monitor sitting on the counter.

Senator Hazelton made room for his wife at his side and kissed her cheek. "All of the dead were patriot marchers, including three mothers and two children."

Drake sat the lunch containers from Hola's on the table and stood behind Liz and watched the news for a moment before asking, "Who were the shooters?"

Secretary Rallings said over his shoulder, "Witnesses are saying the shooters all wore long, black raincoats and covered their faces with masks or black bandanas. It looks like they were Antifa."

"That's quite an escalation from using bats and knives," Liz pointed out.

Drake left the kitchen and called Paul Benning in Portland.

"Are you in Bend?" Benning asked when he saw that it was Drake calling.

"We're at Crosswater. What happened?"

"I called a friend at the Sheriff's Office. From what they can piece together, some of the Antifa black clads had AK-47s under their raincoats. They shoved their way to the front of the protesters and started firing at the marchers ten yards away. The marchers didn't have a chance."

"Did we catch any of them?"

"Portland police were there in the background and had been told not to confront the marchers. They were only ordered to stop the anarchists if they headed downtown. They reacted too late to arrest anyone when the shooting started."

"You said they had AK-47s under their raincoats. Under-folding stocks?"

"That's my guess, on a shoulder sling."

"If you learn anything else, call me."

"I will."

Drake turned on the flat screen in the great room and stood close to it, studying the video from a bystander's iPhone. He hit the pause button when the AK-47 of one of the shooters could clearly be seen.

"Well look at that," he said to himself. "Mark, could I see you in here for a minute?"

Mark Holland was the member of the committee with the most recent first-hand experience with the favorite weapons of terrorists.

Drake led him back to the flat screen and pointed at the frozen image of the AK-47 the black clad anarchist was holding. "What does that look like to you?"

Holland stepped closer to the screen and studied the image of the weapon. "It looks like a shiny new AK-47 under-folder. Where did these guys get brand new toys?"

"That's what I'm wondering. Is there a way to check recent sales of these things?"

"I wish it was that easy."

"There has to be a way to find out where these weapons came from."

"There is a way to do that. There's a company called Conflict Armament Research that traces weapons used in conflict zones around the world. They've published a field guide that interprets the markings on various AK pattern rifles. There are identifying marks on AK-47 fire selectors, rear sights and the receivers all have factory identifying marks. If you identify the factory, you might be able to get them to disclose who their recent buyers are, but I wouldn't count on it."

"But they would have records somewhere in their IT system, wouldn't they?"

Holland grinned. "Yes, I suppose they would."

"If I can get the markings from one of the AK-47s the black clads used, do you have access to this field guide you mentioned?"

"NYPD has one of the field guides. Get me the markings and I'll have a friend there look up the factory that made the weapon."

"I'm on it. Thanks, Mark."

Drake called Paul Benning again. "Send me a clear image of one of the AK-47s used at the march. We're going to find out who bought those rifles for the black clads."

Chapter Fifty-Two

SATURDAY AFTERNOON AT THE HAZELTONS' cabin looked like a command center planning a war against an enemy, which, in reality, it was.

Secretary Rallings was on the phone to DHS staffers he trusted to learn if DHS had intel on Antifa and its anonymous leaders. DHS, he found, had precious little to contribute.

Former DNI Montgomery reached out to former members of his team who were at home for the holiday weekend. They couldn't add to the puny amount of information the committee had already accumulated.

Senator Hazelton and Liz were at the dining room table hunched over the senator's laptop, remotely accessing classified information the Senate Intelligence Committee had regarding domestic terrorist groups. They found there wasn't much that was new, and what there was pertained to patriot and militia groups, not to the anarchists or Antifa.

Senator Montez called staffers at the DNC to ask if any of them had heard anything about liberal or progressive money being funneled to Antifa. No one had heard anything about money for Antifa. They acknowledged that money for the "Resistance", formed to block the agenda of the new president, had been discussed but certainly not money for Antifa.

By five o'clock, they adjourned to the deck for appetizers and a beverage and to say goodbye to the summer and compare notes. They found they hadn't made much progress. After the massacre in Portland, a later confrontation in Seattle had killed a dozen more patriot marchers and one Antifa member, a young anarchist who was well-known in Seattle.

Meredith Hazelton voiced a concern they were all realizing. "Even if you find out that Mikhail Volkov is funding Antifa, that's not going to stop the violence. The patriot groups and the militias will certainly hit back. How will you stop the violence before we reach a tipping point?"

"The president will have to get involved," her husband said. "If there's bi-partisan support condemning the shooting, we might get the patriots and militias to stand down."

"That won't be easy to accomplish," Senator Montez said. "The media's backed itself into a corner by not condemning the previous Antifa violence. It hates admitting it's been wrong."

Drake got up and put a couple of mini quiches and smoked salmon cucumber bites on his appetizer plate. "Then we'll have to hurry up and expose this for what we think it is, another attempt by Russia to meddle in our internal affairs. When the media is faced with the fact that it's been duped and has been carrying water for the enemy, it won't have to admit its mistake, the country will do it for them."

"He's right. I don't see how we can stop this any other way," Secretary Rallings said. "The president might be able to use his bully pulpit to get the patriots to stand down for now, but that won't last forever."

"Then I suggest we make sure we know what we're doing before we leave tomorrow," Senator Hazelton said. "I don't see anyone else doing what needs to be done."

"Unfortunately, neither do I," Senator Montez said.

Senator Hazelton had reserved a table at the Grille in Crosswater for dinner and when Meredith and Liz left to freshen up before leaving, Drake checked his phone and saw that he had a message from Paul Benning.

Drake, this is the best shot of one of the shooter's AK-47 we could find. Hope it's good enough for what you need.

Mark Holland was standing at the edge of the deck, looking at the mountains in the distance when Drake walked over and stood beside him.

"This is the best shot of one of the shooter's AK-47 the Sheriff's Office could come up with. Can you get someone to find out who manufactured it for me?"

Holland took Drake's phone and expanded the photo. "Oh yeah, you can see the marking on the receiver clearly. But I don't need the field guide to identify the manufacturer. See the mark inside the circle on the receiver? That's the mark for the Zastava Military Arms factory in Serbia."

"That's all we needed, thanks Mark. Now let's find out who bought it."

Drake took his phone back and called Kevin McRoberts. "I hope you're not in the office," he said when Kevin answered.

"Hi Mr. Drake. Actually, I am in the office, but I'm not working. I picked up a bucket of ribs at that rib shack Mr. Casey took me to and stopped by to pick up my new laptop. I'm meeting some friends for a friendly gaming tournament at my apartment. Did you need something?"

"When you have time, I need you to pay a visit to a factory in Serbia and find out who's been buying their assault rifles recently. One of their new AK-47s was used in the shooting at the Salmon Street Fountain."

"What's the name of the factory?"

"The Zastava Military Arms factory."

"How far back do you want me to go?"

"Good question. How about one year?"

"Piece of cake, Mr. Drake. I can have it for you when I see you Tuesday."

"Perfect. Good luck with your friendly tournament."

"Luck is what you hope for when you're gambling. I never gamble. Victory tonight is a sure thing."

"You sound pretty confident."

"I should be, Mr. Drake. I created the game. See you Tuesday."

Drake would have considered the young hacker's prediction braggadocio if he hadn't known how good the kid was. By Tuesday, he would know every buyer in the last year who bought AK-47s from the factory, how much they paid, where they were shipped to and probably the name of the buyers' grandmothers.

Chapter Fifty-Three

SUNDAY MORNING AT THE HAZELTONS' cabin at Crosswater bristled with activity as everyone prepared to return to their homes. Each member of the committee had been assigned a task to prove Mikhail Volkov and Russia were funding the anarchist violence to destabilize America.

Senator Hazelton and Senator Montez would request a meeting with the president as soon as possible, to ask him to use his bully pulpit to condemn the Antifa violence. They would also ask him to encourage the states to vigorously prosecute the crimes that were occurring in their jurisdictions. There were far more state and local law enforcement men and women available for the task of prosecuting domestic terrorism than the fourteen thousand FBI agents who seemed to be more worried about foreign terrorism.

Secretary Rawlings would return home to his ranch in Montana to reach out to a man he'd hired to run the Office of Intelligence and Analysis (I&A) at DHS. He wanted to know if he was doing anything to find out where Antifa was getting the money to travel the country and riot wherever it wanted to.

Michael Montgomery, the former Director of National

Intelligence (DNI), volunteered to return to Washington and have coffee, lunch or dinner with old friends in the CIA and NSA, to hear any gossip about Russia meddling again in U.S. affairs. As a former and still interested member of the intelligence community, he assured the others he would find out what the chatter was.

Mark Holland, as a former head of the NYPD counterterrorism division, was tasked with contacting his former colleagues and friends in state and local law enforcement to see if they were planning to prosecute the various crimes being committed by the anarchists; rioting, inciting riots, arson, assault and murder, most recently in Portland, Oregon.

The tasks the committee could not undertake were left to Drake, Liz and PSS; computer trespass both here and abroad and any actions deemed necessary related thereto. Specifically, they were tasked with investigating Mikhail Volkov and Mason Bradley, the donations made by their foundations and anything that would establish their involvement with Antifa.

While technically illegal, Drake had assured the committee that the hacking would not be detected. Everything else they did would be within the letter of the law and/or defensible. He promised that he would take full responsibility for anything he orchestrated.

Drake and Liz left before the others to return to the vineyard and pack the things Liz needed for her first day of work at PSS in Seattle.

On the way, with the snow-capped peaks of the Three Sisters seemingly close enough to reach out and touch just west of U.S. 20, Liz voiced a concern that was bothering her.

"The committee is asking a lot of you and Mike. Have you advised him, as his special counsel, of the risk the company's taking if Kevin gets caught hacking Volkov's computers? A billionaire like Volkov will use every penny of his vast resources to crush PSS if he traces the hack."

Drake just nodded in agreement. "But I know what Mike

will say. He'll say Kevin will have to make sure he's not caught."

"Kevin can't guarantee that, no hacker can."

Drake remembered his friend talking about hearing from Microsoft about the fourteen-year-old hacker who had accessed the Microsoft IT system. PSS was providing security for some of the buildings on the Microsoft campus early on, and Casey had become friends with one of their VPs. He'd suggested letting PSS mentor the youngster as a white hat hacker, someone he'd been wanting to add to his fledgling company for its IT services.

Microsoft had agreed not to press charges against Kevin McRoberts if there was no more computer trespassing until he graduated from high school. That was nine years ago, and Kevin was now recognized as one of the top white hat security hackers in the world. He hadn't broken his promise to Microsoft or Casey while in high school, but Drake knew of several occasions when he had since then.

"Liz, with the way Kevin masks his intrusions, it would take Volkov a long time, and a lot of luck, to trace Kevin to PSS, if he could trace the hack at all. Kevin is driving down to Portland with me on Tuesday to confront a software division of Intel about the attempted hacking of one of our clients. It took Kevin a week to trace the attempts to Intel and what he calls "rookie mistakes". Kevin's in a league of his own. He doesn't make rookie mistakes."

"I hope you're right. I'd hate to see PSS go out of business before I have a chance to work long enough to pay for my move to the Northwest. Speaking of working for PSS, how am I getting to Seattle by Tuesday?"

"I was planning on driving you up tomorrow."

"And leave Lancer alone for another day or so? Why don't you let me borrow your company car and I'll drive up?"

"Oh, I can't let you do that."

"You can't or you won't?"

"You know what I mean. It gives me another day with you."

"Good recovery, Adam. I don't want to take your company toy away from you. I thought it would send a subtle message to Mike if I show up driving your Porsche Cayman."

Drake laughed and turned to see if she was serious. She was. "You want him to buy you a Porsche?"

"No, I was thinking of a new Cadillac CTS-V, like the one I had in Washington. Six hundred and forty horsepower and two hundred miles an hour. Something that you would only see my tail lights pulling away in the distance if you ever raced me in that old Porsche of yours."

Those were fighting words, and he loved every one of them. Even if it did mean there would have to be a few upgrades on his cherished old silver Porsche 993, before then, if he wanted to win.

Chapter Fifty-Four

THE DAY after fifty-nine Free Speech marchers were killed in Portland and Seattle, patriot group leaders met in Boise, Idaho, to plan and organize their response to the deaths of their members. The mood was solemn anger and there was a resolute determination to avenge an eye for an eye.

Antifa anarchist leaders in Oregon and Washington had been identified with social media surveillance tools, the same tools used by law enforcement, and by arrest records in the two states. The locations of the leaders were mapped out. Men were assigned to travel to the various addresses of the leaders and to make simultaneous citizens' arrests on Monday night, Labor Day.

Attorney volunteers prepared charging documents to be served on each of the Antifa anarchist leaders. The felony crimes the patriots had reasonable cause to believe had been committed were listed on the individuals' statement of charges: murder, conspiracy to commit murder, inciting to riot, conspiracy to riot, and hate crimes committed on the basis of race (white men), religion (Christian), gender (male) and sexual preference (heterosexual).

Patriots with law enforcement training and experience

instructed the members of the arresting squads on the legal requirements for a citizen's arrest. Arrests were allowed when there was a reasonable belief that the suspect had committed a felony and the individual making the arrest had a reasonable suspicion about the identity of the perpetrator to justify the arrest.

The squad members were instructed to only use reasonable force necessary to make the arrest. They were also warned that deadly physical force could only be used if deadly physical force was imminent and threatened against a person, themselves or another person.

The first patriot team of three men pulled into the parking lot of the Crest View Apartments on North Columbia Boulevard in Portland, at nine fifty Monday night. They were there to arrest Billy Marquez, a twenty-four-year-old Antifa leader. They waited five minutes in the ten-year-old Ford F-150 extended cab pickup before getting out and taking the stairs to the second floor of the building. They walked calmly down the exterior hallway to Apartment 217 and stopped outside.

One man stood in front of the door with the charging document in his hand while the other two stood to either side with their backs to the wall. They were armed. Their weapons were concealed to avoid escalating any resistance they encountered from anyone coming to the door.

One knock, followed by two more, announced their presence. A television was playing with a soundtrack that sounded like some action movie and a muffled voice asked, "Who's there?"

"Mr. Marquez? Special delivery. UPS."

Someone marched to the door and an eye appeared at the door viewer peephole.

The patriot at the door, wearing a brown T-shirt and a baseball cap, waited for it to open.

"Just leave it at the door."

"It's marked, 'Fragile,' Mr. Marquez. I think you should take it inside."

"All right, just a minute."

The security chain was taken off and the door opened, enough for Marquez to reach an arm out to take the package.

"Sorry, sir. I need your signature first." The patriot held a clipboard with a pen in front of him and waited for Marquez to step out to sign for the package.

When he did, the two patriots on the sides of the door grabbed his arms and pulled him out into the hallway. The patriot with the clipboard closed the door and turned to face the Antifa leader.

"Mr. Marquez, we are arresting you as citizens for the felony crimes of murder, conspiracy to commit murder, inciting a riot, conspiracy to riot and hate crimes against your fellow citizens."

Marquez struggled to free himself from the grip of the two patriots and yelled, "What kind of bullshit is this? You can't arrest me, you fascist pigs! Someone call the cops!"

"The police are on the way, Marquez. They will take you into custody for the crimes you have committed. So just relax until they get here."

Doors opened up and down the hallway, but no one came out to defend Marquez as he continued to yell for help.

Within five minutes of his arrest, a Multnomah County Sheriff's patrol car pulled into the parking lot and two deputies got out to take custody of Marquez. They had been alerted to the pending arrest by law enforcement brothers in Boise.

AN ARREST one hundred and seventy-eighty miles north in Seattle didn't go as smoothly as the arrest of Billy Marquez. An Antifa leader who went by the nickname "Simon", a murdering terrorist character in Joseph Conrad's novel *AN ANARCHIST*, shared an apartment in the University District with other anarchists. The number of his roommates varied from one week to the next.

For that reason, two pickups and six patriots were dispatched to the Tamarron Apartments on Seventeen Avenue Northeast to make the arrest. Simon, whose legal name was Allen Thompson, was a nineteen-year-old student at the University of Washington and was known to brag about his gun collection and his desire to kill cops.

Simon's apartment was a ground-floor corner unit leased in his father's name. In the rear, a sliding-glass door opened onto a small, concrete-slab patio. Music was playing so loudly that stealth wasn't necessary to approach the apartment from the front or the rear. Ironically, given the apartment's location in the University District, the music was from a Pink Floyd album, *The Wall*, and the song "Another Brick in the Wall... We don't need no education..." was playing.

With the frequent traffic in and out of the apartment, the front and the patio doors were not locked. When the patriots took advantage of the fact and entered the apartment, they found half a dozen anarchists and their girlfriends sprawled around the floor in the living room smoking pot.

Several of the women were in various stages of undress. They jumped up when the six men cordoned off the living room and asked which one of them was Simon. The women were allowed to leave the living room to find their clothes, but the men were told to stay on the floor with their hands in plain sight.

Before Simon identified himself, three of the women came down the hall from the bedrooms swinging baseball bats at the patriots. As the patriots struggled with the women to defend themselves, Simon and the anarchist men jumped up and joined the fight.

The mini-riot lasted several minutes until the anarchist

men were moaning on the floor from bleeding noses and sore jaws. The women were herded into a bedroom and told to be quiet if they didn't want to be arrested with Simon and the other men.

When the women were out of sight, it was only Simon who was told he was under citizen's arrest and read the charging document. The other anarchists watched silently as two of the patriots marched Simon out the front door to wait for the police to arrive and take custody of him.

Before the night was over, fifty-seven other Antifa leaders and organizers were arrested in the Northwest and taken into custody by cooperating law enforcement in the various cities.

Chapter Fifty-Five

AFTER FIVE FRUSTRATING hours on Labor Day in bumper-to-bumper traffic on I-5, with all the other end-of-summer travelers driving north, Drake and Liz checked in at the Woodmark Hotel on Lake Washington.

After a glass of wine on their private balcony and a quiet dinner of grilled shrimp in the restaurant downstairs, they celebrated Liz's new job, starting the next day, with a quiet night in the PSS executive marina suite.

Tuesday morning, Drake drove Liz to work and helped Mike Casey welcome the new PSS vice president for governmental affairs to her new executive office, next to Drake's. After a lingering kiss behind her closed office door when Casey left, Drake took the stairs down a floor to find Kevin McRoberts and leave for their meeting with the head of Intel's Software Solutions division in Hillsboro.

Kevin was in his office at the rear of the IT section, standing behind his desk and looking down at the screen of his laptop. When he looked up and saw Drake, he closed the laptop and grabbed the coat hanging on the back of his chair.

"Mr. Drake, is it okay if I ride down to Portland with you?

I can get something from the motor pool and follow you if it's not."

"Are you planning on riding the train back to Seattle, like you told me?"

"Yes, if that's okay. I've always wanted to ride the Coast Starlight, so this is perfect."

"Let's go then. You can tell me how you traced the Caelus hackers on the way."

"Sure thing, Mr. Drake."

They took the stairs down to the underground parking and Drake's silver Porsche Cayman GTS, parked next to Casey's black Range Rover. Kevin ran his hand over the top of the Cayman before he got in.

"Sweet ride, Mr. Drake."

Drake took off his coat and laid it on the rear folded down seat and got in. "Do you have a car, Kevin?"

"I have a bicycle, but I don't have a driver's license. Never really wanted a car, so I never got the license to drive one."

Drake started the engine and listened lovingly to the throaty exhaust bouncing off the cement walls. "I've always liked cars, especially fast ones. Get your driver's license and I'll let you drive this one. You might change your mind about wanting one."

They drove up the ramp and across the overflow parking area to the security gate and a biometric hand reader. It opened when it recognized Drake's handprint and they drove out onto the street. Thirty minutes later, after driving across the floating bridge on Lake Washington, they were on I-5 headed south to Portland.

Settling into the flow of traffic on the freeway, Drake asked Kevin about the Caelus hacking assaults. "What genius tricks did you use to trace them to Intel? If they were illegal, you can tell me. I'm the company's attorney."

Kevin laughed. "I didn't have to do anything super illegal, Mr. Drake. At least, not anything that's likely to get us in trouble. When you asked me to trace the money that Mikhail Volkov gives to the nonprofits he supports, that led me to recipients that weren't nonprofit, two of them. I took a peek at their IT systems and saw that one of them was using a proxy server at Intel to access TOR, the onion router. That made me suspicious, and I looked to see who he was sending messages to when he wasn't using TOR. One of them was someone else who was also using TOR a lot. His use of TOR and the pattern of the packets sent from his PC matched up with some of the hacking attempts through proxies at Caelus."

"Does that mean you can identify the individuals trying to hack Caelus?"

"Not yet, everything that's sent is encrypted. But if we can get the server logs from Intel, I will be able to."

"Is that likely to happen?"

Drake saw out of the corner of his eye that Kevin shrugged his shoulders before saying, "Who knows? It depends on how seriously they respond to one of their employees using an Intel server to access TOR. They'll want to investigate it themselves and I have information they'll need that they might not be willing to acquire for themselves. I thought we could offer them my information in trade for their server logs."

"You mean the information you obtained not 'super illegally'?"

Kevin laughed. "Yeah, that information."

"You said you got on to this while you were following the money from Volkov to two of the recipients who aren't nonprofits. Is Volkov involved in the assaults on Caelus?"

"I can't find that out just yet, but I'll keep looking. It could be that someone at one of these two places is behind the hacking. It doesn't have to mean that Volkov is."

"Keep digging on that, Kevin. Do you like what you're doing at PSS?"

"I'm having a blast, Mr. Drake. I'm doing what I love and

getting paid for it. Some of my hacker friends feel I've sold out, but I don't care. And really I didn't have a choice. It was agree to work for Mr. Casey or Microsoft was going to send me to jail."

"You made the right choice, Kevin. We're lucky to have you."

"Thank you, Mr. Drake. I really appreciate that."

Before Drake had a chance to ask about the Intel manager they were driving down from Seattle to meet, Kevin got a message alert and opened his laptop.

"Sorry, Mr. Drake. I need to deal with this."

"No problem. Go right ahead. I have some things to think about while you're busy."

There was really only one thing on his mind that he was thinking about; it was how he was feeling about leaving Liz in Seattle and heading home to Portland without her. It was one thing when she was on the other side of the country and the distance made it difficult to spend time with her. Now she was a measly one hundred and seventy miles and three hours away up the freeway.

He had obligations in Portland that were important, he told himself, that he just couldn't walk away from. But those obligations weren't all permanent, he knew. Eliminating them would require a major, major change in his life.

Like selling the vineyard. He promised Kay before she died that he would fulfill her dream and restore the vineyard, and he had.

Like closing his law practice and working full time with Casey at PSS. He could lease the office to Paul Benning for his P.I. work and be there with Margo.

As much as he wanted to see Liz more often, the thought of moving to Seattle and leaving the rolling hills of Dundee in the wine country and his old stone farmhouse caused a sick feeling in the pit of his stomach.

Kevin's voice interrupted his train of thought. "Do you think we could stop somewhere so I could pick up an energy drink? I forgot to grab a couple in my office and I need to be sharp when we meet the software manager at Intel."

Chapter Fifty-Six

TWO HOURS, an Ubermonster and a bag of Cheetos later, Kevin was ready to match wits with the Intel manager as they drove through the first layer of security at the sprawling five-hundred- thirty-acre Ronler Acres Intel campus in Hillsboro, Oregon.

Drake was directed to Visitors' Parking in front of RA1, the building housing Data Center Solutions. After entering the red brick building and passing through a second layer of security, before their names were checked off against an approved visitor's list, they were escorted to a small conference room and told that Porter Olsen would be with them in a minute.

The room had a round conference table with four chairs and, on one wall, four flat screens for presentations. There were no pictures on any of the burnt-orange walls. Along the wall opposite the flat screens was an ebony serving cart with two silver carafes, four cups and four water glasses.

The Software and Services Group manager didn't keep them waiting. They had just pulled out their chairs to sit down when he walked in and closed the door behind him.

Drake did a quick assessment of the manager. At five feet

eight and slender, he looked like someone who cycled a hundred miles on a weekend and rode his bicycle to work. His hair was prematurely gray, if he was as young as the early forties that he looked to be. He wore khakis, a white shirt sans tie and a lightweight blue chambray sport coat.

"I'm Porter Olsen, the manager of the Software and Services Group. What's this about someone hacking a client of yours using one of my servers?"

Drake made the introductions. "My name is Adam Drake. I'm special counsel for Puget Sound Security. Kevin McRoberts, the head of our IT division has accompanied me today to answer any questions you might have. Our client is Caelus Research, Inc., a defense contractor working on a DARPA grant. The hacking attempt on our client's system was traced to a server in the group you manage."

Olsen turned to Kevin. "I know your reputation, Mr. McRoberts. I assume you're the one who informed your employer that you believed one of my servers was involved."

"That's correct."

"And I assume, because you're here and not the FBI, that your methods of making this discovery were not entirely legal."

"I'm not at liberty to discuss how we made our discovery."

"Then why are you here? You surely don't expect me to believe one of my servers was involved without some evidence to support your accusation."

Drake decided it was time to level the playing field. "My client is a cooperating partner in the FBI's Counterintelligence Strategic Partnership Program. As such, we cooperate with law enforcement when we have evidence that someone is trying to illicitly acquire sensitive intellectual property or technologies. We have that evidence and we're here to see if you'll cooperate with us to determine if it's someone you employ before we turn this over to the FBI."

Olsen sat back in his chair and looked over their heads out the window before asking, "What form of cooperation are you proposing?"

Drake nodded to Kevin.

"I'd like to review your server logs and compare them to the information I have. We could do that together, if you like."

"That's what you came here to ask me? Absolutely not! There's no way in hell you'll ever see the logs from one of my servers."

"Would you rather have those logs reviewed by the FBI?" Drake asked.

Olsen pushed his chair back and stood, smiling. "Yes, I would, Mr. Drake, because then you would have to tell the FBI how you traced these hacks to one of my servers. I'm not a betting man, but I'm willing to bet that's not something you're interested in doing. I think we're done here. I'll have someone come and usher you out of the building."

The Intel manager turned and opened the door.

Before he left, Drake stood and held out a business card. "If you change your mind, Mr. Olsen, call me."

Standing in the open doorway, Olsen said over his shoulder, "Not necessary. I know where to find you, Mr. Drake."

———

ZAL NAZIR WAS WALKING down the hallway and heard his manager coming out of the conference room saying, "I know where to find you, Mr. Drake."

He momentarily froze and started to turn around before thinking better of it. There could be more than one Drake in the world and, besides, there was no way Drake could know what he looked like.

He needed to know if this Drake was his nemesis because, if it was the attorney who was trying to link to the attacks on the Portland churches and could interfere with his role in the Russian's plan, he had to be stopped immediately. There was too much at stake for Drake to live and mess things up.

Chapter Fifty-Seven

NAZIR CALMLY CONTINUED ON DOWN the hallway pretending to read his iPhone. When he was a step away from the open door of the small conference room on his right, Drake came out and turned left, throwing his shoulder into him as he turned and knocking him back a step.

His iPhone fell to the floor and Drake bent down and picked it up. "Sorry about that. I should look where I'm going."

Nazir took his iPhone from Drake with his right hand and rubbed his shoulder with his left hand. "Rugby or football?"

"Football. Are you okay?"

Nazir forced a smile. "I play soccer and get hit like that every weekend. Thanks for asking, but I'm fine."

When he stepped aside to continue down the hall, Drake said, "Sorry again. I hope your day is accident free the rest of the way."

Nazir nodded and walked past Drake and the young man standing in the open doorway. His pulse was racing, and he felt his face turning red. It was all he could do to keep from sprinting down the hallway. It was the attorney!

Why in the world is he here? Is he searching for me? If he is and doesn't know what I look like, I need to get out of here before he finds out. How could this be happening?

He took the stairs to the floor above and fast-walked to his cubicle to get his laptop and coat. On his way out of the project area he was assigned to, he told the project coordinator he forgot about a doctor's appointment and had to leave for a couple of hours.

When he finally got to his black BMW M5 in employee Parking Lot 1, he slammed the door shut, threw his head back against the headrest and closed his eyes. After taking ten deep breaths, he stared straight ahead and considered his options.

The attorney had to be killed, that was his only option.

When he was dead, he could remain in place and trust Allah to keep his identity, as head of the Council, a secret.

Or he could go underground and direct the Council's activities from a location of his choosing. He was an American and could travel freely in the country. Relocating to another city wouldn't be a problem.

But relocating to another country wasn't an option as far as he was concerned. His Iranian sponsors might want him safely in their custody, but he was accustomed to the American lifestyle. He wasn't eager to trade it for a Persian one.

Weighing the options, he decided to remain in place, at least for now.

His top priority was to eliminate an immediate threat, the attorney named Drake.

Nazir took a BlackBerry KEYone out of his laptop case. It was the smartphone he preferred for security purposes and communicating with encrypted messages to other Council members and BJ.

MEET ME AT MY CONDO IMMEDIATELY

He left the Intel campus and drove as quickly as traffic would allow to his condo in Orenco Station. BJ was parked on the street in front of his building as he drove past and took the ramp down to the underground parking.

When the elevator door opened on his floor, BJ was standing in the door of the stairway and followed him down the hall to his condo. Nazir entered the code on the key pad lock and opened the door. He went inside without looking back, even when BJ closed the door behind him.

When he turned around, BJ had a quizzical look on his face. "You look like you've seen a ghost."

"I wish it had been a ghost. If you'd done what you were supposed to, it would be a ghost. Drake was at Intel today! In my building! He doesn't know who I am, but he has to be getting close to finding out."

BJ held out his hand, palm forward. "Take a deep breath and slow down. Tell me what happened."

"I was coming back from a break and ran into Drake coming out of a conference room. I literally ran into him. He was meeting with my manager about something."

"Do you know why he was meeting with your manager?"

"I don't know."

"Can you find out?"

Nazir threw up his hands. "What difference does it make? He was in my building! Don't you understand? I don't believe in coincidences. He knows something. You have to kill him before he ruins everything."

BJ walked past Nazir to the refrigerator and got them each a bottle of beer. "Try to relax and tell me how you want me to do it. Do you want it to look like an accident? Do you want me to find out what he knows before I kill him? You have a job to complete for us and I can get whatever I need to get the job done, but it might be messy. He seems to have nine lives, like a cat."

"I don't care if it's messy. I just want it done quickly."

"All right. We know where he lives. I'll see if that's a good place to do it. If it is, it will take me a day or so to get what I need. Is that soon enough?"

"What do you need, another drone? That didn't get the job done last time."

"I was thinking of using a grenade launcher and a thermobaric warhead to blow his house up while he's sleeping. I can get what I need from a cell of ours in Canada."

Nazir pointed the neck of his beer bottle toward BJ and said, "Just make sure you don't screw it up this time."

BJ's eyes blazed. He took three quick steps into Nazir's personal space. "Remember who you're talking to, Nazir, and why I'm here. If you don't get the information from Caelus Research you promised, you won't have to worry about Drake. I'll kill you myself and save him the trouble. Do we understand each other?"

Nazir took a step back, but his eyes took on a hard look as he answered. "I understand you. Make sure you understand me. This is your last chance to take care of Drake. I don't think your uncle will tolerate another failure. I know I won't."

BJ set his bottle down and walked out of the condo without saying a word.

Chapter Fifty-Eight

IT WAS four thirty in the afternoon when Drake dropped Kevin off at Portland Union Station for his train ride to Seattle on the Coast Starlight. The train was regarded as one of the most spectacular train rides in the country and the kid was grinning from ear to ear as he waved goodbye and walked into the station.

He wasn't expected in his Portland office, with Wednesday being his day in Seattle for PSS, and Drake decided to head home rather than stopping in to see Margo. On the way, he told the Cayman's Bluetooth audio system to call Liz.

"Hi, gorgeous. How's your first day at PSS?"

"I've taken a tour of headquarters and met with a lot of people, but I know I have a lot to learn before I fully understand everything PSS does. How did your meeting at Intel go?"

"We didn't get what we were after, but Intel will be scrambling to find out why we thought one of their servers was involved in hacking Caelus. I'm hoping the mention of turning what we have over to the FBI will make them change their mind."

"You mentioned that PSS participates in the Strategic Partnership Program, didn't you?"

"Of course. I wanted them to know when the FBI come marching through their doors they should have cooperated with us."

"It's no wonder you're so universally loved."

"Just the way I roll. What can I say?"

"You can say you're rolling my way sometime soon."

"Would tomorrow be soon enough?"

"No, but it'll have to do, won't it?"

"For now. I'm going home early. I'll call you tonight."

"Until then."

"Until then."

Liz was a beautiful woman. He knew she loved him but there was no way he was going to lose her to some Romeo in Seattle who was attracted to her and was there when he wasn't.

To distract his mind from trying to find a solution to his problem, he selected a favorite from his playlist and cranked up the volume. The music from the Eagles didn't help. He turned it off and drove on in silence.

He stopped in Dundee at the Dundee Bistro and picked up the pepperoni pizza he'd called ahead to order and turned up Worden Road to head home. If a pepperoni pizza and a beer didn't help his mood, he wasn't sure what would.

When he turned up the long driveway that led up the slope to the old farmhouse, he saw Lancer running down to greet him. When Lancer ran down and turned to race him up the driveway, Drake rolled down the window. "You sure you want to do this, boy? This car is scary fast."

Lancer turned his head and barked once with his tail wagging.

"Okay, you asked for it. Ready, set, go."

Lancer took off like a shot and was ten yards ahead before Drake spun his wheels in the gravel and gave chase. His dog always won the race and it wasn't because Drake didn't try. The Cayman was no match for his German Shepherd.

He opened the overhead door in the section of the outbuilding behind his house and parked the Cayman. Lancer was standing next to the Cayman with his tail wagging. When Drake opened the door, he barked once and sat on his haunches, watching his alpha.

"You never get tired of racing me up the hill, do you? One of these times…"

Lancer barked twice and got up to walk ahead of Drake into the house. Drake took the barking to mean that 'one of these times' was never going to happen, as far as Lancer was concerned.

He followed with his sports coat thrown over his left shoulder and the pizza box balanced in his right hand. Lancer entered the house through the dog door in the mud room and opened the door for Drake by pulling down on the inside door lever with his paw.

"Thanks, Lancer. You just earned yourself a treat for dinner."

After changing into jeans and a T-shirt, Drake took a Coors Light and a round steak out of the refrigerator, cut the steak in half, and put it on a cast iron skillet to heat. Leaning back against the counter, he opened the beer and took a slice of the pizza out of the box and sampled his favorite from the menu at the Bistro.

Lancer was lying on the floor patiently waiting for dinner. "What would I do without you around to open my doors, buddy? Eat more steak and less pizza you say?"

Drake dripped a drop of water onto the skillet and saw that it sizzled. He sprinkled a little salt and pepper on the steak, seared it and then gave it another two minutes per side before lifting it out to cube and serve it.

"Enjoy it, Lancer, while I eat my cold pizza."

He sat down at the kitchen table with another slice of

pizza on a plate and had the first bite in his mouth when the phone vibrated on the counter behind him.

"Is your TV on?" Paul Benning asked.

Drake swallowed his mouthful of pizza. "Why?"

"Turn it on. You'll see."

He picked up the remote for the small flat screen in the kitchen and turned it on to KGW in Portland. Breaking news was showing running mobs of black clad anarchists smashing store windows and tossing Molotov cocktails in the Lenox Mall in Atlanta.

Drake watched the running black clad mob leave a burning path of destruction behind it.

"It's happening in the capitals of all of the eleven Confederate states. It started symbolically, I guess, in Columbia, South Carolina, the first state to join the Confederacy, and then broke out in the other ten. But it's a diversion, I think," Benning said. "There are reports on several stations that, at the same time the mobs are trashing downtown, smaller groups are pulling down Confederate statues while the police are trying to stop the vandalism in the city centers."

"Antifa's gone back to its playbook to bait the militias and patriot groups. They're trying to escalate the violence."

"That's what it looks like to me."

"Paul, can you check and see if they're arresting any of these black-clad rioters?"

"They usually arrest a few of them. Why do you want to know?"

"This is too well organized, hitting the capitals of all the old Confederate states on the same night. I'd like to know how many of them are being bussed in from other states and who's paying for all of this. I have a hunch it's the same Russian billionaire we suspect is funding Antifa. If we can prove it, we might be able to shut this down before our second civil war breaks out."

Chapter Fifty-Nine

MIKHAIL VOLKOV WAS SWEATING HEAVILY in the exercise room of his eighty-fifth-floor luxury condo in New York. Wearing only a pair of white gym shorts, he was working through the kettlebell training routine he learned while training with Spetsnaz in Russia before his deployment to Cuba.

On the forty-fifth of his daily fifty swings with a thirty-five-pound kettlebell, he was annoyed when his phone started playing the rousing sounds of Tchaikovsky's 1812 Overture. He continued with another two swings, but the phone continued the overture.

Volkov set the kettlebell down between his feet and walked over to the juice bar along one wall and picked up the phone with one hand and a white gym towel with the other to wipe sweat from his face and head.

He moved over in front of the floor-to-ceiling window that looked down on Central Park before accepting the call.

"Congratulations. It looks like you are going to achieve your goal."

"I agree. Perhaps one more push."

"How soon?"

"We will wait to see what the reaction is. We may not need to do much more."

"If we do, what do you need from me?"

"Coordination and perhaps resupply. Our friends will need the necessary tools to carry out our plan."

"The same as before?"

"Increase the number to five hundred. Acquisition plus shipping will cost one and half, say two million to be safe."

"I will arrange the transfer. Call me when the shipment has been distributed."

Volkov ended the call and cursed. Bradley was getting greedy. Zastava AK-47s were only six hundred dollars each, without any discount for a large purchase. Three hundred thousand for the weapons and maybe an equal amount for shipping, if he used the same circuitous route he used before. The total was short of a million by four hundred thousand dollars.

Bradley was asking him to turn a blind eye to a middleman profit of one point four million U.S. He would have to think about how he ultimately would deal with Bradley's greed.

He picked up his water bottle on the juice bar and headed to the sauna at the back of the exercise room to think about a problem that was a bigger concern than the million plus Bradley wanted to steal from him.

Zal Nazir's uncle in Iran had mentioned to his Russian counterpart that the bodyguard sent to keep an eye on Nazir, while he stole some new American military drone technology for them, was asking for a grenade launcher with a thermobaric warhead. Nazir wanted to kill an attorney he thought was about to discover who he was and what he was doing.

If Nazir was exposed trying to kill some attorney, everything he was working on was at risk. He wasn't concerned about Iran's efforts to obtain drone technology. The technology would ultimately be shared with Russia.

He was more concerned about not being able to continue living as a billionaire Russian expat, giving money to worthy socialist and progressive causes in the United States. He would be forced to return home, to a lifestyle not nearly as comfortable as the one he'd become accustomed to.

Volkov closed the door of the sauna and ladled water onto the sauna stones and spread a towel on the wooden bench to sit down and think. He knew that if Nazir was about to be apprehended, the commando bodyguard assigned to protect him would protect Iran first and kill him. It would only be after the civil war broke out and the government investigated its true cause that Nazir's exposure would became problematic.

Once Nazir had served his purpose in their plans, he would have to be eliminated in a way that his role would never be discovered. As he thought about how that could be accomplished, he smiled and got up to throw more water on the stones.

He knew how and where it would happen.

After another fifteen minutes in the sauna, Volkov showered and put on a white, calf-length Turkish Terry robe and called Mason Bradley.

"I want you to casually mention to our young Persian friend, before we ask him to return to social media and fan the flames, that I want the three of us to go to my villa in Hawaii to celebrate our accomplishment, after you make the deliveries we talked about. We need to get him out of the country for a while."

He could hear the wheels turning in Bradley's primitive and cunning mind. "Will all three of us require transportation back to the mainland?"

"I think not."

"Is it something you would like me to take care of?"

"If you like. Be sure that you do not arrange for his travel with small inter-island or private aircraft. They don't have a very good safety record and have been crashing in the ocean frequently, I understand."

"That's good to know. I'll make sure he gets where he's going."

"I'm sure you will. Will you be traveling yourself any time soon?"

"Leaving tomorrow."

"Call me when you return. We need to coordinate our efforts for the rest of the summer. I anticipate it will be an eventful one."

Chapter Sixty

ZAL NAZIR MET the two Hezbollah operatives who were delivering the Russian grenade launcher with the thermobaric warhead he requested on Wednesday at noon. They were waiting for him on the top floor of the short-term parking garage at Portland International Airport.

He didn't know either of them. He knew they lived in Canada, as naturalized citizens, and could travel freely in America. He still watched them for fifteen minutes, sitting in the blue Jeep Cherokee they'd driven to Portland, before he approached.

He waited to walk over to them until he was sure there was no one watching, and then he tapped on the passenger's window.

"Peace be upon you," he said when the window was lowered.

"And upon you, peace," the passenger replied. Wearing a Seattle Seahawk sweatshirt and having no facial hair, he looked like any other young man in Canada or America.

Nazir dropped his right hand to the grip of the Glock 26 in his IWB holster. "Do you have a letter for me?"

The passenger handed a sealed envelope to him.

"Please open it for me."

When it was handed back to him, Nazir took out the letter from his uncle that confirmed the identity of the couriers and the materiel they were delivering.

Satisfied they were the Hezbollah operatives he'd been told to expect, he told them to wait for him to drive his car over before they opened the rear liftgate.

Nazir walked over two rows to his black three-year-old Ford Explorer and drove it around to stop behind the Jeep. He motioned for the courier, standing at the liftgate. He wanted to see how they had concealed the launcher for delivery.

He had to hand it to them, they had been clever. There were three identical pine planter boxes in the back of the Jeep, each four feet long and two feet high. He knew from experience the Russian MRO-A disposable grenade launcher, with a thermobaric warhead, was thirty-six inches long and weighed ten pounds. It was small enough to fit in the bottom of the four-foot-long planter box.

When he got out to load the launcher in his Explorer, he smiled. Each of the planter boxes was filled with planting soil, and there were five-pound containers of Miracle Grow plant food standing next to the three planters. The Hezbollah boys were clever.

"Which planter is it?" he asked.

"The one on the right next to the plant food," the courier said.

BJ pulled the planter box out and loaded it into the back of his Explorer. "Bring two of the plant food containers over and set them along the side of the planter box," he ordered.

When he was satisfied that the launcher was properly hidden from all but a full-on police search of his vehicle, he nodded in appreciation and got in his Explorer. There was no need to thank the couriers. They were under orders. When he had the chance, he would pass on his appreciation for their service to their superiors.

Nazir drove slowly down and out of the parking structure and headed east to I-205 South. He had allowed three hours for the pickup and the drive to Dundee to find the attorney's farm. The launcher had a maximum range of four hundred fifty meters and he wanted to be within the effective range of ninety meters, roughly the length of an American football field, for the kill.

It took him an hour and forty minutes to travel the thirty-nine miles from the airport to the small city of Dundee, Oregon. Proclaimed to be the heart of the Oregon wine country, he hadn't seen any vineyards on the way and was beginning to think the city's PR claims were bogus. That was until he passed through a city to the north called Newberg.

Even then, he saw only a few to the west of the highway until he turned onto Worden Road from Highway 99W. From the highway to the point where the road turned north, he counted eleven wineries along the way. Rows of grapes climbed from the road on south and east facing slopes in the verdant countryside.

It reminded him of the Shiraz region of Iran where his family was from. Once the center of wine making in the country, a tradition and culture that dated back over centuries, it all ended in nineteen seventy-nine with the Islamic revolution. Alcohol was banned, wineries were closed and the vineyards torn up. Iranian viticulture had rebounded since then and was now the eighth biggest producer of grapes in the world, but the production and consumption of wine was still prohibited.

Nazir snapped out of his reverie as he approached the area he'd identified on Google Earth where the attorney's farm was located. He slowed down as he drove past a long gravel driveway that ran along rows prepared for planting grapes, he assumed, that ran laterally across the property. At the top of the hillside was an old stone farmhouse and a long outbuilding behind it.

As he drove past the driveway, he calculated the distance

from the road to the farmhouse to be a little more than two hundred meters. He reminded himself that he would have to aim for the middle of the front door to compensate for the elevation.

Two hundred meters was longer than the effective range of the launcher, and he'd made similar shots before at that range without missing the target, but he preferred to be a little closer. He drove on past the driveway for another hundred yards before pulling into the entrance to a neighboring vineyard and backing up to turn around.

The newly prepared rows, where the grape vines were to be planted, wouldn't provide enough cover for him to move closer to the farmhouse. Still, he wanted to get within ninety meters. Unfortunately, it would be a full moon tonight, but waiting any longer to take care of the attorney would just incur the wrath of Nazir.

He would have to take his chances and make the shot, full moon or not.

Chapter Sixty-One

DRAKE LEFT early Wednesday morning to drive to Seattle, to be in his office before Liz arrived for her second morning at PSS. When he walked past her office next to his, he found that she was already at her desk with a file open and a cup of coffee in her hand.

When she saw him at her door, she smiled and looked at her wrist watch. "Not bad. I didn't expect you until noon."

He knew then that working with Liz at PSS was going to be good for the company, as competitive as they both were. But racing to see who showed up for work first was obviously a competition he was not going to win.

Drake spent the morning reviewing two special projects PSS was considering. One involved the demands of MS-13 for neighborhood protection money for employees who worked for a PSS client in Honolulu, Hawaii. MS-13, the blood-thirsty and sadistic transnational criminal gang, had been keeping a low profile in the islands. Its presence on Oahu, however, in neighborhoods where many of the client's employees lived, was something the client wanted PSS to deal with without involving local law enforcement. It was a big ask, which was why Drake was assigned to review it and recommend a course of action.

After a lunch with Liz at a lakeside bistro, with a French flair that had a terrific chicken salad, Drake visited Kevin McRoberts in his IT division office. He wanted to see if they were any closer to identifying the person, or persons, trying to hack the systems of Caelus Research, Inc., and if there was any new information about the Russian billionaire.

Kevin was staring at one of the three monitors on his desk with his hands locked behind his head, rocking back and forth in his chair.

"Que pasa, Kevin?"

"Mucho, Mr. Drake. That Russian billionaire whose money you asked me to follow just made a two-million-dollar donation to the Students for Social Justice."

"That's pretty generous. Any way of finding out what it's for?"

"I know what some of it's for. I hacked the account of the SST. Three hundred thousand dollars was transferred yesterday to the account of Zastava Arms in Serbia."

"The manufacturer of AK-47s. Can you tell if that's what the three hundred thousand dollars was buying?"

"I could if I hacked Zastava."

"Let me run it by Casey before you do that. Good work, Kevin. This might be the piece of the puzzle we've been looking for. I'll be back after I talk to Mike."

Drake left and took the stairs two at a time up to the executive floor and Mike Casey's office. On the way, he knocked on the door of Liz's office and motioned for her to follow him.

He knocked on Casey's door and entered without waiting for an invitation. His friend was on the phone and covered the transmitter mouthpiece with his hand.

"What?"

"We need to talk."

"Richard, I'm going to have to call you back, say in ten

minutes. Something's developed that needs my immediate attention."

Liz joined Drake at the door and Casey waved her in.

"Kevin found something that I need to confirm. To do it, he'll have to hack into the system of a Serbia arms manufacturer."

"Liz, shut the door, if you will, and both of you have a seat. Does this have to do with the Russian you've been investigating?"

Drake nodded. "Yes, Mikhail Volkov, the billionaire benefactor of all things liberal and progressive. Kevin followed the transfer of two million dollars from Volkov to a group called Students for Social Justice. From there, three hundred thousand was transferred to the account of Zastava Arms in Serbia."

"Do we know what the three hundred thousand is buying?"

"That's what I want to find out, but it will involve hacking the account of a foreign arms manufacturer."

"Liz, any chance we can get someone to do this for us?"

"A government agency? I doubt it, since the money is from Mikhail Volkov. He's too well connected. Someone in the government would tip him off before we could get the information. But if we do it, there could be serious consequences if we get caught. Zastava could argue it has a private right of action against PSS for damages caused by the trespass. The Department of Justice could get involved if Zastava tried to take us to court. That could be an even bigger problem."

"Adam, I know this is important, but do we have any defense to an action by Zastava?"

"Not a good one. Congress is considering a 'hack back' bill that would allow a company to retaliate against hackers, domestic or foreign. We could assert that we were retaliating against a hack attempt we thought was from Zastava, but we would have to manufacture evidence to prove it. I can't recommend that. We'll be taking a big risk in hacking Zastava. But if Volkov and the Students for Social Justice are bringing in AK-47s that could wind up with Antifa and the anarchists, I think it's worth it."

Casey looked up at the ceiling as he considered the risk his company was taking if he approved Drake's request. After a long minute, he dropped his eyes to look at Drake and then Liz.

"We've taken bigger risks before, when it was important, and survived the fallout. Go ahead, tell Kevin he has my approval."

On the way to their offices, Liz put her hand on Adam's arm and gave it a squeeze. "I knew I'd like working here, even if it might not be for very long."

"We'll be fine. Kevin hacked the Pentagon and didn't get caught. I'm more worried about the danger of a shipment of AK-47s winding up in the hands of these mobs rioting down South."

"Are you going to let your father-in-law know about Zastava and what Kevin's doing?"

"The committee knows how we were going to track Volkov's money. It's better if they can deny having any knowledge of how we're going to have a look at Zastava's records."

Drake left to give Kevin the go-ahead and see if there was a way to find out how the AK-47s might be coming to America.

Chapter Sixty-Two

SUNSET WEDNESDAY WAS at 7:36 PM. BJ waited another two hours before he drove slowly past the driveway to the attorney's house on Worden Road. He saw there were lights on at the front porch and in two of the windows on the north end of the house. He drove on to a dirt road leading into a Christmas tree farm a mile up the road. He'd spotted it that afternoon and had driven in far enough to satisfy himself that the place was uninhabited.

He turned off the Explorer's headlights as he turned onto the dirt road and backed in between two rows of six-foot-tall Christmas trees twenty yards in from the road. From there, he was hidden from passing vehicles and could see anyone unfortunate enough to pull onto the access road that night.

He opened the Burgerville sack he'd stopped for in Newberg for his dinner; a Tillamook cheeseburger, a chocolate hazelnut milkshake and waffle fries to go with his coffee in a stainless-steel-vacuum mug. He didn't agree with America's politics, but he sure loved its fast food. Most Iranians did.

Before his first bite of his cheeseburger, his phone vibrated in his shirt pocket. He saw it was Nazir and let loose a stream of expletives. The man wouldn't leave him alone, even when he was doing his bidding, and should know he was trying to avoid being seen or heard.

"What is it?"

"Is he dead?"

"Don't call me again. I will call you when he's dead."

"You said that last time."

"Nazir, you are trying my patience. You do not want to do that. I have two reasons for being here; to protect you, until you finish your work for us, and to make sure you don't expose us. It's my call when I think you're a risk. Don't make me decide that your meddling constitutes a risk. Are we clear on that?"

Nazir huffed and said, "Just don't screw up like you did last time," and hung up.

BJ took a bite of cheeseburger and thought about the ways he would make the man suffer before he killed him. He might be Persian but living in America had made him just as arrogant as all the other Americans.

He waited until midnight before driving back down Worden Road. He slowed down fifty yards from the driveway of the old farmhouse and pulled off onto the shoulder. With the headlights off, it would look like the Explorer was out of gas and he'd left to return with gas later. But what a passerby might think didn't concern him. It would only take five minutes, or less, to get the launcher out, move to a position up the driveway and take the shot. If someone stopped and interfered, they would meet the same fate as the attorney.

The night was still, with a gentle breeze blowing up from the valley below. It carried the scent of freshly mown hay mixed with the smell of fir needles from the trees that bordered the road. Except for the full moon, it was a perfect night and would make the memory of the kill unforgettable.

He listened for a sound of approaching traffic, but the only sound was the whisper of the wind in the tops of the trees.

The launcher was wrapped in a gray blanket on the floor behind his seat. It took only seconds to get out of the SUV and hang it from his shoulder by its sling. With its dark green camo color, it was all but invisible next to the black of the long-sleeved T-shirt he was wearing.

Moving quickly to the bottom of the driveway, he turned right and sprinted up to the position that he'd calculated to be ninety meters from the farmhouse and knelt down.

As he brought the launcher around to lay atop his shoulder, he sighted in on the farmhouse and froze. The porch light and the light in both windows on the north side went off at the same instant. They were on a timer!

If the attorney was home and the two windows alongside the porch were bedroom windows, would the attorney let the timer turn off the light or would he turn the lights off himself when he was ready to go to bed? He knew that's what he would do.

Which meant there might not be anyone home!

He remained kneeling on the soft earth, disappointed and angry at himself. He hadn't taken the time to learn the pattern of the attorney's coming and going. Now he would have to wait for a night when he was certain he was home.

Worse, he would have to tell Nazir the attorney wasn't dead and suffer his criticism. The fact that he'd been rushed into something that would normally take weeks to plan wouldn't placate Nazir. He might know things about computers, but he didn't know the first thing about planning a mission like this.

Moving slowly, he unslung the launcher and backed away. When he was near the road, he turned and listened for any approaching traffic before sprinting back to his Explorer.

Next time, he vowed to follow the attorney home from work and make sure he was home when he vaporized his house.

Chapter Sixty-Three

THURSDAY MORNING DRAKE learned that Liz was a great cook. After showering in her expensive furnished apartment, he found her humming in the kitchen while she fixed their breakfast. He walked up behind her and wrapped his arms around her waist.

"She's beautiful and she cooks. I think I'm in love."

Liz brought her elbow back and gave him a shot in the ribs. "So, beauty isn't enough. I need to cook as well? Sexist!"

"I was thinking about how much fun we could have together in the kitchen."

"Are you sure you were thinking about cooking?"

"I love it when you read my mind. But back to the topic at hand, what are you preparing for our breakfast?"

"I found a Belgian waffle maker, some waffle mix from Williams Sonoma, an egg cooker and eggs. When they said this place was fully furnished, they meant it. We're having Belgian waffles with strawberry jam, soft-boiled eggs and orange juice. Will that get you through the morning?"

"Depends on what we do this morning."

Liz shook her head and pointed to the table in the breakfast nook. "Pour us coffee and then go sit down. "You're distracting me."

Drake did as he was told. "Have you found a condo you like?"

"I've seen several that are okay, but I haven't found one I want to buy."

"You will. Take your time; you can keep your stuff at my place for as long as you like."

Liz brought a plate to the table stacked with Belgian waffles and returned with a small saucer with a cup in the middle holding a decapitated boiled egg.

"What is that?" Drake asked.

"Haven't you ever eaten a soft-boiled egg in an egg cup?"

Drake examined the egg cup set in front of him. "I don't believe I have."

"Then you're in for a treat. When are you leaving for Portland?"

"After I stop at headquarters and see if Kevin has anything new for me."

As if he was summoned to report, Drake's phone vibrated in his pocket. It was Kevin.

"Good morning, Kevin."

"Mr. Drake, I wasn't sure if you were coming back before you left. I thought you might want to know what I found about those items you asked me to research."

He had to smile at Kevin's attempt to keep the NSA from hearing him refer to the 'items' as AK-47s.

"What did you find?"

"Five hundred of them are arriving by ship in Seattle this weekend, straight from the factory."

"Purchased with the money you traced to that student group?"

"Three hundred thousand of it anyway; the rest of the two million is still in the account of that group."

They had found it, a direct money trail from Mikhail

Volkov's billions to the radical professor and his Students for Social Justice they believed were funding the anarchists terrorizing the country.

"I knew you could do it. Great work."

"I'll download what I have onto a thumb drive and leave it on your desk, Mr. Drake."

"Thank you, Kevin."

Drake looked at Liz and grinned. "You have to love that kid. He found that five hundred AK-47s, direct from the Zastava Arms factory in Serbia, are arriving by ship in Seattle this weekend. All purchased with money that Volkov "donated" to the Students for Social Justice and its founder, Professor Mason Bradley."

"Wow! We have to stop the anarchists from getting their hands on those weapons! How are we going to do that?"

Drake shook his head. "I don't know, Liz. Someone on the committee might have an idea. I'd better call my father-in-law and let him get started on this."

He hit the speed dial for the senator with his left hand and picked up his coffee cup with his right. Before he was able to swallow the first sip, Senator Hazelton answered the call.

"Hello, Adam."

"We found the evidence that links our Russian billionaire's money to Antifa and the anarchists."

"Do I want to know how?"

"Not unless it becomes important at some point. He donated two million dollars to the Students for Social Justice. Three hundred thousand of it was used to purchase five hundred new AK-47s from the Zastava Arms factory in Serbia. The weapons are arriving by ship in Seattle this weekend."

"This is rock-solid evidence?"

"It is. Intercepting those AK-47s in Seattle will prove it. Do we have a way to do that?"

"Possibly, but we'll have to be very careful. If we use a

federal agency, we risk them being alerted and the shipment being diverted to another location."

"What about local law enforcement?"

"I'll talk with the others and see if they know someone we can trust. Were you able to find out which shipping company they're using?"

"Not yet, we're working on it."

"Let me know as soon as you learn anything."

"Will do."

Drake ended the call and looked at Liz. "While I'm in Portland today, will you see that Kevin keeps working on this, to find out where and when these weapons are being delivered?"

"Of course. I'll let Mike know what Kevin's found."

He started to get up and sat back down. "I guess I'd better finish the breakfast you made for me. Now, how am I supposed to eat this egg?"

Chapter Sixty-Four

IT WAS noon before Drake got to his office in Portland. Paul Benning was standing in front of his wife's desk reading an open file when he walked in.

"Afternoon Paul, where's Margo?"

"Upstairs, fixing me a sandwich. Want to join us?"

"I had a late breakfast, thanks anyway. Will you be around after lunch?"

"As far as I know. Why?"

"There's something you might be able to help me with."

Benning put the file down on Margo's desk and nodded. "Sure, see you after lunch."

As promised, Margo had left a stack of files on his desk upstairs, with letters and two motions attached that needed his signature. Paperwork is a necessary component of a law practice, he knew, but it was increasingly becoming an annoyance.

He leaned back, rested both hands on his desk and closed his eyes. Inhaling deeply and then exhaling, he rolled his neck to relieve the tension that was building there. His home and practice were in Portland, but his mind and heart were in Seattle with Liz and PSS.

On the dot, an hour later, Benning came up the stairs to

the loft. "Margo said to say hello, and she hopes to see you before you leave, if you have a minute."

"Do I detect a note of criticism in that?"

Benning smiled and shrugged his shoulders before sitting down in front of his desk. "You know Margo. She's just reacting to my being in the office all the time and you being in Seattle more and more."

"Is she worried about me being gone so much?"

"Probably, but she'll adapt. What did you want to talk to me about?"

"If you wanted to intercept a shipment of AK-47s arriving in Seattle, without the feds getting wind of it, how would you do it?"

"You'd have to know someone in local law enforcement you could trust, who would use men he could trust to pull it off. Does this involve Antifa and the anarchists?"

"It does."

"How solid is the information about this shipment?"

"We have the purchase order from the arms manufacturer, and we'll have the shipping instructions maybe today."

Benning thought for a moment and got up to leave. "Let me make a couple of calls."

Adam worked uninterrupted until he closed the last file in the stack and was surprised to see that it was ten minutes to five in the afternoon. Margo wasn't at her desk when he carried the files down to her, but she'd left a note saying she had a doctor's appointment and would see him tomorrow. Her absence didn't concern him as much as her not coming to see him before she left. He was going to have to take time tomorrow to find out what was going on.

The go-home traffic was unusually heavy, and it was after six o'clock when he turned off Worden Road. Lancer was waiting to race him up the driveway. At least Lancer didn't seem to mind how much time he was spending in Seattle.

He opened the overhead door in the outbuilding behind

the house and parked the Cayman beside his cherished 933 Porsche, the last of the air-cooled 911s. Lancer's tail was wagging like a metronome set on allegro when he got out.

Drake squatted down and rubbed behind his dog's ears. "How are you, big guy? Protecting our home while I'm gone? You did, didn't you? Let's go see if we can find a reward for that."

Lancer came to heel and walked with him to the back door and then through the mud room.

"How about your favorite?" Adam asked as he opened the refrigerator and took out a Tupperware container of cooked hamburger meat balls. He picked out two, put them on a plate and popped them in the microwave to warm. A minute later, they'd disappeared from the plate he put on the floor and Lancer was licking his chops, looking up to see if there would be more.

"Tasty, huh? If you're good, maybe another couple later. Right now, I have to unpack and do some laundry."

When his weekender duffle bag was unpacked, and the clothes were in the washer, he poured a glass of pinot and went to the spare bedroom he used as an office. Plopping down in the well-worn brown leather reading chair, he set his glass on the end table next to it and called Liz.

"Lancer says he misses you."

"That's good news. How about Lancer's owner?"

"Lancer says his owner misses you too."

Liz laughed. "He does, does he? Tell Lancer I miss him too."

"How was your day?"

"Mike asked me to find out what we can do to speed up the licensing of our new people in Hawaii. The state "may" issue a concealed carry permit, but it isn't required to, even if you meet all their requirements. I'm trying to make some new friends there."

"If anyone can do it, you can. Have you found a condo?"

"I've found two I'd like you to see. I want to get something you'll like so you can't wait to get up here."

"Where you live isn't what will entice me to come to Seattle."

"Still, I want it to be comfortable for both of us."

"I may drive up tomorrow night. Paul is trying to find someone we can trust to keep the feds at bay when we intercept those AK-47s."

"Anything I can help with?"

"Not now, but you may have to make peace with the FBI or DHS for us if they find out we didn't tell them what we know. Until then, keep a light on for me."

Chapter Sixty-Five

DRAKE'S PHONE vibrated on the nightstand at two o'clock in the morning.

"Adam, there's a guy walking up your driveway with something slung over his shoulder. I think trouble's heading your way."

"Thanks, Chris."

He jumped up, pulled on a pair of hiking shorts, and grabbed the Benelli M4 tactical shotgun he kept next to his bed.

"Lancer, come," he whispered as he ran from the bedroom and out the back door. Outside, he sprinted right to the edge of his property and then ran down along the north side of the vineyard. He didn't know how far up the driveway the person had come, but he wanted to get behind him and make sure he didn't leave without finding out why he was trespassing on his property.

He stopped halfway down to Worden Road and listened. Whoever it was, they weren't walking on the gravel driveway because he didn't hear anything.

But Lancer did. He was still as a statue, looking directly across the soft soil of the vineyard.

Drake followed Lancer's point with his eyes and saw movement. From the light of the full moon, he saw a dark-clad figure stop and unsling something from his shoulder. It's shape and size reminded him of an AT-4 single-shot anti-tank weapon the Marines used.

He had to do something fast before the weapon was on the person's shoulder, ready to take a shot at his house.

"Lancer, *fahs!*"

Given the command to attack, Lancer took off like a rocket toward the person. Drake ran after him.

Running on the soft soil prepared for the fall planting, neither of them made much noise as they closed on the kneeling figure on the other side of the vineyard.

From six feet away, Lancer launched into the air and sunk his teeth into right arm of the person who was holding the weapon on his shoulder. With his speed and hundred-pound weight, Lancer toppled the person over and stood over him, snarling and tearing at his arm.

Drake ran up and pointed the Benelli in the man's face. "Stop fighting and I'll tell him to stop or you'll lose that arm."

The man was wearing a black T-shirt and his right arm was bleeding heavily. As he stared up the barrel of the shotgun at Drake, he stopped thrashing and lay still.

"Lancer, *aus!*"

Lancer obeyed and moved back a step, his lips curling back and showing teeth.

"You again. You tried to get me once at my office, and now this. For a commando, you're not very good at this, are you?"

"What's your saying, 'the third times a charm'?" the man said in accented English.

"There won't be a third time for you. Who sent you?"

"Does it matter?"

Drake reached down with his left hand and picked up the grenade launcher. The lettering on its side was in Cyrillic.

"A Russian grenade launcher, in the hands of an Iranian commando, here in America. A lot of people are going to be very interested in hearing what you have to say. My problem is deciding if I should interrogate you first or wait for the FBI."

Drake looked at Lancer. "What do you think I should do, Lancer?"

Lancer barked twice and took a step closer, growling.

When Drake took his eyes off the Iranian for an instant, to tell Lancer to hold, the man raised his left arm to throw a knife he'd hidden somewhere.

Drake didn't hesitate and shot him in the chest, from three feet away. "I wish you hadn't done that. I really did want to hear what you had to say."

He leaned down and searched the man's pockets. There was no ID, but there was a cell phone in one pocket. Drake slipped it into the pocket of his shorts, just as headlights reached up the driveway to where he stood.

He hadn't heard the approach of his neighbor's Tesla. Chris Conners got out and walked cautiously up the driveway.

"My flight from New Zealand was late and I was driving home when I saw him and called. I turned around at my house when I heard a gunshot. Are you okay?"

"I wouldn't be if you hadn't called. He was getting ready to blow up my house, with me in it."

"His black SUV is parked on the shoulder of the road, up from your driveway. I don't think he heard me coming. He didn't even turn around when I drove by."

"Then I owe you and your Tesla. Thanks."

"Who is he?"

"I think I might know, but I'll let the police see if they can identify him. Would you mind calling them, Chris?"

"Glad to," Conners said and walked back to his car.

It took fifteen minutes for a patrol car from the Village of Dundee to arrive and another four hours before the police completed their initial investigation and left the vineyard. The sunrise was painting the horizon to the east pink when Drake and Lancer got back to the old farmhouse.

"How about steak and eggs for breakfast, Lancer? You earned your keep today."

Lancer barked his agreement and Drake started taking things out of the refrigerator. When two small sirloins were sizzling in a cast iron skillet and a pan was heating for the eggs, Drake called Liz.

"Were you awake?"

"My alarm went off two minutes ago. What's up, other than the two of us?"

"I wanted to make sure you heard this from me first," he said and told her about his night. When he mentioned that the Iranian commando's grenade launcher was Russian, she asked if he was working for Mikhail Volkov.

"I don't know, but I will find out. None of this makes any sense."

Chapter Sixty-Six

PAUL BENNING PARKED his F150 behind the farmhouse and came in through the mud room where Drake was cleaning up after breakfast.

"Thanks for coming, Paul. Did you have something to eat? I can fix something if you didn't."

"Margo still has me drinking smoothies for breakfast, thanks anyway. What the hell happened last night?"

"I got lucky. My neighbor saw someone sneaking up the driveway and called me. We got to him before he had time to launch a grenade at the house. It was the Iranian commando you identified."

"So, this is related to the terrorists who were targeting the Catholic churches? Why now? The terrorists are dead. The FBI closed its file on the matter."

"But we didn't stop looking for the people aiding the terrorists, the owners of that farm. Maybe we're getting too close."

Benning shook his head. "But they wouldn't have any way of knowing we're getting close. We haven't learned anything new lately, except for the identity of the guy you just killed."

"That has to be it. I can't think of another reason." Drake

reached into the pocket of his hiking shorts and took out the smartphone he'd taken off the Iranian. "I didn't give this to the police. Do you have someone who can find out who the commando's been calling?"

"I hope you're on good terms with the police here. They aren't going to be happy if they find out you kept this."

"Then we'll make sure they don't find out. If I told them everything we know, they would call in the FBI, and our federal friends would spend all their time investigating us. We can figure this out quicker."

"I'll see what I can do. Are you going to Seattle?"

"This afternoon, after I wrap up a couple of things in the office."

Benning picked up the smartphone and turned to leave. "I'll try to have something before you leave."

———

ZAL NAZIR WAITED until the sun came up for BJ to call before deciding to leave for the safehouse on the mountain. If his bodyguard had been captured or killed, and the attorney was still alive, he couldn't risk staying around any longer.

He struggled to calm down and focus, driving on US-26 E with the sun in his eyes. He'd planned on going underground if it became necessary. But doing it without Volkov and Bradley finding out why he was doing it wasn't something he'd planned for.

The final phase of Bradley's plan included the manipulation of social media to ignite a civil war with one night of extreme violence across the country. It was designed to replicate *Kristallnacht, the Night of Broken Glass*, in Nazi Germany, the massive coordinated attack on Jews and their property while the police and crowds stood by and watched passively. Instead of attacking the Jews, Bradley would use the anarchists to attack everyone considered to be, or who sided with, the fascists, patriot groups, conservatives and Christian Bible thumpers.

Bradley believed local police would stand down, as they had in San Francisco, Portland and Seattle. The small number of arrests that would follow would convince the other side that they needed to take matters into their own hands if they wanted justice.

To coordinate an assault on social media, to make it look like the anarchists were honorably striking back at the fascists turning America into another Nazi Germany, he had to be actively involved with members of the Council. And in doing so, he ran the risk of someone slipping up and leading the authorities back to him, like the Russians and their troll factory had done in the last election.

If that happened, everything he'd put together to fight America would be jeopardized. It would also make it difficult to deliver the drone software from Caelus Research that he'd promised his sponsors in Iran. That failure would probably be a fatal one for him.

The closer Nazir got to the safehouse, with the morning sun in the east still slanting into his eyes, the darker his mood became. There was no way to slip the noose tightening around his neck. If he reneged on the role in Bradley's plan, he knew the Russian would send Bradley and his pack of anarchists after him. If he failed to steal the drone software for Iran, BJ's uncle would surely send someone to punish him for his failure.

By the time he drove his BMW M5 into the garage of the mountain cabin outside Rhododendron, Oregon, his mind was made up. He would have to keep working with Bradley, steal the software from Caelus and then get out of the country. His work with the Council and his group of genius hackers could be conducted from anywhere in the world.

For now, he just needed to be left alone, with his laptop and the internet, for a few more days.

Chapter Sixty-Seven

DRAKE LEFT the vineyard to drive to his office with Lancer sitting in the passenger seat and extra ammo for his .45 Kimber in his weekend duffle. He didn't expect trouble in Seattle, but he hadn't expected it last night either.

Lancer followed him down the stairs from the parking garage to his office and waited for permission to greet Margo, sitting at her desk.

"Go say hello, Lancer. You haven't seen Margo in a while."

"That's because I haven't seen much of your owner lately," she said while she leaned down and let Lancer nuzzle her cheek. "Paul's in the loft. He's using the phone on your desk to talk with someone at the Sheriff's Office. Don't leave up there until you figure out what you want me to do about the offer on the Chamber's matter."

"Yes, ma'am, the Chamber's matter," Drake said with a broad smile. "Have you already drafted my response?"

"Never know when you'll be around. Someone has to make decisions around here."

"What would I do without you, Margo?"

"We both know the answer to that."

Drake started up the stairs to the loft knowing full well what he would do without the best legal assistant in the world —next to nothing.

Paul Benning was writing something on a legal pad on Drake's desk. "Thanks for getting back to me so soon, Jimmy. I owe you one."

Drake motioned for Benning to stay seated and sat down in a chair in front of the desk with Lancer on the floor beside him. "Did you find out who the commando was calling?"

"All of the calls went to an untraceable prepaid phone," Benning said. "But it gets better. The commando's iPhone, with GPS, identifies two locations, an apartment and a condo, where a number of calls were made. Both are in Hillsboro.

"The apartment is leased to an OSU student here on a visa from Iran, a Bijan Jahandar. His visa photo identifies him as the commando you killed last night. The condo is leased to Zal Nazir, a twenty-seven-year-old software engineer who happens to work for Intel. Mr. Nazir is not at work today. I thought I would go see if he's home with the flu."

Drake nodded and grinned. "Good idea. We could stop and get him some Theraflu. I hear the flu can kill you this season if you're not careful. Mr. Nazir needs to stay alive long enough to answer a few questions I have for him."

It took them twenty-five minutes to drive to Orenco Station in Benning's F150 pickup. Designed as a pedestrian-friendly planned urban community, Orenco Station had light rail access, a town center with retail and offices and eighteen hundred homes, including Nazir's upscale condo.

Benning parked in an empty visitor parking space in front of Nazir's building. "How do you want to handle this if he's home?" he asked Drake.

"We'll let Lancer encourage him to cooperate if he's home and won't cooperate. He won't be a problem."

Unit 209 was on the east end of the second floor. No one answered the doorbell.

Benning looked to see if anyone was down the hall and told Drake to stand beside him. "Hold this while I pick the lock."

Drake hadn't noticed the small Dell XPS 2-in-1 laptop Benning was carrying in his left hand. It had an unusual-looking USB stick with a small antenna plugged into a port. "What's this?"

"Something I got on Amazon. It's a lock picking and hacking program with a computer script that instructs the security system not to create a sound or send a notification when the door opens."

"Something you used when you were a detective?"

"Criminals can't have all the fun."

Fifteen seconds later, they were inside the condo with Lancer searching the place.

Satisfied they were alone, they looked around. A man's clothing was hanging in one bedroom closet. The other bedroom closet was empty. A black quartz countertop in the kitchen had yesterday's Oregonian newspaper lying on it. The sink was empty, but the dishwasher was loaded with dirty dishes. The only food in the refrigerator was Chinese takeout.

Drake opened the sliding door to the balcony that looked down onto a swimming pool ringed with empty lounge chairs. The condo was a perfect place for a young, single software engineer.

Inside, Benning was opening all the drawers and cabinets in the kitchen, wearing latex gloves. "There's nothing of interest in his bedroom and not much in here. Nothing that suggests he's gone and is never coming back."

Drake took a section of paper towel from the holder and opened a drawer on the other side of the countertop. There was a bill for utility services, one for internet service from Comcast and a credit card bill from American Express. He put the Amex bill in his pocket and stood, turning slowly as he looked around for a hiding place they hadn't searched.

"I agree, Paul. He's either very careful or leads a very boring life."

"I saw you put something in your pocket. Anything important?"

"Just an American Express bill. I didn't open it."

"No time like the present."

Drake took out the envelope he'd folded in half and tore off the end to open it. The amount Nazir owed wasn't much, a couple hundred dollars spent at restaurants and for gas from a Standard station. He looked for anything that might tell them where Nazir might be, and then he saw it.

The card wasn't in Nazir's name. It was issued to Chevre Farms, sent in care of Zal Nazir. Chevre Farms was the company registered in Panama that owned the goat farm where Umara and her band of terrorists stayed before attacking the Catholic churches in Portland.

Drake walked over and held out the Amex bill. "We found him, Paul. Nazir's the one who was helping Umara."

Chapter Sixty-Eight

MIKHAIL VOLKOV WAS on his way to the Ethel Barrymore Theatre in the backseat of his Mercedes-Maybach to host the new United States Senator for New York and her husband for a night on the town. His review of the dossier on the senator was interrupted when the Apple Carplay system in the car signaled he had an incoming call on his BlackBerry KEYone smartphone.

He tapped the icon on the console panel to raise the privacy window before sitting back to consider whether to answer a call from an "Unknown Caller". Only a handful of people he trusted had his private number, and their numbers were all known to him.

Curiosity overrode his concern for operational security and he accepted the call.

"Do I know you?"

"All you need to know is that I am a friend."

"How am I to know that?"

"By what I'm about to tell you."

"And what is that?"

"The Seattle Police know the shipment of AK-47s you paid for is arriving tomorrow. Offload them before the ship enters territorial waters or they will be intercepted and confiscated."

"How do you know that? How am I to know you aren't trying to entrap me in something?"

"You have many friends in high places, Mikhail, who are disturbed by the direction the new administration is taking the country. We see what you are doing, with the help of Professor Bradley and Mr. Nazir. We would like to see you succeed, to demonstrate that the president isn't capable of governing this nation. See if the information we gave you is accurate; then decide if you would like our help in the future."

The call ended before Volkov could ask another question. His first thought was that the Americans had somehow learned of his relationship with Bradley and Nazir and were trying to trick him. They could have found out about the money that made its way to Bradley's Students for Social Justice and the arms purchase, but how could they have found out about Nazir?

He'd never met the young man and had never been seen in public with him. The money he provided Nazir, that Iran funneled through him, had been routed through a series of shell companies from offshore banking accounts that could never be traced to him, unlike the donations to Bradley.

Those accounts had been set up before he'd emerged on the world scene as a Russian natural gas oligarch and had no connection to any of his business dealings. When he wanted money transferred to someone that advanced the cause he and his allies in Russia approved of, he only had to make a call and it was done. There was no way his new "friends" could know about the money he'd given Nazir.

They must have been watching Bradley. His involvement with the Antifa anarchists had probably drawn attention that put him under a microscope, causing the FBI or DHS to monitor his movements and activities.

The decision he had to make, and make quickly, was

whether to sacrifice the shipment of weapons and abandon the plan for America's own *Kristallnacht* or give the order to offload the weapons and see if his new "friends" could be trusted.

There was only one way to find out. They might know of his involvement with Bradley, but they could never prove a relationship with Nazir.

He found Bradley's number in his short list of contacts on his BlackBerry and called him.

"We have a problem. Are you in Seattle?"

"Where else would I be?"

"I don't have time for your impudence, Mason. The police know about the shipment. I want you to arrange to offload the weapons before the ship enters territorial waters."

"No way! There's no way the police could know! Who told you the police know?"

"That's not important now."

"The hell it isn't! If they know about the shipment, they know about me. If you trust this source, it sounds like it's time for me to get out of the country."

"Not just yet. Get the shipment off the ship and into the hands of your friends. Then I want you to get our young friend in Portland and go to my villa in Hawaii. I'll have a charter fly you two there and arrange for travel elsewhere if it becomes necessary."

"How am I supposed to offload the shipment? I don't have those kinds of contacts."

"I do. I'll have one call you. Adjust your distribution plan and get those items in the hands of your friends. If they do what we're asking them to do, our work here is done."

Bradley was quiet for a long time before saying, "I guess I don't have a choice, do I? I've worked too long to let this opportunity slip through my fingers."

"Good man. Your favorite Scotch will be waiting for you at my villa."

"Better make it a couple of cases if I'm going to be there for a while."

You won't be there long enough, comrade, to drink a couple cases of my expensive Scotch. Not with what I have planned for you.

Volkov looked at his watch. Time for one more call.

"It's me. I have two problems I want you to take care of. Call the number I'll send you and help the man who answers with something he can't handle for himself. He'll explain. When that's arranged, I want you to take your men and go to my villa on the Big Island. If anyone asks, you are private security I've hired to protect my investment. Wait for the arrival of two men. I'll send you a file on each of them. They've become a problem. Take care of it for me, same arrangement as before."

His driver pulled the Mercedes-Maybach to the curb and came around to open his door. It was time to establish yet another high-level relationship with an official of the country he despised.

Chapter Sixty-Nine

DRAKE ARRIVED in Seattle after the rush hour traffic had thinned out Friday night and spent a quiet night with Liz and Lancer in her apartment. He left the next morning to rendezvous with Paul Benning and a captain in Seattle Police Department's Harbor Patrol for coffee.

Benning and Captain Patrick Lewis were seated at a table in a small Northgate neighborhood café when Drake walked in.

Captain Lewis was a trim fifty-year-old with the tanned and weathered face of a man who spent a lot of time on the water.

"Adam, meet my friend Pat Lewis."

Drake reached across the table and shook hands with Lewis. "Thanks for meeting us, Pat."

"Paul told me about your role in the transit bust of those terrorists here last year. I figured I owed you a listen. Paul's kept me in the dark about what you wanted to talk to me about."

"I think you'll understand why in a minute. Does the Harbor Patrol participate in homeland security matters here?"

"When we're asked, we do."

"How about when you're not asked by DHS or the FBI?"

"Our actionable information usually comes from those two agencies. The information would have to be reliable before we'd act on our own."

"When you say 'we', what does that mean?"

"What are you asking me? I don't understand."

Drake looked at Benning, who nodded. "Paul trusts you, so I'm going to trust you. If you don't feel you can help us, I need to know that the information we're going to share with you won't be passed along to any agency of the federal government. If you determine the information is actionable, I need to know that you will only provide it to people you trust until you act on it. If you decide the information isn't actionable, that you will keep it to yourself."

Lewis signaled for a refill of his coffee cup and waited until the waitress came to the table and left again before he answered. "If you're saying that you have actionable information about criminal activity that you can't trust the feds to deal with, you're telling me this activity is something the feds have jurisdiction over and you want me to poach on their territory, correct?"

"Correct."

"Hell, we do that all the time. What's the likely blowback?"

"If it works out, you'll be a hero. If it doesn't, you can say you were acting on bad information from a confidential informant, you didn't have time to share and you're sorry that it didn't work out."

"What's involved and when?"

"A search for weapons being illegally smuggled into the country on a ship arriving here tonight."

"I don't have authority for a search like that. Paul, you know that."

Benning nodded in agreement. "I also know you work

with U.S. Customs and Border Protection. Someone you know there has the authority."

"I can't organize a search in less than a day, even if I do have friends in CBP. Why didn't you come to me sooner, Paul?"

Drake answered for Benning. "Because I just received the information yesterday. Five hundred new AK-47s, manufactured in Serbia by Zastava Arms, are on the Pacific Moon, a cargo vessel registered in Hong Kong. It's scheduled to arrive tonight. The weapons were purchased with money from a radical student organization, the Students for Social Justice. Those weapons will be delivered into the hands of Antifa and the anarchists if they aren't intercepted. We can't let that happen."

"You can prove all that?"

"I have a copy of the purchase order and the shipping arrangements in my car."

Captain Lewis looked down and drummed his fingers on the table top for half a minute and said, "You're right, we can't let that happen. I don't know why you don't want any federal agency involved, but if your information is accurate, it doesn't matter. The feds couldn't decide to do something in less than a day anyway. Let me have the copy of the purchase order and shipping arrangements and I'll see what I can do."

———

AT TEN THIRTY THAT NIGHT, Drake and Benning stood in the parking lot next to Pier 91, at the Smith Cove terminal, and watched from a distance as Captain Lewis and five members of the Harbor Patrol boarded the Pacific Moon cargo vessel. One hundred and twenty meters in length, longer than a football field, it made everything around it appear small in comparison.

"Do we have time to make a coffee run?" Benning asked. "This could take a while."

"It depends on how cooperative the captain and his crew are. Captain Lewis and his friend from customs will know what to look for. The ship's manifest will identify the containers from companies suspected of smuggling illegal items. Maybe a couple of hours."

"What are you going to do when we've seized the weapons? Let the feds take care of Professor Bradley and Antifa?"

"That's up to Senator Hazelton. He's the one who asked me to investigate this. We'll let him decide."

Benning raised the binoculars hanging from his neck and studied the ship's ladder and the men coming down it. "That didn't take long. Lewis and the others are leaving the Pacific Moon."

Captain Lewis separated himself from the others and walked over to them.

"It looks like someone tipped them off that we were going to search the ship. The ship's master is filing a complete report, but he's telling us they responded to a distress signal from a forty-foot troller in international waters earlier today. They were boarded by six armed men and forced to offload twenty crates listed as furniture on the manifest. Your information appears to have been solid, but we're too late."

Chapter Seventy

MIKHAIL VOLKOV WAS ENJOYING an Arturo Fuente Opus X double robusto cigar on the roof garden of his home in Belgrave Square, London, Sunday morning when he received the second call from his "unknown source". It was the start of a perfect clear-sky day and he was looking forward to conversation with two of his Russian oligarch neighbors at lunch. A call from his new friend in the American government just added to his ebullient mood.

"We see that you made good use of the information we provided you."

"I did. Thank you."

"Here's another bit of information we hope you'll act on as well. Your financial accounts, as well as those of Mason Bradley and his student organization, have been hacked. That's how they knew the weapons were arriving. They followed the money trail to the Serbian arms manufacturer."

"I was promised that no one could hack into my system."

"Then you were misled."

"Who was able to do this?"

"The same man who was at the pier watching when the ship was searched for your AK-47s. He's an attorney who keeps getting involved in things he has no business getting involved in. He's part owner of a very good security firm in Seattle with a lot of defense contractors who are clients."

"But he's not working for the government?"

"Not that we can tell, but his father-in-law is a U.S. senator."

"Then why is he hacking into my accounts?"

"We're not sure, but we recommend that you stop him before he learns anything more about you or what you're doing."

"How am I to do that?"

"We think you can find a way."

"Is it something you could help me accomplish?"

"You need to do this yourself. You have old friends who can help you."

"How much time do I have?"

"Not much. We'll be in touch after you've taken care of your problem."

The call ended along with his ebullient mood.

Volkov left the roof garden and took the lift down to his study; a plan was coming together in his mind.

He did, indeed, have "old friends" who could help him. Six of the best former Spetsnaz soldiers money could buy. Trained to assassinate military and political leaders of enemies of the Motherland, they were headed to his villa in Hawaii and they were more than capable of dealing with the attorney.

All he needed to do was lure this attorney to Hawaii.

He relit his cigar, and when it was burning to his satisfaction, he called Mason Bradley on his encrypted smartphone.

"Where are you?"

"Do you know what time it is?"

"Yes, it's ten o'clock here."

"Yeah, and two o'clock in the morning here, Mikhail."

"It doesn't matter, this is important. Are the weapons distributed?"

"Yes."

"Good. There's something you need to do for us. Today, go to your houseboat in Berkeley. Book a flight to Hilo and write the number of the flight on a piece of paper along with the phone number of my villa there. Crumple it up and leave it in a waste paper basket or somewhere it's likely to be found. Then drive to Portland, collect Nazir and the two of you fly to Hilo in a chartered jet I'll have waiting for you."

"Why should I do that? Has something changed?"

"Because there's someone I want to follow you to Hawaii, someone else who will not be returning to the mainland."

"Who?"

"Someone who found out about the shipment of weapons and was at the pier when the ship was searched last night. Apparently, he's hacked into your SSJ accounts and traced the money you used to purchase the weapons in Serbia. He must be stopped before he gets any closer to us."

"How do you know all this?"

"I have friends in high places. The same friends who let me know the ship would be searched when it docked in Seattle."

"Am I about to be arrested? Because if I am, you can take care of this attorney yourself. I can disappear, they'll never find me."

"Mason, there's nowhere you can hide forever. They'll always find you. The only way to get past this is to get rid of this attorney. Let him follow you to my villa. I'll have him taken care of there."

"I don't like this, Mikhail. We've been too careful. I can't see how anyone found out about the weapons I bought in Serbia. There's a leak somewhere. Have your accounts been hacked as well?"

"Mason, my accounts have not been hacked. I would

know if they had. Do as I tell you and we will finish what we started."

Bradley didn't respond.

"Mason, I need to know that you will do what I told you to do. We can finish what we tried to do in the seventies. We are very close to causing your country to tear itself apart. I know that's what you want. Don't quit now."

He heard his protégé exhale loudly.

"I will never quit, Mikhail. Send me the location of the jet you're going to charter for us. Arrange for it to fly us to Hilo the day after tomorrow from Portland. I'll see you at your villa and we'll finish what we started."

No, my friend, you will not see me at my villa. But you will get to meet some of my old friends.

Chapter Seventy-One

DRAKE, Benning, Casey and Liz assembled in the PSS conference room Sunday morning to discuss their failure to intercept the arms shipment on Pier 91 the night before.

After Drake finished detailing the night's events, he added, "Captain Lewis assures us that no one outside of his team knew they planned to search the Pacific Moon last night."

Casey suggested, "Maybe they planned to offload the weapons out there just to be safe. They didn't have to know you were waiting for them."

"Maybe. But from the way the ship's master described the crates that were offloaded, customs would never have suspected they contained AK-47s without some advance knowledge. They took a big risk by taking them at gunpoint on the open sea."

"If the harbor and patrol captain is right, and none of his people tipped off anyone, don't overlook the possibility that someone found out about the shipment in some other way," Liz suggested. "The U.N.'s International Tracing Instrument Agreement for small arms is followed by most small arms manufacturers.

"Each weapon that's manufactured has an identifying

mark that allows Interpol to trace the source of weapons used to commit crimes. Nation states are required to keep records of the small arms manufactured in its jurisdiction.

"A government agency, like DHS for instance, wouldn't have a problem finding out that five hundred AK-47s were being shipped somewhere if it wanted to. I'm not saying that's what we did while I was at DHS, but it's the kind of intelligence agencies in the intelligence community look for and share."

Benning got up to refill his coffee cup. "Do you really think someone in *our* government would tip these guys off?"

Liz looked to Drake and let him answer.

"From the way *our* government is coddling the Antifa anarchists, yes, I believe someone would. The problem is we may never know if someone did. But we know Professor Mason Bradley and his Students for Social Justice are involved because they paid for the weapons. Bradley might know who the tipster was and, even if he doesn't, he'll know where those weapons are now and why they're here. I'd like to pay the professor a visit and see if we can find out."

"Do we know where Bradley is?" Casey asked.

"We know he lives on a houseboat in Berkeley. We don't know if he's there."

"With the trouble you got me into the last time I visited San Francisco," Casey said with a broad smile, "I haven't been able to visit any of our clients down there since then. If I don't mention to Megan that you're going with me, I guess we could fly down there and see if the professor is home."

It wasn't a laughing matter, but Drake laughed anyway. He'd been helping a PSS client deal with what they thought was industrial espionage but turned out to be an attempt to crash the electrical grid using the client's software. He got in the way and the terrorists had tried to take him out in his hotel room. Casey had turned up in the wrong place at the wrong time and was poisoned, something his wife still blamed Drake for.

"Sooner or later, I knew you'd blame me for that beautiful assassin outside my hotel door who tried to kill me when you got in her way. Don't forget, it was your idea to go out for a late Irish coffee that night."

"Point taken. When would you like to go?"

"Why not now? I need to get back to Portland tomorrow."

Casey checked the time on his watch. "Okay, it's ten o'clock. We can be airborne in an hour. Be down at my car in thirty."

"Can I tag along?" Liz asked.

Benning raised his hand. "Got room for one more?"

"Plenty of room," Casey said. "Now, clear out. I need a moment to think of how I'm going to tell my wife that I won't be home for lunch."

Drake called Carol Sanchez to ask if she would come in and keep an eye on Lancer at PSS headquarters and they were able to leave Boeing Field an hour later.

The PSS Gulfstream G650 landed at Oakland International Airport an hour and a half after that. A black Cadillac Escalade, rented from Hertz, was waiting for the drive to the Berkeley Marina, where Professor Bradley moored his houseboat.

When Casey turned down Marina Boulevard and slowed to a stop in front of Bradley's two-story houseboat, he asked, "How do you want to handle this?"

"Professor Bradley is a well-known lecturer and probably has visitors all the time. He doesn't know who we are. Let's knock on his door and see if he's home," Drake said from the second row of seats where he sat beside Liz.

Benning was riding shotgun and turned around. "What if he isn't? How far do you want to go with this?"

"As far as we have to. That's why you brought your special little laptop, isn't it? We need to find those AK-47s."

"What special little laptop?" Liz and Casey both said at the same time.

"If we need it, you'll see. Let's get moving. Neighbors might start wondering why we're just sitting here."

Drake led the way and stepped onto the houseboat with the others behind him and pulled on the braided cord to ring the brass ship's bell hanging next to the door.

After a minute, he rang the bell again. "If he doesn't answer, get ready to do your thing, Paul."

Stepping next to Drake, Benning opened the laptop with the USB stick with an antenna, plugged in a port and took his lock-picking kit from his pocket. "You do the honors this time."

Drake wasn't as fast as Benning had been at Nazir's place with the coded key pad, but when he opened the door and stepped back, Liz was looking at him with raised eyebrows.

"What, you think I didn't know how to pick a lock?"

"I was hoping you didn't."

Benning stepped inside and waved the others in. "He's a man with many talents. Make sure Bradley isn't asleep somewhere. Then Liz can show us how she searched a place when she was with the FBI."

Casey and Benning went upstairs while Liz and Drake searched the main salon, kitchen and study at the rear of the houseboat.

Fifteen minutes of quiet snooping later, the only thing they found that was of any interest was a wadded-up piece of paper in a hand-woven rattan wastebasket in the study with "UA 1122" written on it and a phone number with an 808 area code.

Chapter Seventy-Two

AFTER VOLKOV'S CALL, Mason Bradley had rushed to catch the early Alaskan Airlines flight to Oakland, made a quick stop at his houseboat and driven north for ten hours in a rented Chevrolet Malibu. He returned his car to Avis and checked into the Embassy Suites, by the Portland airport, shortly before ten o'clock in the evening. He was tired, his back was killing him, and he was tired of taking orders from Volkov.

As soon as he finished talking to Zal Nazir, he was going to call a cab and go somewhere for a late dinner and a Scotch or two.

"What is it this time, Bradley?"

"Our friend wants us fly to Hawaii tomorrow morning. Pack a bag and meet me at the Atlantic Aviation terminal at Portland International Airport by eight o'clock tomorrow. He's chartered a jet for us."

"My work is done for him. Why should I fly to Hawaii?"

"Nazir, I'm tired and I don't have time for this, but I'll give you two reasons. First, you don't say no to Mikhail Volkov. Second, you don't say no to Mikhail Volkov."

"What's changed? I thought we were supposed to go our separate ways."

Bradley considered telling him about the hack into the SSJ account and the attempted interception of the weapons shipment, but he didn't want to answer questions about it right now.

"You didn't have a need to know, but it's happening tomorrow. Being off the mainland when it does is smart."

"What's happening tomorrow?"

"Use your imagination. Multiply what we've done so far by a factor of ten."

"Is he meeting us there?"

"He'll be there sometime, maybe not to greet us. Just be at the airport by eight tomorrow."

Bradley ended the call. He wasn't looking forward to flying with the kid, but maybe he could help him figure out how someone found out how the SJS account was used to buy the AK-47s. Volkov implied that it was his fault, but it could just as well have been something Volkov did or didn't do. It also could have been Nazir that screwed up. Either way, it looked like someone was on to them. Hawaii was as good a place as any to hide out for a while.

———

NAZIR SET his phone down and stared out the window in the kitchen. He'd been getting another beer from the refrigerator when Bradley called. There was something Bradley wasn't telling him. He'd known the Russian wanted something big to happen, but going to Hawaii, when it happened, didn't make sense. If someone had found out that they were involved in the anarchist violence, being in another state, even one twenty-six hundred miles away, wouldn't make a difference.

It would help him, however, with BJ failing to kill the attorney, if he left Oregon. But his plans for going underground and establishing another base of operations didn't include a trip to Hawaii.

He was tempted to let Bradley fly to Hawaii by himself. But Bradley was right about one thing; the Russian was a hard man to say no to. He was former KGB and Nazir knew about his work in Cuba. It wasn't that hard to discover.

He didn't trust the Russian or Bradley, and he didn't want to go to Hawaii, but it looked like he didn't have a choice. In case there was something going on, that they weren't telling him about, he needed to be careful. He'd considered the possibility that they would think he was disposable. When he'd completed his work, he put together an insurance policy to protect himself, just in case.

On his laptop was a detailed account of his involvement with the Russian; the meeting, the money he'd received, his contacts with Bradley and the time of each recorded were saved on his computer. It was all there. If an attempt was made to access the file on his laptop without the encrypted password, the file would automatically be forwarded to the FBI tip line.

The Russian and Bradley might know how to use violence to advance their cause, but he knew how to use information and technology to advance his.

Chapter Seventy-Three

DRAKE RETURNED to Portland Sunday night with Lancer and was in his office early the next morning. The only file on his desk had a Post-it with red writing saying the file needed immediate attention.

Caelus Research had called and wanted to know if he'd been able to find out who had been trying to hack their IT system. The cyber assaults were continuing, and they were getting tired of it. They wanted to know what defense they would have if they launched a counterattack in retribution against the hackers.

He wanted to tell them to go for it, to take the offense, but until Congress acted to protect companies like Caelus Research, a counterattack would constitute a federal crime under the Computer Fraud and Abuse Act of 1986. It would subject them to a possible fine and up to twenty years in prison.

A better response for them would be to be patient and let him continue working to identify the hackers. The FBI could take it from there to punish their tormenters. He'd started to dictate a letter with that advice when Margo let him know Senator Hazelton was calling.

"It's not in the news yet, but a new wave of violence has started. It's a coordinated attack on individuals and their property and it's happening all over the country. Homes and businesses are being set on fire and people are being shot by the anarchists with AK-47s when they try to defend themselves. It's like the Night of Broken Glass in Nazi Germany against Jews in 1938. Except here the victims are people being identified as fascists, white nationalists, Nazis and like-minded conservative sympathizers on a list that Antifa posted online."

Drake was stunned. The violence of the anarchists had risen from smashing windows and setting cars on fire to shooting marchers in Portland and Seattle and now this. Maybe it should have been expected, as divided as the country had become. But murdering mobs killing people they didn't agree with wasn't the way America settled its differences.

"What's being done to stop this?"

"There's not much that can be done. Governors are activating their National Guard units, but it will take time to get them deployed. How close are we to having evidence that Mikhail Volkov and Bradley are behind this?"

"We can show Volkov gave money to Bradley's SSJ that was used to buy a shipload of AK-47s. We were waiting to search the ship they were on, but someone tipped them off and offloaded the weapons before the ship docked in Seattle. We flew to Berkeley, looking for Bradley, but he wasn't on his houseboat. I have no idea where Bradley or Volkov are right now."

"Volkov is in London; Michael Montgomery is in D.C. and he just told me where he is. Can you find Bradley? You have evidence his money bought these AK-47s. We can have him arrested for that. At the very least, we have reason to believe he's traveled in foreign commerce to aid and abet the anarchists in this rioting."

"Let me work on that. I may know where Bradley is."

"Find him quickly. We don't have a lot of time if we're going to stop this."

Drake took the remote controller from his desk drawer and turned on the flat screen TV mounted on the wall to his right. KPTV news had a reporter standing on the street in front of a burning house. Police cruisers, with red and blue lights flashing on their light bars, blocked the street on either side of an ambulance. In the background, a body covered with an emergency blanket lay on the lawn.

He didn't need to turn up the sound; the breaking news bulletin running across the bottom of the screen told him all he needed to know.

…alt-right Free Speech leader gunned down by black-clad anarchists.

He turned his chair to continue watching the news and called Liz.

"Are you in your office?"

"I just got here. Are you watching the news?"

"Yes. I wanted to know that you made it there safely. Is Mike there?"

"He's in his office."

"See if you can get him to join us in a conference call. We need to decide what we're going to do."

"Give me a minute."

While he waited, he took the crumpled piece of paper he found on Bradley's houseboat out of his wallet. He googled UA 1122 and saw that it was the flight number of a United Airlines flight from Oakland, California to Honolulu, Hawaii.

"What's up, Adam?" Casey asked when he came on the line.

"I want to go to Hawaii to find Mason Bradley. Remember the crumpled-up piece of paper we found on his houseboat? UA 1122 is the number of a flight from Oakland to Honolulu. 808 is the area code we used when we were on the Big Island of Hawaii. Bradley's there, I know it. We can have him arrested for providing the AK-47s to the rioting Antifa anarchists. When he's arrested, it might help to stop the killing."

"We don't know the AK-47s that were purchased with money from the SSJ account were given to the anarchists. How are you going to convince anyone to arrest him? He can say he didn't know what the SSJ was going to do with the money he gave them."

"It won't make any difference. I can make a citizen's arrest. I have a reasonable belief that he's aiding and abetting the anarchists. Once we have him in custody, he'll tell us what we need to know."

"Liz, what do you think?" Casey asked.

"It's risky, but I agree with Adam. Bradley had to know how the AK-47s would be used."

"Hawaii's a big island. How are you going to find him?"

"We'll ask your friend, Riley Bishop, to help us," Drake said. "He knows every inch of that island and we have a phone number. We'll find him."

"I suppose you want to use the Gulfstream to get there?"

"Sure, and I thought you might want to go. Give you a chance to see your old Night Stalker friend."

"And the reason we're doing this…"

"Is to stop the killing before this gets any worse."

"Since you put it that way, I'd better call Megan and tell her I won't be home for dinner tonight."

Chapter Seventy-Four

BY THE TIME the sun set on the West Coast Monday evening, two hundred and seventy-four men and women had been killed by the Antifa anarchists. Their names had all been posted online by Antifa, where they were branded as fascists, racists or Nazis for having marched in a Free Speech parade, being a member of a patriot group, the NRA or a Republican.

The country was shocked and paralyzed. People watched the horrific news and saw homes burning and bodies being lifted into ambulances in their cities. Law enforcement advised citizens to shelter in place; no one knew if the killing would continue throughout the night or the next day.

The PSS Gulfstream G-650 was halfway to Hawaii with the PSS team before the network anchors had time to agree on a narrative that excused their previous support for the antifascist anarchists. Politicians on the left were suddenly unavailable for comment and politicians on the other side of the aisle angrily blamed their opposition for refusing to call out the anarchists sooner as the domestic terrorists they obviously were.

Casey was on his smartphone, using the G-650's IP Swift-

Broadband system to coordinate a search for Mason Bradley with Riley Bishop in Hilo.

Bishop had a friend in the State Prosecutor's Office who had been able to trace the (808) area code number they found in Professor Bradley's houseboat to a villa on the Hamakua Coast, north of Hilo. After two sightseeing flights with tourists as he circled the Big Island that afternoon and flew along the coast close to the villa, he reported they might have a problem getting to Bradley. He'd seen a security guard smoking outside the guard shack at the entrance to the ten-acre estate and other guards patrolling the perimeter of the villa.

He couldn't say that Mason Bradley was on the estate, but his office manager/girlfriend at Royal Bishop Helicopter Tours was calling car rental agencies and cab companies to learn if anyone had seen him or taken him to the villa.

Casey walked back to the rear cabin and sat in the recliner across the aisle from the light beige leather sofa, where Liz and Drake were sitting.

"We may have a problem getting to Bradley. Riley says the villa has security guards. He says they don't look like rent-a-cops. They're wearing black tactical clothing and Riley swears he saw a Krink slung over one's shoulder."

"What's a 'Krink'?" Liz asked.

"It's a short barrel AKS-74U carbine, favored by Russian Spetsnaz soldiers," Drake said. "How many guards did he see?"

"He spotted one on the roof of the villa, one at a guard shack near the road outside smoking and two others patrolling the perimeter."

"Do we know who owns the villa, Mike?"

Casey took his phone out of his pocket and stood up to leave. "I didn't ask. I'll ask Riley if he can find out."

Liz put her hand on Drake's leg. "I don't like the sound of this."

"We don't know if he is staying there. Even if he isn't, I'd like to know why Bradley had the number for the villa. I'm going to get a beer from the galley, do you want something?"

"A Perrier, if it's available. A diet Pepsi if it's not."

Drake got up and walked forward to the galley. When he passed Casey's chair, he heard him say, "You have to be kidding!"

Casey followed him to the galley.

"You aren't going to believe who owns the villa. It's the Russian oligarch, Mikhail Volkov."

Drake grinned. "And Mason Bradley just happens to have the phone number of his villa."

"I didn't think it would be this easy to get the goods on Bradley and Volkov, did you?"

"We're not there yet. We still need something that conclusively proves Volkov and Bradley are responsible for the Antifa violence."

"How we do that? We don't even know if Bradley's there."

"He's there, Mike. We just have to figure out how were going to get in to see him."

"Those armed guards aren't going to let us just walk in and arrest him."

"Maybe, maybe not. I have an idea that might work."

"Which is?"

"An emergency landing at the villa tonight. Riley's going to fake an engine failure and autorotate us down somewhere on the estate."

Chapter Seventy-Five

AFTER TOUCHING down at the Hilo International Airport, the G-650 taxied to the Royal Bishop Helicopter Tours hangar, where Riley Bishop was waiting for them.

"Impressive," Casey said, admiring the interior of the hangar as he walked across the tarmac to shake hands with his old friend. "Business must be good to support a fleet of Airbus H130s."

Bishop pointed with his thumb over his shoulder. "Don't forget the H145 in the back I use for emergency evacuations from the lava flow. Flying tourists around isn't as exciting as flying Delta Force missions, but the pay's better."

"Then tonight just might be an exception. Is there someplace where we can have a private conversation and go over what we're planning?"

"Sure, there's a conference room inside. This used to be the DEA's hangar before they closed up shop to save money."

Casey turned and waved to Steve Carson, his pilot, to let the others on the plane know it was okay to deplane and join him. Bishop watched with him as Liz and Drake came down the air stairs, followed by Marco Morales and the two former SEALs, Dan Borden and Nick Manning.

After the introductions and handshakes, they followed Bishop to a conference room on the south side of the hangar. On the wall, at the end of a long conference table, was a large map of the Big Island of Hawaii.

"Beer and soft drinks are in the refrigerator through that door, if anyone's thirsty," Bishop offered.

Drake walked to the end of the conference table and stood in front of the map on the wall. "Can you show me where Volkov's villa is?" he asked Bishop.

Bishop joined him in front of the map and pointed to a spot on the coast. "It's north of Ninole, twenty miles from here."

"That's not far from where Liz and I stayed earlier this month."

"It's about two miles on up the highway from where you stayed."

Drake turned away from the map and took a seat next to Liz at the conference table. "Were you able to find out if Mason Bradley is staying there?"

Bishop nodded. "He rented a charcoal-gray Jeep Wrangler from Hertz, Sunday afternoon. He had another fellow with him and asked for a map of the island. When I flew over the villa this afternoon, the gray Jeep was parked next to the tennis courts."

Bishop looked around the table and then back to Drake. "How are you planning on getting in to see this guy with armed security guards there?"

Casey smiled and said, "Remember the night we lost power in that Black Hawk in Helmand Province? Drake wants you to fake engine failure tonight and autorotate us down somewhere on the estate."

"Then what? Those guards aren't going to let you in to see Bradley."

Drake turned to Liz and raised his eyebrows. He waited for her to flash him a smile before asking, "Ever known a man to refuse a woman when she asks to use the restroom in an emergency?"

Bishop laughed and shook his head. "That's terrible, using this pretty lady to gain access. What if they say no?"

"Then I'll have to convince them that's not the right answer."

For the next hour, while they waited for the pizza and wings Bishop had ordered, they hashed out contingency plans in case the security at the villa overreacted to their emergency landing.

Bishop recommended flying the H130 because it could carry all of them and any equipment they might need. But Marco Morales, the former reconnaissance ranger, wanted to position himself and the two SEALs somewhere just outside the estate in case things went sideways. That way, they wouldn't be trapped in the helicopter.

Drake insisted that Liz carry her Glock 19 when she left the helicopter to use the restroom. She argued that the clothes she planned to wear wouldn't conceal much of anything, not even a compact Glock pistol. Drake agreed that she didn't need to carry her Glock herself but said he'd carry it for her under his Hawaiian shirt.

And Casey wanted to make sure Bishop's prosecutor friend and the Hawaii County Police Department were prepared to take custody of Bradley after Drake made a citizen's arrest. Bishop assured him that his prosecutor friend was prepared to take custody of Bradley and turn him over to the HCPD.

While the others were sitting at the conference table, finishing off the pizza and wings, Drake walked Liz out into the quiet of the hangar.

"We don't know how these guys will react when we drop in. I would never forgive myself if something happened to you."

"Adam, I'm the one who suggested using the restroom ploy to get inside the villa. I can take care of myself."

"You won't be wearing body armor if bullets start flying."

"Neither will you. This will work. Besides, it's exciting working with you to get the evidence we need. I never had a chance to do undercover work in the FBI. This is kind of like that."

"If you're determined to go unarmed, you have to promise me you won't go Wonder Woman on me. If we can't get in to Bradley, we leave and find another way."

Liz put her hand on his chest and pushed him back against the maroon helicopter they were standing next to. "I'll promise that if you'll kiss me and make me the same promise."

Drake kissed her, knowing he'd just made a promise that would be hard to keep. If they didn't arrest Bradley tonight, they probably wouldn't get another chance.

Chapter Seventy-Six

ZAL NAZIR RAISED his head and opened one swollen eye to look over at Mason Bradley and see if he was conscious. They were both secured with duct tape to solid wood kitchen chairs, sitting atop clear plastic sheeting in the villa's kitchen.

Within minutes of entering Volkov's villa, they'd been marched to the kitchen at gunpoint and forced to sit in the chairs with black bags put over their heads. When they tried to speak to their captors, or each other, they were hit in the head with something that felt like a thick phone book. Nazir felt that his right eardrum had probably been ruptured by one blow to the side of his head.

They were left alone in the silence of the kitchen all night. In the morning, the beatings resumed. He knew he had lost track of time. He thought it was an hour or so each time before his hood was pulled off. As soon as the hood was off, he'd been pummeled in the face and chest by a bear of a man who introduced himself as Demetri and kept asking where the money was. He didn't know what money the man was talking about, and when he said so, the beatings resumed until he passed out again.

Nazir, however, thought Bradley did know what money

Demetri was asking about. After an earlier bout with Demitri, he'd regained consciousness while Bradley was still being beaten. He heard Demitri ask him repeatedly about "the money for the weapons."

Now Demetri was kneeling in front of him with a smile on his face. "I am told you are smart guy and great hacker. Your friend won't tell me where he has money that doesn't belong to him. He may not live much longer, so you will help me find it. I know the account the money was sent to him. I want you to tell me where it went from there. If you do that, I will let you live."

Nazir's lips were cracked and swollen, and his throat was parched. It was all he could to whisper, "Water."

"Sure, sure, I will get you water."

Dimitri stood and got a glass from a kitchen cabinet near the sink and filled it from the faucet. He returned and poured water from the glass into Nazir's open mouth. Most of it went down his throat, causing him to choke and cough.

"You want more?"

Nazir shook his head. "Why are you doing this?"

"Why do you think?"

"It's hard to think with my head throbbing and my ears ringing, but you want the money Volkov gave Bradley?"

"You are smart. But it's my money, if I find it. Volkov doesn't know I know about the million dollars Bradley kept for himself."

"How did you find out about it? Bradley never said anything about it to me."

"Bradley offered it to me if I let him go."

"Then why not let him go? You'd have your money."

"He wanted to go with me, to get the money from his bank. I can't let him leave here."

"But you will let me leave? How can I know you'll keep your word?"

"You can't, but what choice do you have? All you have to

do is work your magic with your computer and get the money from Bradley's account into my account in Singapore. When you do that, I will let you go."

Nazir knew Dimitri was lying. Volkov had ordered them to go to his villa to have them killed. That was the only reason for Dimitri and the others to be at the villa. He and Bradley could have entertained themselves on the estate without armed security hovering over them.

If he could use his laptop without Dimitri looking over his shoulder, there was a chance he could get someone to rescue him. Maybe even the police. There weren't any warrants for his arrest that he knew of, and the police wouldn't have any basis for holding him. It was worth a try.

"I will need my laptop and internet access if I'm going to help you. I want out of this chair and out of this kitchen, also something to eat and time for the swelling to go down so I can see."

"I can move you to another room, but you stay in chair. I will get you food and let you have some time. But I want the money in my account before the sun comes up tomorrow. That's all the time you get to save your life."

"Move me out of this kitchen, get me something to eat and let me rest awhile. I'll get your money."

The sky was painted a soft purple outside the kitchen windows. Nazir knew he had ten hours or so before sunrise. It wouldn't take him that long to trace the money Bradley had stashed somewhere. But Dimitri didn't look like he was going anywhere, and he needed to be left alone long enough to send an SOS. Then it would just be a matter of waiting for help to arrive before the sun came up, if he was going to live to fight another day for Allah, *inshallah.*

Chapter Seventy-Seven

BY NINE O'CLOCK MONDAY NIGHT, a plan was finalized for an incursion into enemy territory at Volkov's estate.

Riley Bishop would fly his H130 Ecostar helicopter and follow the coastline to a point north of the villa. He would then turn south as if he was returning from a late sightseeing trip around the island with Liz and Drake. When he faked engine failure and autorotated down, he would land somewhere on the ten-acre estate as close as possible to the villa.

Liz and Drake would pretend to be stunned and act like they were trying to get as far away from the helicopter as possible. Bishop would get out to inspect his helicopter for damage, while they would likely be greeted by the security guards or even Mason Bradley himself. Liz would ask to use the restroom and Drake would insist that he had to go with her.

With any luck, they would find Bradley in the villa and make a citizen's arrest. Bishop would notify his prosecutor friend to come and take custody of their prisoner, after they'd had a chance to ask him a few questions.

Drake would have his Kimber .45 in a paddle holster on his hip, concealed under a Hawaiian shirt Bishop loaned him, and the Glock 19 Liz favored inside his waistband in the small of his back. Casey would have a HK416 and a SIG and stay in the helicopter to cover Liz and Drake, if necessary, to get them in the villa.

It wasn't the greatest plan. In fact, it wasn't much of a plan at all, but they didn't have time to come up with a better one. They were private citizens, and none of them relished the thought of going to prison, but they were determined they wouldn't leave the island without finding Bradley.

They would only use the amount of force reasonable and necessary to make the arrest. But if physical force was used against them, they would defend themselves.

Morales and the two SEALs would park near the entrance of the estate to provide backup. They each had an HK416 assault rifle and a SIG 320 pistol, plus a two-way radio with a single wire earpiece and PTT button and microphone, to keep in touch with Casey and Bishop.

Hopefully, the security guards wouldn't overreact when the helicopter made its emergency landing. With at least one of the security guards armed with an assault carbine favored by the Russian Spetsnaz special forces, however, you couldn't count on it.

After a comm check with Casey and Bishop, Morales and the SEALs left at nine fifteen in one of Bishop's people haulers, a white Ford Transit Passenger Van. They had forty-five minutes to be in place at the side of Highway Belt Road, Highway 19, out of sight from the guard shack.

At nine thirty, Casey and Drake rolled the Airbus H130 Ecostar helicopter out of the hangar on a landing platform and helped Bishop prepare to lift off. Liz had returned to the PSS Gulfstream to change clothes and came back wearing a tight-fitting pair of denim short shorts and a revealing white halter top.

Drake stood with his mouth open watching her walk out to the helicopter. He was wearing a tan pair of cargo shorts, a red-and-white floral Hawaiian shirt and sandals to look like a tourist. He hadn't expected Liz to dress as she had, but he appreciated the distraction she was going to provide when they landed.

"The guards at the villa don't stand a chance," Casey said.

"Just doing my part to contribute to the effort," Liz told them.

Bishop walked around from the other side of the helicopter on his preflight inspection and whistled. "Forgive me for staring, but I'll have to concentrate extra hard to fly this thing with you in the cockpit, miss."

"I'll take that as a compliment, Riley. But I'm not worried about you flying your helicopter. I'm worried about how you're planning on landing it."

"Nothing to it. You just let it fall out of the sky."

Drake saw that Bishop's assurance hadn't helped her much. "He's a former Night Stalker, Liz. We'll be fine. Ready to go?"

"Ready as I'll ever be."

Liz opened the door on the passenger side of the helicopter and slid over to the middle seat, next to Bishop, and put on her headset. Drake let Casey slip into his seat in the rear and then climbed in to sit next to Liz. When he closed the door, he signaled thumbs up and Bishop powered up the H130's turboshaft engine.

When he had his seatbelt and headset on, he asked Bishop if it felt like old times taking off on a night mission.

"A little, but I always got to drop you guys off and fly away."

"Yeah, but you had to come back for us. This time we're just saving you the return flight."

Bishop opened the throttle slowly until the engine was at its operating RPM and pulled the collective gradually up until they lifted off the ground. When he pushed the cyclic forward, the H130 moved forward above the tarmac.

They flew out over the beach parks, on the southwest of Hilo Bay, and then gained altitude over the Pacific.

The lights of Hilo disappeared on their left and then narrowed to a scattered strand of lights from homes along the coastal highway.

After twenty minutes of flying at two thousand feet above the ocean, shimmering under the illumination from a waning gibbous moon, they began a gentle turn west and then flew south along the Hamakua Coast.

Bishop descended to fifteen hundred feet and pointed ahead. "That's the villa. Let's see who's home."

Chapter Seventy-Eight

AUTOROTATION IS FLYING a helicopter when the rotor blades are turned by air moving up through them as the aircraft glides down, without engine power turning the rotors. A controlled landing without engine power is something every helicopter pilot must learn to get his pilot's license. It can appear to be as smooth and safe as a full-powered landing, but Bishop wanted his emergency touchdown to look dangerous. It had to be rough enough to cause his two passengers to run for safety as soon as they got out of the helicopter.

"Hold on, I'm going to make it look like we're going to crash land," he said.

Bishop rocked the helicopter from side to side as it descended to a hundred feet at fifty knots airspeed and flew over the northern end of the estate. When they were fifty feet above ground with a large grassy area west of the villa in their path, he flared the nose of the helicopter up, to reduce speed, and leveled off just before landing. They hit hard, with the skids tearing through the soft earth.

The only sound Drake heard when he threw open the passenger door was the ticking sound of the hot engine cooling in the night air. Then the guards started shouting as they ran toward the helicopter.

Adam jumped out and fell to his knees. Liz remained in her seat, appearing to be stunned with her hair messed up, staring straight ahead in shock.

"Liz," Drake shouted, "get out before it explodes or something!" He got to his feet and reached in to unbuckle her seatbelt.

Liz kept staring straight ahead for a minute then shook her head and jumped out into his arms. Then she pushed him away and started screaming. "I told you I didn't want to go! I told you I wanted to stay at the hotel! We could have been killed!"

Drake led her away from the helicopter and started walking with her toward the villa. Floodlights had come as soon as they hit down and were flooding the area with a yellowish sodium vapor light.

A guard ran toward them from the villa, shouting for them to stay where they were. As he got closer, he raised the short barrel of the AKS-74 he was carrying and pointed it at them.

"This is private property!" he shouted. "You can't be here!"

Drake looked over his shoulder and saw the guard from the guard shack running across the grassy area toward them from the west. He was motioning with his hands to two other dark forms vectoring across the estate from the north and south.

Drake and Liz raised their hands above their shoulders and stopped.

"We didn't have a choice," Drake said and pointed with his thumb over his shoulder. "The pilot said it was engine failure. We had to land."

Bishop got out and was walking around the helicopter to inspect it for damage.

They were now surrounded by three security guards, all dressed the same and carrying assault carbines.

Liz lowered her hands and held them palms together at chest level with her fingers pointing up in a praying gesture. "Please, before we go, I have to use your restroom. This has really upset me."

"We're sorry for all this," Drake said. "I understand that you want us to leave, but my wife had surgery recently. She's not well and needs to use your bathroom before we leave."

The guard looked away from staring at Liz's visible cleavage and sneered. "Why should I care? You can't be here."

"Just let me walk her to a restroom in your villa and we'll leave. You guys have the guns, what are you afraid of?"

The guard from the villa lowered the barrel of his AKS-74, let it hang across his chest and smiled. "It is you who should be afraid. But you are right, we have the guns. I will let her use the bathroom, as soon as I make sure you do not have guns, if you will promise to leave when she is finished."

Liz wrapped her arms around herself and rocked from one foot to the other. "We promise. Can I please use the restroom now?"

The guard said something to one of the other guards standing behind them, who moved forward and quickly searched Liz for a weapon. When he didn't find one, he continued more slowly a second time, with a more thorough and lingering search.

When he was satisfied she wasn't hiding anything under her skimpy attire, he moved over behind Drake. When he found Drake's .45 in the holster on his hip, he stepped back and held it up for the other guard to see. Handing the .45 to the guard closest to him, he returned to Drake and quickly found the Glock 19 in the small of his back.

When the lead guard saw the second gun, he started

waving his AKS-74 widely back and forth at them and shouted, "Down on your knees, now!"

Drake and Liz did as they were told and dropped to their knees.

"Look, I can explain," Drake said. "I have a permit, I—"

"Stop talking," the lead guard ordered.

Drake and Liz watched the guard jog to the front door of the villa to talk with another guard standing there. After a brief conversation, he jogged back and motioned for them to stand up.

The lead guard looked behind them to where Bishop was standing next to his helicopter. One of the other guards was covering him with his assault carbine pointed at his chest.

"Keep the pilot there," the guard shouted. "Demitri wants to talk to these two."

Motioning with his weapon to walk ahead of him, Drake and Liz started walking toward the villa.

Volkov's villa was a three-story concrete superstructure built on the edge of a tall cliff. As they walked across the lawn toward the front door, Drake saw a guard looking down at them from the villa's flat roof where the helipad was located. He'd counted five guards so far and wondered if there were more inside the villa.

The entrance to the villa consisted of a twenty-foot expanse of glass. In its center was a frameless glass door with a large etching of a sea turtle. A sixth guard stood in the salon beyond and walked over to open the door for them. Drake spotted the Spetsnaz tattoo of a black bat on the back of his left hand that he recognized.

"I wondered when you would come see me, Mr. Drake. My name is Dimitri. You were very clever, faking an engine failure in your helicopter."

At the sound of his name, Drake's mind raced to the obvious conclusion. He had taken the bait hook, line and sinker. That scrap of paper in Mason Bradley's houseboat with the United Airlines flight number and the (808) area code had been left there to lure him to Hawaii.

"How did Volkov know we were on to him?"

"You would have to ask him that."

"Why bring us here? Volkov could just scurry back to Russia. Bradley's the one we want."

"You don't expose a king when you can sacrifice a couple of pawns."

"And we're the pawns?"

"No, but you got to close to him."

"Is he here?"

"And you would like to meet him, yes?"

"Might as well, since I'm here."

Liz raised her hand, like a schoolgirl wanting to use the hall pass. "The engine failure was faked, but I wasn't faking when I said I needed to go to the bathroom."

Dimitri smiled salaciously at Liz wearing her short shorts and white halter top. "I'm afraid I can't let you do that, Ms. Strobel. Vasili is a good soldier, but he's also a man. I wouldn't want you to distract him and try something foolish."

Chapter Seventy-Nine

THROUGH THE DARKENED rear window in the helicopter, Casey saw Drake and Liz standing inside the main salon in the villa with a guard behind them carrying his AK-74S at port arms. Drake was leaving the room, walking ahead of the guard who had stayed in the villa when they arrived.

He pushed the PTT button on his headset and radioed to Morales out on the highway. "Marco, you three meet me at the helicopter on my command. I don't like the looks of this."

"Roger that."

Three guards were clustered around the helicopter. The one guarding Bishop kept his assault rifle trained on him as he continued checking every inch of his helicopter for damage. The other two stood on the other side of the helicopter with their backs turned toward the highway, smoking and talking softly.

Casey's concern was the guard on the roof. He had an unobstructed view of the helicopter and the area around it. He seemed more interested in smoking a cigarette than keeping watch from above. Even so, if he saw Morales and his mates crossing the estate from the highway, he would have an easy time picking them off. He needed to get out of the helicopter and neutralize the rooftop guard.

He waited until Bishop moved along the side of the helicopter, continuing to look for damage, and knocked on the interior wall softly. He saw Bishop stop to locate the sound and then he knocked once more.

Bishop looked up at the rear window, nodded once and moved to the pilot's door.

Before he opened the door, he said to the man guarding him, "I need a flashlight to inspect the undercarriage. It's inside."

Bishop opened the door and leaned inside.

"We need to get Drake and Liz out of there," Casey whispered. "You subdue the guard closest to you when I jump out. I'll take care of the guard on the roof."

Bishop nodded once and reached for the flashlight in its holder mounted under his seat.

When Bishop closed the door, Casey picked up his HK416 and pushed the PTT button on his headset to call Morales out on the highway. "Marco, move in and meet me at the helicopter. Take the guards out, on my count, then we'll go get Liz and Drake."

"Roger that. Moving now."

Thirty seconds later, Morales whispered, "We're here."

"Whenever you're ready."

"Roger that."

Casey watched through the opposite rear window of the helicopter as three shadows rushed forward. The two SEALs moved in unison around to the right, behind the two guards who were smoking, and applied rear choke holds, exerting pressure on their carotid arteries until both men slipped down, unconscious.

Morales moved around the helicopter to the left, coming up behind the guard covering Bishop. As the startled guard turned his head to look to see his comrades being attacked,

Bishop sprang forward and knocked the assault carbine aimed at him to one side as Morales threw his right arm around the man's neck and used a rear choke hold to take the fight out of him.

In ten seconds, three of the four guards outside of the villa were unconscious and on the ground.

The fourth guard on the helipad saw the movement below and hesitated a few seconds too long, waiting for a clear shot at the intruders. When he fired a short burst at Morales, who was now running toward the villa, Casey jumped out of the helicopter and returned fire.

When the man spun around and fell to the rooftop, Casey shouted, "Morales, hurry around back. Find a way in. We'll move in from here."

———

AT THE SOUND OF GUNFIRE, Demitri calmly told Vasili to find out what was going on outside.

"It sounds like your pilot may have done something stupid," he said. "Don't worry, you won't need him. Let's move into the kitchen. You wanted to meet Mason Bradley, and so you shall."

Dimitri pointed with his 9 mm GSh-18 pistol to an area beyond the main salon. "Bradley's through there."

Drake exchanged a look with Liz and shrugged his shoulders. "Why not?"

They walked ahead of the Russian across an expanse of rose travertine tiled floor and turned right into the kitchen. An oval granite-topped breakfast table had been moved aside to make room for a large sheet of clear plastic. It was splattered with blood and vomit from the man duct taped to a wooden chair.

Mason Bradley's battered head hung down with his chin resting on his bruised and bloody chest.

"Is he alive?"

"Don't know, I haven't checked recently."

Drake saw that there were two distinct areas of blood splatter. Five feet away from Bradley's chair were four indentations where another chair had been.

"Who else did you kill?"

"No one, yet."

Drake turned to face Dimitri and leaned back against the kitchen counter. "You're Spetsnaz, right? Why is Russia willing to risk your capture on U.S. soil?"

"Was Spetsnaz, now just private soldier, like military contractors your country uses in the world."

"Don't glorify what you're doing, Dimitri. You're just a hired killer, not a soldier."

"Same work, better pay."

The Russian was leaning against the counter across the kitchen, facing Drake and Liz. His pistol was pointed at the floor, held loosely in his left hand against his leg. Confident in his ability, as the trained soldier that he was, he was clearly not worried about Drake's own lethal skills. But the distance between them was too great to cross before Dimitri could get off a shot at one of them.

Drake was searching for a way to distract the Russian and gain an advantage when he heard someone walking toward the kitchen.

"I found your money, Dimitri," a young man said as he entered the kitchen looking down at the screen of a laptop held out in front of him.

"Hello Nazir. Fancy meeting you here," Drake said.

A deer-in-the-headlights look gave way to a look of disbelief as Nazir recognized Drake. "You! How did you find me?"

Dimitri brought the pistol up and pointed it at Drake and then at Nazir. "How do you know this man?"

"Nazir's been trying to kill me, Dimitri. He's just not very good at it."

"Explain," Dimitri demanded.

"Zal Nazir is a terrorist, hiding behind the skirts of young girls to kill Americans. He killed a friend of mine, an FBI agent, and I killed the Iranian commando he sent after me. You're not very selective in the losers you choose to work with, Dimitri."

Chapter Eighty

THE RUSSIAN POINTED his pistol at Nazir and then back toward Drake and Liz. "Move over closer to them, Nazir, and explain. Does VolKov know this about you?"

"It didn't involve anything I was doing for him, so I didn't tell him."

"But now it has. I should have killed you when I had you in the chair."

"If you had, I wouldn't have been able to find your money."

Drake had to laugh. "Don't tell me he told you he would let you live if you found his money and you believed him?"

Nazir smiled and looked at Dimitri. "He won't kill me. He doesn't know it, but I have insurance. If I don't reset the alarm on my laptop on schedule, a file that has everything I've done for Volkov and Bradley will automatically be sent to the FBI tip line. So now that you know that, you won't kill me, will you, Dimitri?"

"If you have this file, why didn't you tell me about it? Why did you let me beat you? I don't believe you, Nazir."

"You can't take that risk, Dimitri. I'll show you the file if you want. To answer your question, I didn't know Bradley had stolen money from Volkov. I wanted to hear what he had to say so I could get to it when I leave here."

Drake didn't think Nazir's bluff, whether it was real or not, was going to work. But the longer it kept Demitri from wondering where Vasili was, and what was going on outside, the better the odds were that the cavalry would reach them in time.

Drake moved away from Liz a couple of steps and said, "Maybe you should work together and split the money. You seem to be at checkmate."

Dimitri smiled and pointed his pistol at Drake's head. "I don't need your advice, attorney, and I see what you're trying to do by moving away from your wife. You think maybe I can't shoot you before one of you gets to me, yes?"

He took three quick steps and grabbed Liz by the wrist and spun her around. With his right arm around her neck, he held his pistol to her head with his left hand. "Now we're at checkmate."

"Take it easy, Demitri. You can walk away from this. I came here for Bradley, but I'll settle for Nazir. You can have his laptop and the money, I don't need it."

Nazir moved away from Drake and Liz and started to leave the kitchen.

"Do not leave this room, Nazir," Dimitri said over his shoulder. "We have business to finish."

Drake looked at Liz to reassure her that they were going to get out of this and saw that she was blinking both of her eyes rapidly. He blinked back to signal that he was watching.

Liz blinked her right eye quickly three times, followed by two slower blinks.

She was signaling to him using Morse code, the number three.

She then blinked quickly twice, followed by three slower blinks for the number two.

She was getting ready to try something and wanted him to be prepared.

With the flash of a smile, she blinked quickly one time and then four times more slowly for the number one.

Spinning to her left, she shot a lateral elbow strike to Demitri's stomach.

Drake sprang forward, pivoted on his left foot and followed with a rear straight offensive kick to Demetri's solar plexus, knocking him back.

Before Demitri could bring his pistol up, Drake hit him with a slashing strike to his throat with his right hand. He followed that with a rapid one-two palm heel strike to his nose with his left hand and a palm heel strike to the right side of his face with his right hand.

Demitri crumpled to the floor, lights out.

Liz kicked the pistol out of Demetri's hand and leaned down to pick it up. "That was fun."

"That's not how I was going to describe it. Are you okay?"

"I'm fine."

"It's quiet outside, but be careful and go see how the guys are. I'll see if I can find Nazir."

Drake stopped when he heard someone coming toward them from the back of the house. He pulled Liz back into the kitchen and listened. Footsteps were marching across the tiled floor from the rear of the main salon and then they stopped.

"Boss, it's me," Morales shouted. "It's okay to come out. Eagle Warrior."

'Eagle Warrior' was the all-clear code to be used when the giver was not under duress.

Drake stepped out of the kitchen ahead of Liz and saw Morales standing with one hand on the shoulder of Nazir and a laptop in his other hand.

"I ran into this one trying to sneak away out back."

"Where are the guards?"

Morales grinned. "They're taking a little nap, except for

the one on the roof. They didn't hear us coming until it was too late. If these guys were Spetsnaz, they're not training them like they used to.

Chapter Eighty-One

DRAKE APPROACHED Nazir and stood in front of him. "I came here to arrest Bradley for inciting riots on the mainland with Volkov's money. Now I find the man who's been trying to have me killed was also working with Volkov. That's killing two birds with one stone, wouldn't you agree? But before I decide what we should do with you, were you bluffing about having a file on your laptop set to go to the FBI?"

Nazir blinked several times before answering. "Would it make a difference if I did?"

Drake knew what he was being asked. He'd negotiated plea deals when he was a prosecutor. "Are you asking, if you give us the file, would your cooperation get you a deal?"

"Something like that."

"We have your laptop. Why do we need your cooperation? I'm guessing your laptop is booby-trapped. If we try to open the file, it will automatically be sent to the FBI."

"Because I didn't put everything you might want in the file."

"What else is there?"

Nazir leaned forward and whispered, "Not until I have a deal."

Drake held out his hand to Morales. "Let me have his laptop. Take him to the helicopter and keep him there while I talk with Liz."

She waited until Morales left with Nazir before asking, "What are you thinking?"

"Let's go out on the lanai. I want to call Senator Hazelton."

"Why? Aren't we going to turn him over to Bishop's prosecutor friend?"

He led her out to the cliff-side lanai and looked out down at the waves surging against the bottom shore.

"What if we take Nazir somewhere to question him without getting the government involved? We could leave the others with Bishop's friend and have them arrested for killing and torturing Bradley."

"You mean take Nazir to a black site?"

"Not exactly but a private place where we can find out what's on his laptop and any other information he might give us. We started working with the committee because they needed to work outside normal channels. I think we should keep doing that a little longer."

Drake took out his smartphone and called his father-in-law in Washington, D.C., knowing it was three o'clock in the morning there.

"Senator, I'm sorry for waking you at this hour, but I need your advice."

After explaining where they were and what they had found at Volkov's villa, Drake asked, "What should we do with Nazir?"

"I have an idea. I'll call you back in a few minutes."

Drake and Liz were still on the lanai discussing their options when Senator Hazelton called back five minutes later. Drake put his phone on speaker.

"Take Nazir to Secretary Rallings' ranch in Montana. He'll arrange to have Nazir questioned by special agents he trusts from the Homeland Security Investigations' field office in Denver. But take the laptop to Seattle. Let your young IT guru see what's on it. As soon as we have the evidence that Volkov and possibly Russia itself are sponsoring the violence, Senator Montez and I will request an emergency meeting with the president. It shouldn't be too hard to convince him to call the governors and ask them to arrest the Antifa leaders in their jurisdictions and have them tried in state court for inciting the riots."

"We can do that. Liz and I will have to stay a little longer to straighten things out with the local authorities. They'll want our statements about what happened here."

"Understood. If there's anything I can help with, call me."

Drake put his arms around Liz and pulled her close. "Shall I see if we can still use the villa where we stayed earlier this month? I have no idea how long they'll keep us here."

"If we must."

"Yes, the things we do to serve our country."

Chapter Eighty-Two

BY THE TIME they left Volkov's villa, the sky at sunrise was splashed with vibrant pink and purple and yellow, as if it had been painted by Monet.

After being interviewed, Drake and Liz more thoroughly than the others, by Bishop's prosecutor and the detectives from the Hawaii Police Department, they left the crime scene that was still being processed to rendezvous at Bishop's hangar.

Casey and Morales had slipped out with Nazir and driven to the airport in Bishop's people hauler before the police arrived. Morales had then returned to give his statement, and neither his nor any of the other statements mentioned Casey or Nazir ever being on Volkov's estate.

Bishop, Morales and the two SEALs were eating donuts and drinking coffee in Bishop's hangar while Drake and Liz met with Casey in the PSS Gulfstream.

Nazir was flex-cuffed and sitting with duct tape across his mouth at the rear of the plane with Casey.

"Sorry about you having to babysit him all the way home," Drake said, "but the rest of us were told not to leave the island."

"It's better this way. You get to stay in paradise and I get to keep my involvement out of the police reports. I think I can handle Mr. Nazir for a couple of hours."

"Were you able to get a hold of Secretary Rallings?"

"He's going to meet me at the airport at Bozeman and take Nazir to his ranch. I'll return to Seattle with the laptop and let Kevin work on it. If he gets what we need, Senator Hazelton will send someone to take it to Washington."

"Thanks for doing all of this, Mike."

"God's blessed me with the wherewithal to help where I can. It's the least I can do. Are you able to stay at our client's villa?"

"He was just leaving his house when I called him and said, 'It's vacant, go ahead and use it.'"

"What about the others?"

"Bishop called and reserved rooms for them at the Grand Nanilo Hotel on the bay. We'll keep an eye on them."

"Please do. I guess that's it then. Tell Carson on your way out to take off as soon as he's ready. I want to get back to Seattle from Montana in time for dinner at home tonight."

Drake and Liz watched the PSS Gulfstream take off and then reminded Morales to call if the prosecutor or HPP wanted to talk with any of them. He was the company attorney and needed to be present at all future interviews of any of the PSS employees.

When the red Mustang convertible Drake rented for the second time from Hertz arrived, he carried their weekend duffel bags out and loaded them in the trunk.

"Are you hungry?" he asked Liz.

"I could eat something light, maybe a pastry and a good cup of coffee."

"Bishop told me about a place on our way to our villa, it's not far."

Drake drove them to the Moonstruck Patisserie in historic downtown Hilo, just off Kamehameha Avenue, where they had croissants and coffee before driving north up the Hamakua Coast.

They had just driven across the Singing Bridge over the Wailuku River when Liz mentioned something that was troubling her. "I get that Volkov has the money to own villas and give away millions to charities and nonprofits, but how did he find out you were waiting for the shipment of AK-47s in Seattle? That's the kind of information the federal agencies didn't even have because you worked around them."

"That's been bothering me too. If he's smuggling drugs or something, he might have people at ports that could have tipped him off. But by the time they could have learned anything, the ship would have already been in our territorial waters. They had to know we were waiting to search the ship before it reached the twelve-mile limit."

"That could have been the plan all along, like Mike said, or maybe he just got lucky."

"He wasn't lucky today, though, was he?"

"No, we were. But he found out that you were on to him and lured you to Hawaii. He needed more than luck to do that. He needed inside information. Where did he get it? How did he get it?"

"I don't know, Liz. Maybe Nazir knows. I'll call Secretary Rallings to make sure the investigators ask him."

They drove on in silence, tired from being up all night, and too distracted by the lush scenery to worry about Volkov's omniscience on the way to their villa and a couple hours of sleep.

The key was where the property manager said it would be, hidden behind a metal sea turtle mounted on the wall above the doorbell.

Drake carried their duffel bags to the master bedroom, took his sandals off and lay down on the bed. "Wake me up in a couple of hours."

"What makes you think I'll be awake in a couple of hours? I'm going to take a shower and join you."

When he woke up four hours later and was greeted with the fresh scent of coconut from her hair, he realized how tired he'd been. Liz was lying beside him with only a towel wrapped around her beautiful body and he didn't remember her returning from her shower.

But he wasn't tired now.

Drake turned on his side to look at her and saw that she was awake with a smile on her face.

When she sat up and let the towel drop off, he smiled too.

Chapter Eighty-Three

THE CLOUDS that had captured the colors of the sunset so brilliantly the night before brought rain squalls sweeping over the island the next morning.

Drake was drinking his second cup of coffee in the kitchen when Liz walked in wearing a black halter-top bikini.

"Did you notice that it's raining outside?" Drake asked.

"I did. It's also seventy-two degrees. I plan on making the most of my time here before we leave."

"I can't find anything for breakfast. Looks like we have to drive to Hilo if we want something."

"That's fine, after I finish swimming."

He watched her walk out to the pool and gracefully dive in when his iPhone started dancing across the counter. Caller ID told him Casey was calling.

"I hope this isn't too early. I keep forgetting about the time difference. Were you awake?"

"Awake and having my second cup of coffee while I watch Liz swimming in the pool. What's up?"

"Quite a bit, and I'm not sure what to make of it. Kevin couldn't open the file with the initials MV he found on Nazir's laptop. When we tried to open it, he triggered a "Share" order and the file went straight to the FBI tip line."

"So, Nazir was telling the truth. Now we don't have anything for Senator Hazelton to show the president."

"That's not the worst of it. When I landed at the airport in Bozeman, I expected Secretary Rallings and investigators from HIS to be there to take Nazir off my hands. Instead, the FBI were there and took custody of him. We never had a chance to interrogate him about Volkov or Bradley."

"How did the FBI find out you were flying Nazir to Montana?"

"I don't know. The only person I talked to was Secretary Rallings. I don't know if Senator Hazelton talked with him before or after I did."

"The only person I talked with was Senator Hazelton. If he didn't talk with Rallings…"

"Exactly, someone's monitoring our phone calls."

"Could Volkov do that?"

"Maybe, I don't know. But we both know there's someone else who could."

"Why would the government be monitoring us?"

"Why did you work around the feds in Seattle when you wanted to intercept the AK-47s?"

"For the same reason Senator Hazelton wanted us to help the committee; there are people he doesn't trust in the government."

"Bingo. That's how I think the FBI found out we had Nazir and were waiting for him in Bozeman."

Drake let that sink in. "We have a big problem then. The FBI has whatever it received on the tip line and they have its author. We have zip, nada, and Senator Hazelton and Senator Montez have nothing to show the president."

"We took Bradley and Nazir off the table, but Volkov's probably in Russia by now. We need to be very careful from now on. I think we need to get all of you back to Seattle, as soon as possible, and regroup."

"Bishop's prosecutor friend hasn't told us we can leave yet."

"As soon as she does, have Bishop fly you to Honolulu. I'll have the G-650 there, ostensibly on business for our new office we're opening. Our 'friends' in government won't expect you to be leaving from Honolulu. The less they know the safer I'll feel for all of you."

"I need to let Senator Hazelton know what's going on, but I don't have a secure way to contact him."

"I do. I'll call him."

"All right, I'll see you in Seattle as soon as we can get there."

Drake walked out to the lanai and stood in the rain watching Liz swim laps. He wasn't on the best terms with the FBI office in Portland, but if they were monitoring his phone calls, it was going to get a lot worse.

He was thinking about that when Liz called to him from the edge of the pool.

"The water's great. Coming in?"

"No, you finish your laps. I'm going to call Riley Bishop and see if he can meet us for breakfast."

Forty-five minutes later, they found Bishop sitting at a window table at Hulu Hulas, the restaurant and bar in the Grand Naniloa Hotel on Hilo Bay.

Bishop stood as they approached and greeted Liz with a kiss on her right cheek. "Aloha, you look beautiful, as always."

"Mahalo, Riley," Liz said and turned to look out at the bay. "What a beautiful place."

Drake's greeting was just a handshake, after he pulled out the chair for Liz. "Thanks for meeting us. Have you had breakfast?"

"Just coffee."

Their waiter, a young Hawaiian boy, brought menus and promised to be right back with their coffee.

"Have you heard from our friendly prosecutor?" Drake asked.

"I thought you might ask me that. I called her just before I drove here from the airport. She's meeting us here."

"Why?"

"She said there was something you needed to know. She didn't tell me what it was."

"That sounds a little ominous," Liz said.

Bishop stood up on the other side of their table, looking behind them. "Here she is now."

Drake stood with Bishop and turned to see Ms. Kukana Taupou walking toward them. She wasn't smiling.

"Mr. Drake, Ms. Strobel, thank you for seeing me," she said and sat down on the other side of the table with Bishop.

"Would you like some coffee?" Drake asked.

"No thank you. I only have a minute. I thought you should know. Two FBI agents from their Kona office came to see me. They asked about my investigation of the murder of Professor Bradley and wanted to know if I would be arresting any of the Russians or any of you. I don't know how they found about it so soon, I haven't completed my investigation. I told them I would probably arrest the five Russians for their role in the torture and murder of Professor Bradley. They seemed to be disappointed to hear that I wasn't planning on arresting you and your friends as well. They're requesting my file and all of the evidence we collected before I make any arrests or let you leave Hawaii."

"Why are you telling us this?"

"Because I would like you to leave before I comply with their request."

"Why?"

Ms. Taupou smiled and nodded toward Bishop. "I trust Riley, and I don't like what the FBI is asking me to do. If they want to detain you, they can. Instead, they're asking me to do it for them. If they want my cooperation, they need to tell me what they're up to, and they haven't. I don't want to be involved in whatever they're planning. If you're not here, I won't have to."

Drake liked her honesty, as well as the courtesy she was extending to friends of her friend.

"We'll make sure you don't have to be then," he said. "Mahalo, Ms. Taupou."

She nodded and stood up to leave. "Mahalo, Mr. Drake. I hope you've enjoyed your time in Hawaii."

When she had left, Drake asked Bishop, "Can your Airbus H145 get all of us to Honolulu?"

"It can carry eight and Honolulu is within its range. How soon do you want to leave?

"As soon as we have breakfast and I get the guys checked out of their rooms. Give us an hour to get our stuff.

Chapter Eighty-Four

THEY LEFT Hilo International Airport at ten o'clock that morning for the two-hundred-twenty-mile flight to Honolulu with Drake and Liz, Morales, the two SEALs, Borden and Manning as passengers in Bishop's Airbus H145.

In chasing Mason Bradley to Volkov's villa on the Big Island, they had hoped to confirm that Bradley and Volkov were working together to incite riots in America and have Bradley arrested. Instead, Bradley was dead and the Russians, who were believed to have killed him, were either dead or being held for trial. It was unlikely any of them would provide the evidence that was needed to prove what Volkov, and perhaps Russia, had been doing.

The serendipitous discovery of Zal Nazir at the villa was a plus. But the file he claimed to have on his laptop was in the hands of the FBI and might not ever be available to them. And Nazir was in the custody of the FBI instead of the investigators Secretary Rallings trusted. How that had happened suggested the FBI, or some other government agency, was monitoring their phone calls.

As they flew out over Hilo Bay, Drake fought to control the

anger he felt building within himself. It was one thing to butt heads with the FBI when he was representing a client. It was something else to think the FBI had him under a microscope when he was doing its job and trying to protect the country he loved.

Senator Hazelton and the other members of the committee were right; the government, or at least some parts of it, could not be trusted to faithfully serve the people it was intended to serve. Instead, it served its own interests.

What he couldn't understand was how turning a blind eye to, or even defending, the violence of the anarchists served anyone. Worse than that was the possibility that someone in the government was aiding Volkov and Russia; helping someone who was funding anarchy in the country was, in his mind, the worst kind of treason.

Drake took a deep breath and sat back in his seat. They had a long flight home and plenty of time to think about unmasking the person or persons aiding and abetting the anarchist violence. He didn't know how he was going to do it, but he was damn sure going to find a way.

After waiting four hours in the passenger lounge of the Signature HNL FBO at the Honolulu airport until the Gulfstream G-650 landed, Drake thought he knew where to start.

A hand-written letter their pilot handed him from Mike Casey had informed him that Senators Hazelton and Montez were able to convince the president to activate the National Guard to detain the Antifa anarchist leaders and not wait for the states to do it for him.

They'd done it without the benefit of the file Nazir had sent to the FBI because the FBI was saying it wasn't convinced the tip line information they'd received was credible. The FBI was telling the president that it had no idea who had sent the file to them.

Someone in the FBI knew who sent the file and that

someone was responsible for making sure Nazir wasn't interrogated by the HIS investigators in Montana.

Identifying that person would lead him to the person, or persons, in the government aiding Volkov and the anarchists.

That's where he would begin. God help the betrayers when he found them.

Next in the Adam Drake series

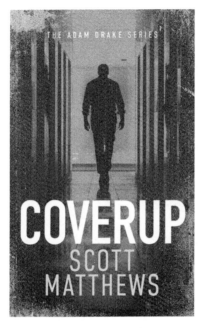

http://vinci-books.com/coverup

A dark secret lurks within the U.S. intelligence community. Those involved will stop at nothing to keep it buried.

Drake, convinced he knows the truth behind the coverup, is determined to expose the treachery that has cost countless lives, including that of a trusted FBI agent.

It's time to take the fight to the Deep State.

Printed in Great Britain
by Amazon